VIOLET MOON SERIES
BOOK 1

Alisa Hope Wagner

F'lorna of Rodesh
Violet Moon Series Book 1
Marked Writers Publishing
Copyright 2018 by Alisa Hope Wagner
www.alisahopewagner.com
Written by Alisa Hope Wagner
Art by Albert Morales
All rights reserved.
ISBN: 978-0-578-21503-7

F'LORNA OF RODESH

VIOLET MOON SERIES
BOOK 1

ACKNOWLEDGEMENTS

The idea of a story starts at conception in the writer's heart with the Holy Spirit's touch of approval. The process of birthing the story is lonely, but the process of bringing it to life takes a team.

Without the expertise and talents of those God has gifted me, this book would not be here. I want to acknowledge their hands in making this book come to life.

To my editing team, Patricia Coughlin, Joanne Sher, Jennifer Smith, Daniel Wagner and Bernadine Zimmerman, thank you for your encouragement, comments, corrections and suggestions.

To Albert Morales, your talent and diligence has allowed F'lorna to leave the imagination, so she can dance across the page.

To Shay Lee, your formatting expertise have created excellence in my publications, and to Holly for your graphic help and encouragement. I am so grateful for both your work in this book. And to my twin, Crissy, for always seeing the best in me.

Most importantly, I am blessed to have the best investor and awesome encourager, my husband. Without you, this book would not be possible.

Finally, I want to thank God for dead-ends and detours—all of which have led me directly into His will and favor. I pray this book opens the eyes of many to see God's majesty and tenderness through the Person of Jesus Christ.

DEDICATION

To my high school sweetheart and husband, Daniel, my stories live because you cherish me.

To my three loves, Isaac, Levi and Karis Ruth, I write with excellence to make you proud.

To Julia, Kiki, Megan, Reagan and Brooke. I pray the courage of F'lorna emboldens you to take risks for your Heavenly Father. And to Noah, Nathan and Brody, may you live like warriors for God.

To all the children, youth and young adults who desire a world of beauty and strength, may this story inspire you.

Thank You, Father, for giving me purpose.
Thank You, Son, for redeeming my world.
Thank You, Spirit, for guiding my journey.

"Behold, I am doing a new thing; now it springs forth, do you not perceive it? I will make a way in the wilderness and rivers in the desert." – Isaiah 43.19 (ESV)

MAP OF RODESH

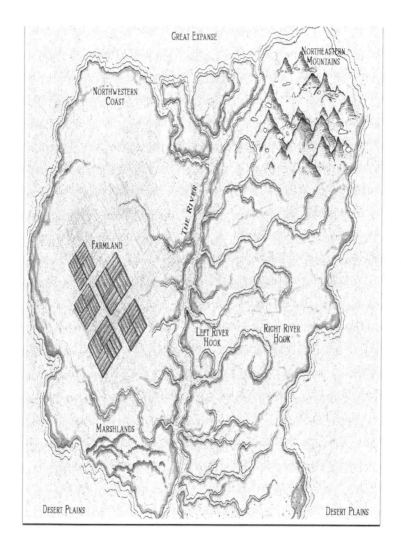

TABLE OF CONTENTS

Prologue

Taken from Within

L uminous, silent swells of the Seventh Indigo
Moon drenched the open belly of F'lorna's
Achion tree. She and Raecli lay silently side by
side on the fiber-filled mattress. F'lorna knew her time
spending the night with her best birth friend in her
Achion tree was diminishing like the Indigo Moon. The

next turn of the moon would introduce the Violet Moon. The blue light would pass away with F'lorna's youth—not to be seen again until F'lorna was the age of her father. She and Raecli would perform their Doublemoon Ceremony under the First Violet Moon and become Novice Elders of Right River Hook.

"Are you still happy you chose dancing as your Adoration for our Doublemoon Ceremony?" she heard Raecli ask from beside her.

F'lorna said nothing for several seconds. Her birth friend knew her too well. She had felt what F'lorna was silently thinking.

"Yes," F'lorna said, trying to sound confident.

"But you are a singer," Raecli said. "Your mother is very upset that you still dance. She believed you would have given up many moon rises ago."

"Dancing is a difficult Adoration for me," F'lorna admitted. "But my body is finally learning the forty-four *Images of Jeyshen*. Besides, singing offers me no challenge." F'lorna forced a smile and gently nudged her friend with her shoulder. "Your mother was right. You are the best singer in all of Right River Hook. Our village doesn't need another beautiful voice. I will stay with dancing as my Adoration."

Silence filled the Achion tree once more. Raecli shifted on the mattress. "The Violet Moon will greet us soon and we will no longer be younglings."

"I wonder if the Violet Moon will match the color of your eyes," F'lorna said. "You and your mother are the only ones with such a color in our village."

"And you and your mother are the only ones with grey eyes," Raecli added. "A sign that our mothers are Sand-shapers."

F'lorna sighed. "My mother is ashamed of who she is. She weaves twigs through her hair to look like us. I believe she would change the color of her eyes too if she could. She only wants to be seen as a River-dweller."

"I understand why she would," Raecli added. "Our village has always been uneasy about our mothers being Sand-shapers. They speak acceptance with their words, but their actions say otherwise."

F'lorna pushed up against the side of her Achion tree and leaned upon one elbow. She looked down at Raecli. "I don't sense any misgivings from them."

"That is because your father is both the Healing and the Spiritual Elder of our village. They hide their feelings well before your family. But me with a single mother—it is different. It doesn't matter now, does it?"

F'lorna noticed the slip of tears sliding down Raecli's cheeks. "Your spirit still aches for her."

"I couldn't make her better. The Smoke Sickness slowly stole her away from me, and I couldn't stop it."

"She is in her Eternal Dwelling now with Ra'ash under all the Six Colored Moons. No more coughing up blood and staying in her Achion cluster from the rise to the fall of the Heat Source. She is at peace," F'lorna said, pulling words from her Eternal Memory that now held the *Divine Oracle*.

"I know your words are true," Raecli nodded. "But her absence is like an empty Achion hole in my spirit."

"I am here," F'lorna whispered.

Raecli gave a wisp of a smile. "I know. And you are squashing me into my side of the Achion tree. F'lorna, you are so tall that you have to sleep with bended knees that poke into my side. You need a bigger tree."

"It is a curse having a father is who is so tall," F'lorna laughed softly. "I give many voiceless words to Ra'ash that I am done growing."

F'lorna heard movement. "What was that?"

A yellow torch hovered just outside her hole.

"Someone is out there," Raecli whispered.

"I have found the location!" a shout ricocheted through the forest.

"I don't recognize that voice." F'lorna looked through the Achion hole. Streaks of yellow light interrupted the indigo glow outside. "I see torchlight." She crawled out of her hole and Raecli followed. A man with tan skin and dark hair stood in front of the dwindling hearth fire. His horns had been extracted. He was a Sand-shaper.

He pointed his torch toward F'lorna's face and she blinked from the brightness. Then he moved the torch to Raecli's face and stared intently. "She is here!" he yelled again. "I have found her!"

"What is going on?" F'lorna's father said once he crawled out of his Achion tree. "What are you doing on my land?"

"I was sent by my master to find his granddaughter and I have found her. My master demands that she be returned to him."

F'lorna's mother crawled out and stood beside her husband. "He is a servant of Sahara's father. It is as we feared. I see more torches along the River." She looked toward Raecli. "Your grandfather has sent his servants to take you back to him."

Raecli stumbled back. "I will not go to the Northwestern Coast! I am not a Sand-shaper!"

F'lorna grabbed her friend's hand. "I will not let them take you."

The torchlights in the distance grew brighter. The lights traveled away from the River's edge and upland toward F'lorna's Achion cluster like a band of glowing-eyed predators. F'lorna squinted. "What is that they carry?"

"I can't believe it!" T'maya said. "It is his traveling case. Raecli, your grandfather has come himself to fetch you!"

F'lorna watched the faces of the Sand-shapers grow clearer as the yellow light from their torches overpowered the glow of the Indigo Moon. The traveling case rested upon two great poles protruding from the back and front of the case. Two men on each of the four corners carried the weight of the poles. A large portion of fabric hung on the side of the case, hiding whatever was within. Hornless men walked around the traveling case carrying torches. The heat of their fires became uncomfortable as they entered her Achion cluster. In a moment, F'lorna and her family were surrounded.

The traveling case stopped and the man who had shouted walked to the fabric and slid it to the side, revealing the opening. He reached in and grasped the arm of another. F'lorna watched as an aged, hornless man was carried out of the traveling case and onto the grassy land of her Achion cluster. The servant brought him directly to Raecli. She knew instantly that he was Raecli's grandfather. They had the same light tan skin and violet eyes. His hair had turned silver, though. Raecli's hair had the youthful dark luster of the River flowing at night.

"Did you check her eyes?" the old man asked.

"Yes, they are violet like yours," he said. "The other girl has grey eyes. Did you want them both?"

The aged man looked at F'lorna and shook his head. "No. She is no kin to me." He looked back at Raecli. "It is time for you to come home."

F'lorna desperately held onto Raecli's wrist. "No! You can't take her!"

The grandfather leaned toward F'lorna, his face only a finger's length away from her own. "I was told about you," he whispered, staring into her eyes. "Such a waste."

"Do not speak such words to my daughter," Jaquarn said stepping beside F'lorna.

The grandfather straightened his stance. He looked from Jaquarn to T'maya and then pointed at F'lorna. "Make sure this girl doesn't go to the coast looking for my granddaughter. She's better off staying in this petty village." He looked to his servant. "Get her and put her in with me."

The servant walked to Raecli and stole her into his arms, but F'lorna clutched her wrist.

"No, Father! Stop him!"

"There is nothing I can do, F'lorna," Jaquarn said. "He is her grandfather. She no longer has family in the village. He has the right to take her."

F'lorna looked to her mother, but she had covered her eyes and begun weeping. Suddenly, F'lorna's feet began to slide along the ground as the servant started walking back to the travailing case with Raecli in his arms. "No! She is a River-dweller! She will get Smoke Sickness on the coast. Don't take her from me! Don't take her!" F'lorna held on tighter.

The servant tried to put Raecli into the traveling case, but he couldn't lift the weight of both her and F'lorna. "You must let go!" he shouted.

"Never! Ra'ash, help me!"

"Let go of my granddaughter," the aged man shouted. He looked to Jaquarn. "Make your daughter let go!"

Jaquarn shook his head. "I will not be the one to separate them."

"Fine," he said. Then he pointed at two servants nearest him. "Release this girl's fingers from my granddaughter and keep her away from us."

Two men came up and pulled F'lorna's fingers from Raecli's wrist, releasing her grip. The servant holding Raecli immediately put her in the case. Then he hoisted the old man into the case after her. The men carrying the poles moved quickly away from the Achion cluster.

F'lorna tried to run after the traveling case but the two men blocked her way. Every time she tried to get around them, they would move to prevent her from getting by. "Raecli, come back to me! Don't let them take you away! Find a way to come home! Don't forget me!" She finally fell to her knees weeping. The yellow lights of the torches dissipated and the glow of the

Indigo Moon returned. Raecli and the Sand-shapers were gone. F'lorna felt an ache in her heart, like a giant Achion hole had been dug deep within her.

Chapter 1

THE BUDDING ACHION CLUSTER

F'lorna carefully walked passed the budding Achion trees that marked the entrance to her family's land. Her almost knee-length leather foot coverings padded nimbly along the mossy forest floor, and her

1

lightweight tunic shirt swayed noiselessly against her taupe skin. She wore a muted yellow vest tucked under her tunic belt. It was dyed from the underbelly fibers of the Achion tree. F'lorna reached her right hand along a smooth tree before continuing her walk. Her father had planted these Achion trees on the perimeter of their land during the First Green Moon, the time of her birth. At fourteen, the trees still had a long way to go before reaching their zenith. She envied their lengthy adolescence.

She balanced the tightly woven basket on her head with her left hand, priding herself on the fact that she no longer lost any of the precious water from the River. Her two bound horns had recently stopped growing, so the basket lay steady on their edges. Their light almond color contrasted against her wavy, waist length amber hair, the color of Achion tree sap. The top half of her hair was braided around the horns, keeping them protected and preventing long tendrils of hair from falling across her face. The two braids united under her horns, and the thicker, single braid slid down her back. She could feel the calcification of her horns along the hairline of her scalp, and she looked forward to finally unbinding them.

All too quickly, F'lorna's feet brought her into view of the four large Achion trees that made up her family's hearth. No one knew the exact age of the larger trees, but her father estimated that they have seen several folds of the Six Colored Moons. F'lorna looked up into the Upper Realm and gazed at the First Violet Moon still lingering in the horizon. She loved when the Heat Source and the Violet Moon faced each other every morning and night in their special greeting. She had only seen three colors out of the six moons, since they each circled Rodesh for seven turns, but she decided that the violet color would be her favorite—it matched the hue of Raecli's eyes. Knowing that it would hover over her for one full cycle of seven turns gave her a small sense of peace. She wondered if her friend enjoyed the moon from where she now lived.

"How did the River look, F'lorna?"

F'lorna looked toward the cooking table placed in front of the largest Achion tree where her mother was preparing the morning meal. She liked how her mother's tan shoulders looked against the deep green of her tunic dress dyed from the leaves of the Zulo vine. Her father's skin was paler than hers, and it reddened under the Heat Source's gaze. He wore his tunic sleeves long and stayed under the shade of the Achion trees when the Heat Source progressed across the Upper Realm. Her mother also had linear facial features that reminded F'lorna of the large predator cats that roamed toward the Desert Plains. F'lorna's features were rounder and softer like her father's. She looked a lot like him, although she had her mother's translucent grey eyes, rather than her father's deep blue.

F'lorna noticed that her mother had put down the utensil and was now staring at her. "I think it looked well enough, Mother," F'lorna finally said.

Her mother frowned and stared at F'lorna. "I was hoping you would have a special moment with the Help of Ra'ash while you were out. I sent voiceless words to Him on your behalf. I know He is pursuing you. I sense a powerful destiny for your life beyond what you will allow yourself to envision."

F'lorna sighed. As of late, her mother looked expectantly at her every time she entered her family's Achion cluster. She knew she was disappointing her mother, but there was nothing she could do to change her feelings. The past could not be undone. F'lorna had no answers to offer, so she tried to distract her mother's thoughts. "I saw Father and the Circle of Elders testing the River. I believe there were some Elders from Left River Hook with them as well."

T'maya looked away distracted. "Yes, the River is not as healthy as it should be. Your father is trying to discern if our village is causing the sickness or if the River, as a whole, is not well. They are comparing Left River Hook with Right River Hook to see if the water samples are similar."

F'lorna veered off the feelings of guilt. She hoped that the pain of Raecli being taken from her wasn't causing unease in their village. She had been honest about her feelings; but after almost a full moon turn, she hadn't found resolution. She still longed for her friend, and she struggled with anger against Ra'ash for allowing Raecli's mother to die. If the Smoke Sickness hadn't consumed her, Raecli's grandfather would have had no right to take her best birth friend to the Northwestern Coast to live as a Sand-shaper. She wondered if Raecli's horns had been extracted. She feared that the rest of her Eternal Memory would be wasted on the written symbols.

F'lorna looked at her mother and tried to mask her thoughts. Her mother grew up as a Sand-shaper, and

her Eternal Memory did not hold the *Divine Oracle*.
Instead, it held the written symbols that the Sand-shapers
used to record their Sand-shaper methods. She had
watched her mother try to memorize the *Sacred Songs of
the Prophets and the Holy Images and Chants of
Jeyshen*, but no matter how many times she repeated
them, she could not retain the divine words. F'lorna's
eyes glanced at her mother's two hornless chestnut
braids that traveled the slope of her head to her neck. Her
horns had been extracted when she was a youngling—
another obvious sign that she wasn't raised a River-
dweller. With water and pressure, she had shaped two
smooth branches from the Achion tree to resemble the
horns' descent down the back slope of the head and had
braided her hair around them.

"F'lorna, how is Ra'ash supposed to guide and
help you if your thoughts are not open to Him?" T'maya
asked, pulling F'lorna out of her thoughts.

Wanting to ignore the question, F'lorna slowly
knelt down and slanted her head toward the ground,
lifting the water-tight woven basket off of her bound
horns. "My thoughts are open to Him," she finally said.

"Yes, they may be," T'maya said, as she
retrieved the basket from her daughter's arms and set it
on the cooking table. "But not enough. Your thoughts
dwell with Raecli more."

"I miss her, Mother. She was my closest birth
friend," F'lorna said, hating that tears threatened to
reveal themselves in her eyes.

"Don't you think I miss Raecli's mother? When I
came to Right River Hook, she understood me. She
helped me find my way with Ra'ash. We sang the

Sacred Songs and the Chants of Jeyshen. She tried over and over again to help me memorize the parts of the *Divine Oracle* that she knew. She was taken away from the Sand-shapers by her mother before her Eternal Memory was totally consumed. Even though she still had her horns and I did not, she could relate to the Sand-shaper I once was. We were with child together, and we gave birth to girls in the same week of the First Green Moon—" T'maya paused, taking a few deep breaths in order to calm the tension rising in her throat. "The inhabitants of Rodesh, both Sand-shapers and River-dwellers, cause many wrongs, F'lorna, but the help of Ra'ash always remains good."

F'lorna saw the tears filling her mother's grey eyes. She knew this conversation would lead to sadness. She couldn't understand why her mother kept reopening old wounds. There was never healing—only layering of scars.

"Mother, do you remember the *Sacred Song of Shilon*? She was a prophetess who waited a long time for Ra'ash to give her understanding. You can't rush me, Mother. I can't smile without joy, and I can't rest without peace. I can't pretend that I'm healed—that would be deception. I don't understand why Raecli's mother died of Smoke Sickness. She was a Sand-shaper for not even one full moon cycle. You were a Sand-shaper for over two moon cycles and there is not one drop of Smoke Sickness in you. I'm so grateful that you are well, Mother, but I'm confused why death chooses one and passes over another."

"Don't you think I asked Ra'ash that same question, F'lorna? I don't understand it all, but I know

Raecli's grandfather owns many Sand-shaper mills, and he lives in the most crowded parts of the Northwestern Coast. The smoke is thick there and the waters of the Great Expanse are very sick. I grew up in the Northeastern Mountains where the air was thin and clear. I lived in a little village and shaped small ornaments and jewels, using simple flames for my work. The shaping mills on the Northwestern Coast have raging fires that are difficult to contain. I left the mountains when my mother died and made my way south along the River. I was able to avoid much of the Sand-shaper's smoke."

"And that's where you met Father?" F'lorna asked, probing her mother for details.

"Yes," T'maya whispered. "He was on a spiritual journey being mentored by several Spiritual Elders of different tributary villages along the northern River. He was on his last stop. He didn't like being so far north. He says it is too cold for him. I'm thankful he saw me there at the Pillar of the village. I was lost and alone, and I heard the River-dwellers talk of the Pillar and the voiceless words of Ra'ash. I went to ask Ra'ash if I should try to make a life with the River-dwellers or go to the Northwestern Coast and offer my services at a shaping mill. Ra'ash answered my question by sending your father to me. He asked me if I had received the Indwelling, and I told him that I didn't know what that was."

F'lorna stared at her mother. "I see how Ra'ash has sent His help to you. Dad gave his heart to you that morning."

"Yes, he did. And I gave him mine," T'maya said, wiping her tears. "F'lorna, I understand that healing

7

takes time. But I also know that healing quickens when you seek it. I was asking for help right before I met your father and received the Indwelling. You must do the same." With that she began to scoop water from the basket into three bowls filled halfway with dried grain. She added two colors of small berries and mashed the mixture together. "Here is your morning meal, my daughter," she said, picking up the bowl from the cooking table and presenting it to F'lorna. "Will you be practicing your dance for your Doublemoon Ceremony today?"

"Yes, but I wanted to ensure that I may use my horns. My final dance expresses the Holy Image of the Rebirth of Rodesh," she said, as she received the bowl.

"Which image is that one?" T'maya asked without hesitation.

F'lorna's cheeks immediately flushed and her grey eyes stared into the bowl that she held in her hands. "It's the final image of *Jeyshen Riding the Swarve through the Sphere*, symbolizing when He'll finally come back to declare His rightful place as King of Rodesh." She looked into her mother's eyes. "I offer you my apology of healing, Mother. I should know better."

"Don't be," T'maya said, walking toward her only child and gently clasping her willowy shoulders. "I am forever grateful that your Eternal Memory now holds the *Sacred Songs of the Prophets and the Holy Images and Chants of Jeyshen*. This is the Truth for River-dwellers, and for all Rodeshians, and it must be passed on to each generation of moon children. The *Divine Oracle* will bear much fruit in you. Now, why don't you sit down, so I can take a look at your horns."

8

F'lorna crossed her legs and sat on the ground with her bowl. She quietly ate her food with her washed fingers as her mother unbraided her hair and unwrapped the binding. She knew her mother took much pride in her horns. She painstakingly monitored their growth and adjusted the horn binding to make sure they flattened perfectly—they were a thumb's length above her scalp and a palm's length apart from each other, gliding down the back of her head until they reach the nape of her neck.

"The calcification is not permanently set, F'lorna. How much weight do you intend to put on them?" T'maya asked.

F'lorna took the last bite of her food and chewed slowly, trying to quickly think of a way to present the answer positively. She set the bowl on the ground beside her and cleared her throat. "The weight of my body will be on my horns, but only for a few seconds."

"Dancing is done on the feet, F'lorna, not on the head," T'maya said.

"I know, Mother, but my offering of Adoration tonight at our ceremony is different. I am establishing my maturity and marking my individuality as a Novice Elder. I'm supposed to compose a dance that blends traditional moves with new ones of my own creation. The move I have envisioned has never been done before, but I know it will be the perfect statement for the Holy Image that I have chosen."

F'lorna waited patiently for T'maya's reply. She knew her mother was considering her father's opinion in the matter. T'maya only burdened her father with questions when she was unsure of how he would respond. She didn't want to add to his responsibilities as both Healing and Spiritual Elder of the village.

"You can do the move only if I can braid the horn brace under your horns. You are tall, F'lorna, and strong. You don't have the petite stature of the other dancers. Your horns are still setting, and too much pressure will cause movement and possible bleeding and tearing. I've worked too hard to make your horns perfect, and I won't allow one dance to ruin it."

"I know, Mother. I'll be careful," F'lorna said, hoping the subject would end on the favorable reply.

"Hurry up and get the brace for me, so I won't have to re-braid your hair later," T'maya said.

F'lorna quickly got up and went to the Achion tree that held her sleeping quarters. She jumped into the burrowed hole at the base of the wide tree and felt through the triple layer of shelves chiseled over her fiber-filled mattress. When she found the brace, she crawled back out of the tree and handed it to her mother and sat back down on the ground.

"I know you dislike when I bring this up, F'lorna," T'maya said, tightly weaving her daughter's hair around the brace and her horns. "But you are a singer, not a dancer. You should be singing the *Sacred Songs and the Holy Chants* as your Adoration. Ra'ash has given you a beautiful voice, and I'm saddened that you have taken it for granted. I miss hearing you sing the songs like you did before you began dancing."

"I chose to glorify Ra'ash through dance, Mother. You know," F'lorna said. "You can watch me dance the *Holy Images*. They are just as important as the *Chants and Songs*."

"They are not the same because you have to explain to me which image they represent. You and I both know that you chose dance only because Raecli wanted to sing. F'lorna, you don't squander a gift simply to alleviate tender feelings of a friend. But none of that matters anymore. You should have started singing a turn of a moon ago when she was taken away from us."

"Mother, why are you bruising her memory? Raecli meant more to me than singing. Besides, it was too late for me to train fully in song," F'lorna said, trying to keep her voice calm.

"You are a smart girl. You would have caught up easily," T'maya replied sternly.

F'lorna heard footsteps walking along the forest floor and looked up to see her father stepping into their Achion cluster.

"My wife and my daughter—the echoes of your subtle argument are sure to bounce off every Achion tree in Right River Hook. Are you trying to make the River sick?" Jaquarn said, entering into their cluster of aged Achion trees. He was one of the tallest River-dweller of Right and Left River Hook. F'lorna was already a palm length taller than her mother, and she fervently hoped her height would not match her father's. He wore simple fiber pants and tunic the color of the sunlit Upper Realm on a cool morning.

T'maya sighed and finished tying up her daughter's hair. She walked to the cooking table and mashed up the berries in her husband's bowl of grain. "I offer you my apology of healing. I only wish that F'lorna could see through my eyes."

11

"I also offer you my apology of healing, Father. I had no right to become upset with Mother. I am thankful for her presence in my life, and I don't want to dishonor her," F'lorna said, getting up from the ground and checking the stability of her heavy, amber braids. "But I too wish you could see through my eyes."

"It is impossible to exchange eyes, but Jeyshen has offered His eyes to all of us." Jaquarn smiled. "And only when we see what He sees will we ever have the clear vision of Ra'ash."

"So be it," T'maya said, handing Jaquarn his bowl. "How is the River? Do we need to have the village meet at the Pillar?"

"No, Left River Hook's water samples match ours. The Circle of Elders has also received word that other villages have similar sickness in their tributaries. Some of the North River-dwellers are leaving their hearths to reestablish them further south just before the River disappears into the Desert Plains where the River is the healthiest. The water is becoming too sick along the North River Banks. The Sand-shapers are affecting the waters of the Great Expanse. They are polluting the River with their smoke, and Ra'ash hasn't sent the rains in many phases of the moon. Our tributaries need healing waters to overcome the River's sickness."

"What if Ra'ash doesn't send rain?" T'maya asked. "We can only move so far south until the River fades into the Desert Plains. Nothing lives beyond the desert. How can we survive without healthy water?"

"There is no need to worry, my wife. Ra'ash has His purpose in withholding the rains. But I have a feeling that our next downpour will come in the midst of a mighty storm, so we must be ready."

"Father, is the River's sickness going to affect the Doublemoon Ceremony tonight? My birth friends have all been working so hard on their Adorations for Ra'ash. They would be devastated if the celebration was postponed," F'lorna said.

"F'lorna, there is no need to be alarmed. The River is a little sick, but it doesn't warrant making any immediate changes. When the Heat Source descends from the Upper Realm and the First Violet Moon awakens, we will rejoice over you and all the First Green Moon Children."

F'lorna's worried expression was replaced by a look of urgency. "Father, I need to practice my final dance. May I go to the Village Achion cluster to prepare? I have finished my morning duties."

"Yes, you may after you tell me what the Help of Ra'ash has done for you today," Jaquarn said.

F'lorna faltered. "Father, you know I dislike when you ask me this question."

"I know you do, but it doesn't stop me from asking. I want you to be aware of His help. I don't want you to take His care and guidance for granted."

"You and Mother have both stated that I am taking Ra'ash for granted, and the light has just begun to brighten," F'lorna said, irritably.

"You might want to receive our correction," Jaquarn said, embracing his daughter's chin and tilting it up. "Ra'ash has a wondrous purpose for you, my daughter. But you will miss it if you are not paying attention to His movements. Jeyshen continually offers voiceless words on your behalf."

F'lorna gazed into her father's cobalt eyes. "When I was filling the basket in the River, the current pulled harder than usual. I almost lost the basket, but the River pushed it against a nearby rock hidden just under the water, and I was able to adjust my grip. I filled the basket and returned it back to our hearth undamaged."

"You see, my child, there is no such things as a coincidence. The Help of Ra'ash is always there to guide and help us."

F'lorna smiled up at her father and allowed him to kiss her forehead on the supple skin between her two horns. She got up and placed her bowl in a large, hollowed out Achion stump near her mother's cooking table. She turned to leave, when her mother called to her.

"F'lorna, would you mind dictating a few of the *Sacred Songs* to me when you return to our hearth? I would like to hear them before the ceremony tonight. I know you are busy, but Kytalia is helping with the Doublemoon Ceremony preparations and is unable to come to me today. And your father is meeting with families all afternoon for the individual blessings of your birth friends."

F'lorna saw the resolve in her mother's expression. Her mother always had to ask other Rodeshians to recite the *Divine Oracle* to her. As a child, F'lorna remembered her mother crying to her father when he didn't have time to recite any songs or chants. F'lorna had memorized them early, listening to her father say them to her mother, so she could also bear the burden of reciting them. As F'lorna grew up, her mother had gotten better at asking others, especially when F'lorna's study of dance intensified. Her mother's desire for the *Divine Oracle* had become stronger than her shame of not knowing it.

"Yes, Mother. I'll come back and recite as many as you need," F'lorna said and turned to leave once more. As she walked away from her parents, her mind centered on her father's final words: *"There is no such thing as a coincidence."* She could not prevent the image of Raecli being taken by her grandfather from entering her mind. She was brought to the Northwestern Coast before she had all of the *Divine Oracle* memorized. Had some of her Eternal Memory been given over to the Sand-shapers' symbols? Would she too have to beg like her mother for others to recite the rest of the songs and images to her? If there was no such thing as coincidences, then Ra'ash was to blame for Raecli sudden departure and her mother's lack of the *Divine Oracle*.

Chapter 2

THE WHITE DIAMOND STAG

F'lorna walked briskly away from her family's
Achion cluster, not wanting to hear the call of her
mother demanding for her return. When she finally
made it to the rocky walking path that wound its way to
each Achion cluster of Right River Hook, she slowed her
steps. She had practiced many moon phases on her

16

dance, and she needed only a sliver of the morning to rehearse the final move. Today, she sensed that she needed to encourage her birth friends and diffuse their anxiety. She had been the unspoken leader of the First Green Moon children since before the Green Moon retired to Indigo. She would try to visit them and speak affirmation into them.

The further she walked along the path, the softer the sound of the rushing River became in the distance. She had slept to the gurgle of the River almost every night since her birth. During the few times she had stayed in Raecli's Achion tree, she had difficulty sleeping for lack of the River's noise. Right now, though, the noise of the forest came alive, and she rather liked the distraction. The leaves of the Achion trees softly brushed up against one another, and the wind whispered a secret song along the forest floor and through the shrubs. For a moment, she almost felt completely whole again for the first time since the loss of her best friend.

Suddenly, F'lorna heard a familiar hooting sound resonating through the trees. She instantly stopped. Two seconds later she felt the tickle of a thin airstream zip past her face, and an arrow plunged itself deep into the chest of a White Diamond Stag that was hiding in the thicket to the left of where she stood. The large beast's front legs buckled, and his great spread of horns tangled themselves in the dense netting of underbrush. He tried to release his wide rack, but he only dug the ivory points deeper into web of branches and vines. F'lorna had only seen a White Diamond Stag roaming the lower hills from a distance, and she was surprised that one would wander so close to their village.

As the White Diamond Stag whined and kicked his hind legs, F'lorna heard a soft thump hit the forest floor and quick footsteps racing toward her direction. Lemmeck's black, braided hair flashed into her view. He swiftly grabbed his crystal blade from his tunic belt with his left hand and straddled the beast's back. He put his right forearm under the stag's large jaw and sliced the throat from right to left with his blade, quieting the animal's whines with one rapid movement. He wore russet colored pants and tunic to blend in with the outer bark of the Achion trees. His tawny skin was only a few shades lighter than the color of his clothing.

F'lorna listened as Lemmeck chanted Jeyshen's words of sacrifice. She liked to hear the bass voice of her birth friend. He had the finest male voice in both Left and Right River Hook, though he would never embrace such a title. Lemmeck was a hunter, and, unless his voice was required for ceremony, he only used it to offer up the life-source of his prey. F'lorna noticed that he no longer wore his horn bindings. His dark, thick hair was divided into thin braids, pulled back and bound tightly together at the nape of his neck, exposing the full distance of his two flattened, almond-colored horns. River-dweller males did not hide the tops of their horns under braids as the females traditionally did. F'lorna looked back at the beautiful beast lying on the forest floor. This kill would solidify Lemmeck's Adoration to Ra'ash as a hunter and his position as a Novice Elder of Right River Hook.

"So may it be," Lemmeck finally whispered.

18

"So may it be," F'lorna repeated and waited a moment while Lemmeck dismounted the animal. "Ra'ash has honored you with a rare animal. I have never seen one so close. Its silver mane is more beautiful than I realized. I can see the Six Colored Moons shimmering on the strands like translucent crystals. Your offering of Adoration tonight will be truly favored."

Lemmeck's calm smile could not hide his excitement. "I have been trailing this animal since before the Violet Moon started its descent yesterday evening to the lower hills. The Help of Ra'ash has guided me, though my patience was greatly tested. As he came closer into our village, I worried that another hunter would harvest him. I was pleased he came past your family's Achion cluster first because I know your father does not hunt."

"Why is he so close to the village? They usually stay protected in the lower hills," F'lorna asked. She knew the White Diamond Stag would create much discussion at the Doublemoon Ceremony tonight.

"I don't know why he came so close to our village except that it was the Help of Ra'ash. He drank the River's waters near the Pillar and continued through the brush. He is full grown, but not toughened like the older Diamond Stags. I am glad I will not have to dry his meat. I will offer it to the village for our Doublemoon Ceremony this evening," Lemmeck said, wiping his blade on a large leaf, exposing the rare violet color of the Tarnezion crystal. "My father will be well pleased that I have solidified my Adoration as a hunter with such a beautiful and mighty animal. The Help of Ra'ash has been especially good to me."

19

"Yes," F'lorna agreed. "I assume that you have received your Doublemoon gift," she said, motioning her chin to the blade he held.

"My mother and father gave it to me almost a moon phase ago when I began hunting for my offering of Adoration," he said, holding up the blade. "It matches the color of the Violet Moon under which we will celebrate."

"Your father will be honored that you used the Tarnezion blade on your first kill as a hunter," F'lorna said. "I believe this stag will more than feed entire village tonight at the ceremony. They may have to dry some of the meat after all."

"Twice I owe you my deepest gratitude," Lemmeck said, placing his blade back into a small, thin pouch on his tunic belt. His booted feet tread softly toward F'lorna, and he reached out his left hand to gently squeeze her right shoulder in greeting.

F'lorna usually felt uncomfortable about her height, but Lemmeck stood several thumb lengths above her. She enjoyed not having to slouch or look down during their conversation. "Why have I received your gratitude twice?" she asked, curious of how her presence played into the hunt.

"My eyes tried to get a secure aim on the stag, but he continued his walk along the brush, and I was unable to find a clear shot. I knew this White Diamond Stag was strong, and he would overpower my arrow if I didn't achieve a direct hit to the heart. But my view was blocked, and I didn't want to waste my arrow on chance," Lemmeck said, his emerald colored eyes reflecting bright against his tawny skin. His eyes were the color of his grandmother's—a color that was rare since *The Great Engulfing,* which took a fourth of all Rodeshians. "But you came through the clearing and startled him right as he walked into a line of low brush. He froze long enough for me to let my arrow fly."

"I'm glad the Help of Ra'ash sent me your way," she said in earnest, receiving the compliment with a slight bow of her head. "How have I helped a second time?" she asked.

Lemmeck exhaled and grinned. "You stopped when I hooted the signal. I hooted just before I released my arrow, so I was not sure whether you had heard and reacted. I gave voiceless words that Ra'ash would halt your feet, and He did just that."

F'lorna's smile faded slightly. Although the hooted signal to stop was well known even to younglings, the signal was not always received, since the wind could capture the sound and disperse it amongst the leaves. Usually, the signal was given several times before the hunter released the arrow. "You put a lot of faith into my ears for hearing your signal and into Ra'ash's ears for hearing your request," she said, noticing that Lemmeck's eyes did not flicker from her subtle rebuke.

"I offer you my apology of healing. I know I may appear careless, but, somehow, I knew Ra'ash would protect you. I've never felt a certainty about the unknown before, and if the peace hadn't been so real, I might have not trusted it. I felt Ra'ash giving me permission to let the arrow fly."

"You have become confident in hearing from Ra'ash. This is not the friend that I have known who

21

struggled to hear His voiceless words," F'lorna said, "You have changed." She felt a swimming feeling in her mid-section. "Have you received the Indwelling?"

Lemmeck hesitated a moment before speaking. "Honestly, I'm a little embarrassed to discuss my struggle, but if Ra'ash would use my journey to help you, so may it be. You know how I look up to my older brothers?"

F'lorna nodded. She knew that Dashion and Rashion were twins of the Yellow Moon Children. They were notorious along the South River tributaries as two of the best huntsmen around. The girls of Left and Right River Hook and of surrounding tributaries admired them. Their height, handsome looks, tawny skin and golden eyes and superior marksmanship fueled the esteem of others and caused their names to be well known for a great distance. But instead of shining under such praise, the twins were happy to lead quiet lives hunting or resting in the Achion cluster of their family's hearth. Their hearth and surrounding lands stretched out a walk that would take the full rise and fall of the Heat Source. They lived on the other side of the River and the farthest from the Village Achion cluster.

Lemmeck thought for a moment and continued. "They received the Indwelling at a very young age—before they started training their Eternal Memories on the *Divine Oracle*. Mother and Father were discussing *Jeyshen and the Holy Chants*, and Dashion received the Indwelling and shortly after Rashion did as well. All my life, I've felt this need to be like them, and when I began training my Eternal Memory, I did everything possible to force the Indwelling. I carried much heaviness, and I feared the River would become sick from my worry. Almost a moon phase ago, I finally went to the Pillar and confessed my anxieties, but instead of feeling dishonor, I felt peace and acceptance, like Ra'ash was drawing me to Him. I told Ra'ash that I could never be my brothers, and I felt His voiceless words whisper that He created me for a different purpose."

Lemmeck paused and reached for his blade and carefully handed it to F'lorna. "Later that evening, I went back to my Achion cluster, and my father and mother had my Doublemoon gift waiting for me in my Achion tree. My father made me the blade from the Tarnezion Crystal that my uncle brought back from his travels to the Northeastern Mountains. I knew it was the Help of Ra'ash letting me know that He was pleased with me. The next morning, I went back to the Pillar and sang Jeyshen's Chant of Rebirth. Then I continued my hunt, passing up many animals in order to find a truly special offering for my Doublemoon Ceremony. And finally, on the last rise before our ceremony, I have shot a White Diamond Stag. I know of no one who has ever presented one as their Adoration to Ra'ash at their Doublemoon Ceremony."

"Nor have I," F'lorna agreed, returning the blade back to Lemmeck. "I didn't realize that you were struggling. I should have noticed."

"Please do not claim my heaviness," Lemmeck said, placing his left hand on F'lorna's shoulder again. "The process of receiving the Indwelling is different for all of us." Lemmeck's emerald eyes centered on F'lorna. "My biggest mistake was trying to walk down my brothers' path to Jeyshen."

"I wish you would speak so to my mother," F'lorna whispered.

"Your mother loves you greatly. We all see it. Maybe that is why she pushes you. Allow her to unburden the weight of her worries, but make sure to give the heaviness to Ra'ash. He is very patient, and His moment with you will come when it's time."

F'lorna was surprised by Lemmeck's words. She realized how his struggle with heaviness had affected his confidence in Ra'ash over the last few phases of the moon. Lemmeck now talked with certainty and boldness, and F'lorna felt awkward under his assertive gaze. She looked down, feeling her cheeks heat with color. "Thank you for your kind words. I set out to encourage my birth friends, but instead I have been encouraged."

Lemmeck smiled. "Allow me to dedicate the White Diamond Stag to you and your family tonight, for without your assistance, I would not have such a grand offering of Adoration at our Doublemoon Ceremony."

F'lorna's blush deepened. "I would be honored," she said, turning her eyes to the stag. She felt a cool breeze ascend from around the Achion trees and hoped it would taper the color rising in her cheeks. "Would you like help skinning the stag?" she asked.

"No, this stag represents my Adoration for Ra'ash. I must do it alone."

"Yes, I offer you my apology of healing. I know that hunting is your Adoration. You have your blade and now you have your stag. When my mother discovers she will have White Diamond Stag to prepare for the Doublemoon feast, she will be well pleased," F'lorna said.

"It will not be too late for your mother and our cooking birth friends to prepare it?" Lemmeck asked.

"No, but we need to let her know soon. I am sure she will enjoy helping her cooking pupils create a new recipe for it. I will tell her when I return from practicing my final dance," F'lorna said. "She has asked me to recite some of the *Sacred Songs* to her when I get to our hearth."

"Thank you for alerting her of my harvest," he said. "Have you not received your Doublemoon gift yet?" Lemmeck asked, looking over F'lorna's body for something he hadn't noticed.

F'lorna shook her head. "No, they have said nothing of it. I know my parents believe that my offering of Adoration to Ra'ash tonight should be singing. They are still disappointed I chose dancing when all of the First Green Moon Children selected their Adorations. During the Sixth and Seventh Indigo Moon turns and now even into this First Violet Moon turn, my parents have resisted dancing as my Adoration."

Lemmeck said nothing and looked back down at his White Diamond Stag.

"Why do you say nothing, Lemmeck? Do you agree with my parents?" F'lorna asked.

Lemmeck looked back into F'lorna's grey eyes. "Do you remember when we and our birth friends were eleven turns of the moon, and we were being mentored in each of the Adorations for a time? It was during the Fifth Indigo Moon turn."

F'lorna felt the swimming of anxiety in her stomach again. "Yes," she whispered.

"Raecli was not with us that morning, and you seemed so lost without your closest birth friend. The mentor asked you to sing one of the *Sacred Songs of the Prophets*, and you chose the *Foreshadowing of Jeyshen*," Lemmeck paused watching F'lorna's reaction. "When you sang, all of the mentors and our birth friends stopped to listen. And the Elders of our village made their way to your voice. I remember seeing tears— even the younglings stopped playing, soothed by the sound of your voice. As I reflect on it now, it was as if the breath of Ra'ash descended on us."

"Yes, I remember that moment. Raecli stayed at her Achion cluster with her mother. It was the first sign that she had Smoke Sickness."

Lemmeck shook his head. "You see what you are doing? I'm speaking of a spiritual moment with Ra'ash and all you focus on is your pain. The Adorations are not for us to choose. Ra'ash knows what we were created for. He designed each of us to serve our village in a special way."

"Your voice is the best of all the male First Green Moon Children, yet you are to be a Hunting Elder," F'lorna said defensively.

"Singing is my second Adoration to Ra'ash, and I do use my voice when asked. Someday I may use it more, but now I know Ra'ash has chosen me to be a hunter," Lemmeck said and pointed to the fallen stag on the forest floor. "You see this White Diamond Stag? It may be my Adoration to Ra'ash, but it is for the entire village. You must choose the Adoration that will best serve those around you, not just a single friend."

"But I can dance the *Holy Images of Jeyshen*. They are an important part of the *Divine Oracle*," F'lorna stated, forcing her voice to stay steady.

"Yes, you are a good dancer, but we do not feel the breath of Ra'ash like we do when you sing."

"I feel nothing of Ra'ash," F'lorna said. "Not when I dance, sing, eat, nor when I go to the Pillar—He's nowhere for me."

"Was He there for you when you sang the *Sacred Song* when we were eleven?"

"I don't know," F'lorna whispered. "All I remember is that Raecli was not there, and I was sad."

"You are a good friend, F'lorna. But Raecli has been gone since the Indigo Moon began its final turn across the Upper Realm."

"Is it wrong to love a friend?" F'lorna asked.

"No, Ra'ash wants us to love. I just feel that there is no room for Ra'ash when your eyes are full of Raecli."

F'lorna looked toward the north. She felt the pain of her loss more deeply now than ever. The sadness no longer felt like a sharp wound as it had before. It was now a deep throb. She wanted to be angry with Lemmeck, but she knew her birth friend spoke to her with his heart. She wouldn't rebuke him after he had shared his own heaviness with her. "I must go practice my final dance one more time."

Lemmeck nodded his head. "But before you go, may I request you as a witness for my kill? Report it to your father and mother as my witness."

"Yes," F'lorna said, finally able to return the stare of Lemmeck's penetrating, emerald eyes. "I will

27

confirm the news to my father and mother, and I will be honored to be your witness."

"Thank you," Lemmeck said and turned toward the White Diamond Stag lying motionless where it fell. He squatted next to the ivory rack and carefully sectioned out three fingers thick of the stag's silver mane, slicing the hair just above the animal's neck. He knotted the hair in the middle and walked back to F'lorna. "I hope that you will accept this gift of my gratitude."

F'lorna's eyes widened, and her body momentarily froze. She had to force her hands to receive the gift. The silver main of the White Diamond Stag was greatly valued because of its beauty and scarcity. "Thank you, Lemmeck," F'lorna managed to say in a hushed voice.

"Ra'ash has provided favor to us both today," Lemmeck said, obviously pleased with his decision. "I will see you when the Heat Source whispers goodnight to the Violet Moon. May the Help of Ra'ash always be with you," he finished and turned back toward his stag.

"And may the Help of Ra'ash always be with you," she whispered back to her birth friend who had transformed in a single phase of a moon.

F'lorna gently placed the precious silver mane into a pouch on her tunic belt and continued her walk. When she looked at the morning horizon, she no longer saw the Violet Moon. She realized that she needed to move quickly. She wanted to get to the Village Achion cluster before the other dancers of the First Green Moon Children got there. She didn't want them to see her final dance that she had created to honor Jeyshen. They had agreed to offer their Adorations alone on the village platform. She wanted to practice her dance uninfluenced by the opinions of others. The secret of her dance felt beautiful and pure, and she would offer it to Ra'ash as a symbol of the trust that she desired but couldn't seem to maintain. Maybe then He would answer her pleas for the return of her birth friend.

Her pace quickened on the dense forest floor, and she easily jumped over the large Achion roots that threaded through the top layer of earth. Although she enjoyed the physical elements of dance, the free-flow run through the woodland breeze caused her eyes to brighten and her expression to relax with enjoyment. She heard the soft whistle of an Achion bird and noticed its yellow feathers streaking through the forest pallet of browns and greens next to her. When her eyes captured its tiny frame, the bird fluttered up into the gold rays of the Heat Source.

F'lorna stopped and gazed in awe as the yellow of the bird connected with the blue of the Upper Realm, and she wondered how it would feel to fly into the vaulted heights above. Her mind suddenly stumbled on an image of Jeyshen strapped to the expanding Sphere, rising into the Upper Realm. She thought of his limbs ripping slowly apart just before His body plummeted to the watery Great Expanse below, painting the blue horizon with the red of His blood. How could she embrace beauty within such a horrible death? What did the others see in the blood-mixed waters that moved them to gratitude and joy? She tried to quiet the heaviness that Lemmeck's words created within her. Her journey to Ra'ash was at a standstill.

29

Chapter 3

A HURTING WHISPER

As F'lorna neared the Village Achion cluster, she heard the voices of her three singing birth friends gliding through the branches. She was disappointed that she hadn't been the first to arrive for practice but honored to hear each tender note rise into the air. Even though the voices rolled together like liquid, she could identify every intonation and imagine each singer's face in her mind. She didn't want to interrupt them, so she treaded quietly along the tree line that circled the large Achion cluster. She would sneak into the back of the partially enclosed wooden platform and quietly rehearse her final move as her birth friends continued to sing. Hopefully, she would only need a few practices, so she could make herself available to her friends for encouragement and support before their offerings of Adoration tonight. She knew that if she could focus on her friends, she would push the hurt of Raecli to the aching backdrop of her mind.

F'lorna took off her tunic belt and gently laid it on the floor next to the wall. Then she leaned forward extending her arms to the floor. She needed to stretch the long muscles of her legs before she began to use them in her complicated final move. She had always been the tallest of her female birth friends and taller than many of her male birth friends. Many of them, especially the girls, stopped growing several moon phases ago. Some had even stopped more than a moon turn ago, but she kept rising upward. Each night she had to monitor how far she bent over to get into the burrowed hole of her Achion tree. She struck her horns too many times to count because she underestimated her height. She feared that her body still had several finger lengths left to climb, but she was relieved to notice that many of the boys, like Lemmeck, still continued to grow as well.

She brought her torso back up and rolled her shoulders several times. She was glad that she had retrieved the water from the River earlier that morning. Her limbs felt warmed from the exercise. She finally stilled her body and quieted her mind. She began to envision each dance move of her offering from the beginning to end, but she didn't move her muscles. Every movement was etched in the Eternal Memory of her mind and her body would respond exactly. As the

31

dance unveiled itself in her imagination, she felt her pulse begin to rise. The final move was close—the image of *Jeyshen Riding the Swarve through the Sphere.* This is the move that she needed to practice—it was one of her own design. She would place her horns to the floor of wooden platform and use the force of her legs to spin her inverted body. After crossing her feet at the ankles and bending her knees into the shape of a sphere, she would push her arms away from her torso, symbolizing Jeyshen's flying Swarve. Finally, the Sphere would explode, and her feet would uncross in one decisive move. Then she would push off the ground with her hands and whip her legs back to the floor in her closing stance.

The dance in her mind came to the final moment, and she leaned forward pressing her flattened horns firmly on the wood planked floor. She spun her legs and crossed them at the ankles, keeping her knees bent. As she pushed her arms horizontally, the spin of her body slowed until at the right moment she pressed her palms to the ground and forced her legs back, landing nimbly on her feet. Her final move played out perfectly and the brace for her horns had taken much of her weight. She felt breathless yet elated. She quickly looked toward the opening to see if anyone had seen her. She noticed that the singing hadn't yet stopped. Her body made very little noise, which was a sign that she was ready for her offering of Adoration to Ra'ash tonight. She would honor her family at her Doublemoon Ceremony and prove to everyone including herself she would become a Dancing Elder. She could lead many spiritual meetings with that skill and mentor the younglings how to display the *Holy Images of Jeyshen* with their bodies.

F'lorna slowed her breathing and thought about practicing the final move again, but she heard the singing had finally stopped and she could hear her birth friends chatting at the entrance to the enclosure. She wanted to greet them before they ran off to their Achion clusters to get ready for the ceremony tonight. She quietly walked to the entrance but stopped when she heard the name of her stolen friend being whispered.

"I wish Raecli hadn't left," a voice that F'lorna knew to be Sage said. "Our harmony sounds too light. We need a deeper voice to balance us." F'lorna envisioned Sage in her mind. Her skin was a darker shade than Lemmeck's—more like an umber color, but her hair was a silken burgundy, like the reddish-purple veins threading through Coleus leaves. And her eyes were the light green color of the moss that padded the forest floor.

"Too bad Lemmeck doesn't want to sing with us. His voice would pair nicely with mine," laughed Zelara.

F'lorna cringed when she heard Zelara's voice. She was new to Right River Hook, and no matter how F'lorna tried to be nice, Zelara was never more than indifferent toward her. Zelara's family was wealthy and moved to Right River Hook from the northern tributaries. She and her family had taken Raecli's Achion cluster after her grandfather took her away. F'lorna had heard from her father that Zelara's family moved when the River up north became too sick. Raecli's land was small, so Zelara's father demanded more acreage along the River. He was a Fishing Elder

33

and brought a variety of fertile eggs and small fish to populate the tributaries of Right River Hook with new, hardier species. The Elders conceded and gave him several communal acres along the River—land that was meant for the entire village to enjoy was now privately owned. F'lorna wouldn't admit it, but her family had acquired the most land along the River up to that point, and she thought it was unfair that newcomers could take so much so quickly.

The conversation continued, and F'lorna fixed a serene expression on her face. She would not allow one Rodeshian to destroy her desire to encourage her birth friends. She waited patiently for a pause in the conversation, so she could enter the group nonchalantly.

"You just like him, Zelara. We all know how you swoon over his emerald eyes and his dark, handsome features. Besides his Adoration is hunting, not singing," said Shalane.

"I know he's a hunter. Anyway, we don't need his voice. I think we sound wonderful. In fact, I think we are the best singers in all of Right and Left River Hook," Zelara said, confidently.

F'lorna heard Shalane agree with Zelara's self-assured statement.

"You haven't heard F'lorna sing. She has a deep voice like Raecli's, except hers radiates like the Indigo Moon at its zenith," said Sage. "Or at least that's what my older sister, Blaklin, says. She's a storyteller and is staying at Left River Hook because she's being courted by a young villager there. She tells me the story whenever the villages get together and she sees F'lorna dancing instead of singing. When we were in our eleventh moon turn, I remember when she sang one of the *Sacred Songs*—or *Holy Chants*—I can't remember which, and it was as though even the River hushed to hear her voice. We were sure she was going to be a singer, but Raecli wanted to sing, so F'lorna chose to dance instead."

"Why would she care what someone else chose? If she was that good, she would have chosen to sing as her Adoration," Zelara said. "I think you were young and foolish when you heard her sing—and your sister is prone to exaggeration—she is a storyteller. That is not an official Adoration of Right River Hook. Your childish memory has amplified her talent."

"It is an Adoration," Sage protested. "We just don't have a mentor for it in our village, which is why she went to Left River Hook."

"I was bored and being mentored in the Cooking Adoration," Shalane added. "I remember our mentor stopped in the middle of her cooking demonstration with a boiling pot when she heard F'lorna's voice."

F'lorna was relieved when she heard Shalane agreeing with Sage's statement. She hadn't realized that her birth friends had so many opinions about her and her voice. No one had mentioned her singing, and she never thought to discuss it. The past moon turn was difficult without Raecli, and she realized that due to her sorrow, she had neglected many of her other friendships.

"Raecli's mother got the Smoke Sickness just before we chose our Adorations to Ra'ash. Some of our birth friends think that F'lorna chose to dance so that she wouldn't overshadow Raecli's voice," Sage added. "She had already lost her father, and now she was losing her mother. F'lorna might have not wanted to cause her friend any more pain."

Zelara laughed. "That's why she chose the Dancing Adoration? She looks so silly when she offers her Adoration. She's too big. I keep waiting for her to strike the other two girls in their noses or knock them on their horns when they practice."

F'lorna froze when the other girls laughed.

"She is very tall," Shalane agreed. "But I do think she dances well for her size."

"You're are just saying that because her father is the Spiritual Elder and Healing Elder. If he didn't have two important roles in this village, the villagers would not allow F'lorna to dance. She takes up too much space and the other girls have to be a tree's length away from her just so they don't get in her way," Zelara said.

"Jaquarn is one of the most respected Healing Elders in our area, but I do not believe that it changes how we treat F'lorna," Sage said.

"He may be a good healer, but my father doesn't believe he should be the Spiritual Elder. It is not right that he can offer two such important Adorations for the village. His wife is a Sand-shaper. She doesn't even have her horns. I know she braids her hair over long sticks to look like us, but her Eternal Memory is lost. She has to beg the widow to describe the *Holy Images* and recite the *Chants of Jeyshen* and the *Songs of the Prophets* to her. How can she be the wife of a Spiritual Elder? I'm surprised she hasn't fallen to the Smoke Sickness, like all Sand-shapers do."

F'lorna could no longer listen to the Zelara's hateful chatter. She came out from her hiding spot. "You utter hurtful words about my family," she said to Zelara. "I have only offered you peace and kindness, yet you never receive my gestures of goodwill."

Zelara swung her long ebony braids behind her as she turned to stare at F'lorna. Her dark, soil-colored eyes gleamed like the River at nightfall and her skin was the exact shade as F'lorna's mother's skin. She wore a lavender tunic dress—a color only possible with the petals from the flowers found in the northern tributaries. She could see why the boys were taken with Zelara's beauty.

"You think you offered me goodwill, yet you only wish to make me one of your subordinates. I see how you walk around the Achion clusters like you are the Elder of your birth friends. But you are not the leader of me or my family. Where I come from, my father has always been in charge."

"But your father is a Fishing Elder, not a Spiritual Elder," F'lorna said.

"My father says that Spiritual Elders are antiquated and have no use in the villages today. We don't need a Spiritual Elder if we have our Eternal Memories. There is no need for a communal Shoam-sha. We can do them in our own Achion clusters."

F'lorna couldn't believe what Zelara was saying. "The Shoam-sha is the core of Jeyshen's teachings. We can't simply change His words to suit our own desires."

Zelara crossed her arms. "You simply have one interpretation of His Chants, which suits your family because your father is the Spiritual Elder. Of course, he would teach that the Shoam-sha was still necessary. But our village in the north did not require it. In fact, our

Spiritual Elder was content with the offerings the villagers gave him and he left us alone."

F'lorna's grey eyes burned at what she heard. "Then maybe that is why your family had to move. Your village built up so much disorder that you tainted your tributary, and now you are making the rest of the River sick!"

Zelara leaned her head back and laughed again, letting her long ebony hair sway against her lavender tunic. "We can't make the River sick simply by carrying negative feelings. It's the Sand-shapers fault for polluting the waters of the Great Expanse that feed the River. And now some of those very same Sand-shapers are moving away from the Northwestern Coast and into our Achion clusters. If anyone is causing disorder, it is them! In our old village, they were always begging villagers to recite the *Divine Oracle* to them. My father finally took a stand against them. If they don't have the Eternal Memory, they can't be Children of Ra'ash!"

"How do you say all this? All Rodeshians are Children of Ra'ash if they have the Indwelling. My mother doesn't have the Eternal Memory, but she is a Child of Ra'ash. She hears His voiceless words and offers up her own to Him!" F'lorna yelled.

"The Indwelling was a myth created by Rodeshians during a time of hardship and separation. That myth is not needed today. We can use our Adorations for Ra'ash without such fables. There is no need to distinguish ourselves from others if we have the Eternal Memory of the *Divine Oracle*. That is the real proof that we are truly Children of Ra'ash."

"You may have the Eternal Memory and my mother may not, but she knows more about the *Holy Images and Chants of Jeyshen* than you ever will!" F'lorna shouted. She hovered over Zelara and for the first time she embraced her full height. Zelara flinched back in surprise.

F'lorna continued to yell. "The Eternal Memory is a matter of the mind. We can activate it or not. But the Indwelling is a matter of the heart. It is why Jeyshen was strapped to the Sphere and Expanded, so we could be Ra'ash's Children and have His Indwelling."

"If you know so much about this Indwelling," Zelara touted. "When did you receive it?"

F'lorna paused and her face flushed with guilt. She stepped back away from Zelara.

"F'lorna, you should calm down," whispered Sage, walking in between F'lorna and Zelara. "I've never seen you so upset."

"Yes, F'lorna," Zelara interjected. "You need to be open-minded, but I know it may be difficult because your father is the Spiritual Elder of Right River Hook. My father speaks openly about those childish myths, like Indwelling and the communal Shoam-sha. I don't need those things to know who Jeyshen is. I have the *Divine Oracle* stored right here," Zelara said, pointing to her temple. "In my Eternal Memory."

"My parents have been listening to Zelara's father," Shalane said. "Much of what he says has opened their eyes to different possibilities. Maybe there isn't an Indwelling. Maybe we don't have to listen to voiceless words from Ra'ash. If that's true, all we need is our Eternal Memories."

39

"Either way, we are all entitled to our own opinion, and we must respect the opinions of others," Sage added, staring from Zelara to F'lorna. "And we should not be offering these mean words at the Village Achion cluster just before our Doublemoon Ceremony."

"What good is the Eternal Memory and the *Divine Oracle* if we don't have the Indwelling to lead us in them?" F'lorna asked, not wanting to give up. "Having something doesn't mean we will know how to use it."

"I would prefer to do my own Shoam-sha by myself. I don't want a Spiritual Elder to lead me," Zelara said and smiled. "That way I can do what I want with my Eternal Memory and choose the parts of the *Divine Oracle* that I like most. Honestly, some of it just seems like rubbish to me."

F'lorna faced her birth friends. She had never heard them talk like this before. She didn't know if Zelara had been influencing their thinking or if they never discussed their true thoughts around her. She knew that she needed to neutralize the situation, so her birth friends wouldn't carry turmoil into the ceremony tonight. She had always felt responsible for them, but after today, she didn't know if they needed or even wanted her concern. "I offer you my apology of healing. I should have never allowed these words to wander so far. Please do not carry any ill feelings from this moment. I look forward to watching your Adorations to Ra'ash when the Violet Moon ascends tonight. I know you will each please Jeyshen. I ask that the Help of Ra'ash guide you."

F'lorna did not wait to listen the responses of her birth friends. She stepped passed the village Achion

cluster and disappeared into the foliage surrounding
them. She veered off the main walking path of the
village, so she could avoid running into others. She
didn't want to talk. She had very few hours left to sort
through her feelings. She tried to locate why she felt
hurt. Was it Zelara's words about her mother and father?
Was it Shalane's defense of Zelara's new ideas? She
needed to find the reason why her spirit saddened so
quickly or it would nag at her, inhibiting her best
offering tonight. She paused for a moment and leaned
against the large, old Achion stump. *What was it? Why
did her spirit grieve?*

She replayed the conversation in her mind, and a
thought suddenly rose up like an air pocket bursting
along the water's current. Her birth friends used their
Eternal Memory of the *Divine Oracle* as a means to feel
superior. The image of her mother came to her mind's
eye. Her mother longed to have the *Divine Oracle* etched
into her memory, so she could meditate on the *Sacred
Songs and Holy Images and Chants* without assistance
from others. But her mother's memory had been filled
with the Sand-shaper's written symbols, so now she was
dependent on others. She could never worship Jeyshen
alone, which was exactly what Zelara wanted to do.

Chapter 4

THE DOUBLEMOON CEREMONY

F'lorna followed her father and mother's methodical footsteps down the stone path to the village Achion cluster. She wore a grey tunic to match the color of her eyes and a red vest jacket tucked under her tunic belt. No one spoke. Her parents had given her a Doublemoon gift, and after her Adoration tonight she would be a Novice Elder as a dancer. When she came back to her Achion cluster from that morning's final practice for her Adoration, she found the gift on her mattress, and her father gave her the Doublemoon blessing. It was a new pair of leather foot coverings for dancing. They looked so long and thin compared to the other dancers. She looked down at her feet while she walked behind her parents. Her feet seemed huge next to the small rocks that lined the path. She wondered why she had never noticed before. Zelara's words continued to penetrate her mind. She was a big, silly dancer.

"It looks like it may rain tonight," T'maya said. "Thanks to Ra'ash we do need water to purify the River, but I fear it may interrupt the Doublemoon Ceremony. I know that your birth friends have been working diligently on their offerings of Adorations to Ra'ash."

"T'maya, my dear, we must never fear. We can believe that Ra'ash knows exactly what He is doing even if it doesn't make sense to us. Tonight, we will honor the First Green Moon Children as Novice Elders of our village, and Ra'ash will bring forth their Doublemoon Ceremony as He wills it. Besides," Jaquarn said looking up. "I doubt the rains will come until we are all asleep in our Achion trees."

"I hope you are right," T'maya said with uncertainty in her voice.

Trying to ease the tension, her father spoke again. "I'm honored by Lemmeck's expression of dedication to our family. I know that the White Diamond Stag he harvested will add great favor to the First Green Moon Children's Ceremony tonight. I must say that I gave many voiceless words to Ra'ash on his behalf. His brothers are so well known, and I know personally what it feels like to be a sapling in the shade of a greater sibling. But I concede that the twins have never killed something as rare as the White Diamond Stag. Ra'ash must have great plans for Lemmeck."

"Will my father's sister be able to attend the ceremony tonight?" F'lorna asked. Her aunt had never joined with a mate and had no younglings of her own, and she had replaced F'lorna's lack of grandparents in her life.

"Yes, Eline sent word that she would be here. She made it to Left River Hook three moon rises ago to help the Healing Elder there, but she'll be here for your ceremony. She is probably already seated at our table at the Village Achion cluster. This is also a special night for her. Today she will celebrate a life of Twofolds of the Six Colored Moons. She is a child of the First Violet Moon two Twofolds passed," Jaquarn said. "She will have acquired eighty-four turns. My mother was well past her Onefold when I came along, and Eline was already a renowned Healing Elder by then. My father was very surprised when Mother became heavy with me."

"She does not appear to be as aged as other Twofolds I have met. She says that the plants she eats help her to stay strong and youthful. I know my Eternal Memory doesn't have the *Divine Oracle*, but it would be so nice to at least have something useful there, like Eline's plant knowledge. Anything would be better than the useless Sand-shaper symbols," T'maya said.

"My dear wife, you act like you have no memory at all. You have your daily memory that comes with habit and environment. You are a Cooking Elder, you have gained much knowledge already about plants and their flavors and uses. In fact, I believe you are the best Cooking Elder in all of Right River Hook."

T'maya smiled. "The villagers like the interesting blend of flavors that I use. Mixing what I know as a Sand-shaper and what I learned as a River-dweller has allowed my cooking to be distinctive. But I would give up all my daily knowledge just to have even one of Jeyshen's chants memorized."

"Do not say that, my wife. You know that F'lorna and I are here to recite them to you, and Kytalia looks forward to offering you chants in exchange for your meals," Jaquarn said.

T'maya nodded. "I know, but without the *Divine Oracle* in here," she said pointing to her hornless forehead, "understanding of Ra'ash is much harder to maintain. It is like I am missing the vine that binds everything together. I feel as though I have to hold all the knowledge with my own strength, constantly having to organize and stack the memories, like stacking the washed soup bowls after a village Shoam-sha. And only when I beg someone to tell me the *Divine Oracle* does everything make sense. And for the short moment as they speak the *Sacred Songs of the Prophets and the Holy Images and Chants of Jeyshen* everything becomes clear and beautiful and easy. And when I lost Sahara, I lost the only one who understood my struggle."

F'lorna stared at her mother. She rarely mentioned Raecli's mother's name, but she knew she grieved her loss. When she died, F'lorna watched her mother lose consciousness the moment she heard the news. The following morning, F'lorna chose dance as her Adoration to Ra'ash. Raecli was taken away less than a moon phase later.

F'lorna stopped walking when she saw the light of the Doublemoon Ceremony ahead. "Why must we decide on our Adorations at such a young age? Can we really know how we will best serve our village with only fourteen turns of the moon?"

Jaquarn stopped and walked toward his daughter. Her bound horns were just under chin level to him. "Usually, the gifts of Ra'ash can be seen in each youngling if we look closely enough. They are drawn to different Adorations because they are passionate about them or the Adorations are offered in their own Achion clusters," Jaquarn said. "But is it not unusual for someone to change their Adoration after their Doublemoon Ceremony. Some villagers have several Adorations, like me. The Doublemoon Ceremony is simply the beginning—a demonstration of love to Ra'ash and the community."

"You sang at yours, father?" F'lorna asked, knowing the answer but needing to stop time. She didn't want to enter the Village Achion cluster with so much confusion in her spirit.

"Yes, because singing was easy for me, but I wanted more than to simply sing, which is why I became a Spiritual Elder and now a Healing Elder thanks to my older sister who practiced teaching plants on me when I was a youngling. Ra'ash takes your gifts and your study and your labor and brings you onto a path that only you can walk," Jaquarn said.

"And that is why I wanted you to choose singing as your Adoration, F'lorna," T'maya interjected. "You have a voice like your fathers, but you take it for granted because it comes so easy to you. You don't realize the gift that Ra'ash has bestowed upon you."

"I understand, Mother. I can sing very well— probably better than Raecli could sing. But I didn't choose dance to avoid hurting my friend's feelings. I chose dance because I saw Raecli's passion for singing—like the passion of a new colored moon taking over the Upper Realm—and I didn't have it," F'lorna said.

"And you have that passion for dance?" T'maya asked.

F'lorna looked down at her long, thin feet. "No," she whispered.

Jaquarn placed his hands on his daughter's shoulders. "Then what do you have passion for?"

F'lorna looked up and gazed at her mother. "I feel this urgency to help Raecli. She was taken before she had memorized all of the *Divine Oracle*."

T'maya exhaled. "F'lorna, we've gone over this—"

"No, Mother. You don't understand. It is not just Raecli. It is you. It all began with you. I feel this need to help you. You are so burdened by the lack of the *Divine Oracle* in your Eternal Memory," F'lorna said, as tears stung her eyes. "I want you to have *the Divine Oracle,* but how can I give it to you? There has to be a way."

T'maya's eyes filled with glittery liquid reflecting the light of the descending Heat Source and the rising Violet Moon. She walked toward her daughter and wrapped her arms around her. "You cannot save my Eternal Memory. It is lost. But you can help yourself,

47

and that is what makes me happy. You have your horns, you have the *Divine Oracle*. You have everything I never had, and that knowledge gives me peace."

F'lorna bent down several inches to allow her mother to embrace her. When her mother loosened her grip, she stood straight and stared into her mother's grey eyes that matched her own. "Yes, Mother. That may be. But your peace in what I have does not satisfy my passion for what you do not have."

F'lorna followed her parents the rest of the way to the Village Achion cluster, lit up with dozens of small torches. The Heat Source was now almost gone. Many long tables and benches had been placed in the clearing surrounded by trees. Each table was decorated with white and green foliage from the surrounding forest.

The wooden platform that would showcase all the offerings had also been decorated with the blooming Zulo vine that was lined with green blossoms, representing the Green Moon Children. There were bouquets of green draping grasses, spotted with small white Rivervalley flowers. Ralona, another of F'lorna's birth friends whose Adorations was creation, walked up to her and placed a necklace made of the Zulo vine around her neck. Her own curly, dark brown hair draped like vines around her pale face, which contrasted nicely against her mossy green tunic dress with golden stitching. Her pale blue eyes sparkled with delight. She was several palms shorter than F'lorna, so F'lorna widened her stance and curved her knees to shorten the distance between their heights.

"I hope you like our beautifications!" Ralona said excitedly. "We have been planning so long with hopes to honor our birth friends and all the villagers of Right River Hook at our Doublemoon Ceremony!"

F'lorna looked around in awe. "You have offered well and have honored us with your Adoration. I believe your creations of beauty will be a cherished memory for us all," F'lorna said. "I never thought of making bouquets with the long grasses, but they turned out beautiful."

"We also used the same grasses as centerpieces for each table. We had so much to do that I needed to create a simple design for the table decorations to save time and energy. I am quite pleased with the end result," Ralona said, grinning.

"You and the other creation birth friends have done a fine job, Ralona," Jaquarn said, squeezing the shoulder of the young Novice Elder. "I have been to many Doublemoon Ceremonies—celebrating the life that has now seen two cycles of our Six Colored Moons— and I can honestly say this one is my favorite…though, I may be biased," he said, smiling at F'lorna.

"Thank you, Spiritual Elder. I am grateful for your generous words," she said. "You will find your seat of honor next to the platform over there." The girl pointed to a long, decorated table near the right front of the wooden platform.

F'lorna looked to the table and saw Zelara and her parents. She waited for her parents to make their way to the table before turning her attention back to Ralona. "I see that Zelara and her family are sitting at our table," she said, trying to sound nonchalant.

The young girl leaned into F'lorna. "I heard that Zelara's father insisted on having the best view of his daughter's offering of Adoration."

"Yes, but there are families who have lived much longer in Right River Hook who also have First Green Moon children offering tonight," F'lorna said. "Why was a new family given priority over families that have contributed longer to our village?"

Ralona shrugged her shoulders. "I asked my mother the same thing. I may not be offering my Adoration on the village platform, but I also wanted my parents to have a good view of all that we created for the benefit of the Doublemoon Ceremony tonight. It doesn't seem fair. My mother told me that the Fishing Elder is contributing a lot to our village, so we must extend leniencies to him and his family."

F'lorna noticed her birth friend's cheeks reddened. She didn't want to cause her friend to be upset. "Also, Zelara and her family have never experienced a Doublemoon Ceremony at Right River Hook, so maybe they were given a place where they could really appreciate it," F'lorna said with an overconfident tone.

Ralona nodded her head. "You may be right. Our village is very good at not playing favorites and welcoming guests and newcomers," she agreed.

F'lorna bent down and embraced her birth friend. "You have outdone yourself. I know you were chosen as the leader the Creation Adoration, and I do believe that you and our birth friends have marked our celebration as one of the most beautiful."

Ralona's cheeks became a deeper shade red, and her pale blue eyes sparkled. "Thank you, F'lorna. We truly wanted to honor our birth friends and their families with our efforts. When I looked at the horizon today, I began offering many voiceless words to Ra'ash that the rains will hold back until the last offering of Adoration." She looked at the Upper Realm and back at F'lorna. "I know that dancing was chosen to be the final Adoration, so I hope your offering will not be eclipsed by a storm."

F'lorna smiled. "Thank you for your concern. I trust that Ra'ash will do what is best for the First Green Moon Children. The River is sick, and the rains will bring healing to the waters," F'lorna said.

Ralona looked away and stared briefly at Lemmeck who had just come into the Village Achion cluster with his family. She leaned in toward F'lorna. "I think Lemmeck harvested a large animal for his offering of Adoration. When the Heat-Source was still low in the morning horizon, I saw the Cooking Adoration digging a cooking pit in the ground. Later that afternoon as we were decorating the Village Achion cluster, I saw him and his twin brothers carrying something under a large fabric cloth. No one said anything because we know it's a surprise for his Adoration, but I am so excited. I overheard some of the elders saying that his kill was bigger than his brothers' offering at their Doublemoon Ceremony," she said and stopped. "See! Smell the air! I have not smelled anything like it before."

F'lorna nodded and sniffed the air. "Lemmeck is a skilled hunter."

51

"I am sure you already know what it is, so I won't ask. Your mother is the main Cooking Elder of our ceremony. It is just so exciting to think about it. Plus, we will be eating new species of fish from the Fishing Elder! I remember when we were just younglings, learning from all the elders. But here we are—Novice Elders offering our Adorations to Ra'ash," Ralona said excitedly.

"What was your Doublemoon gift?" F'lorna asked, enjoying her friend's excitement.

"My mother had a set of creation tools made for me from a Creation Elder in Left River Hook who specializes in it. They are beautiful, but there are many tools that I don't know how to use. I am thinking about staying with my cousins who live there, so I can learn more from other Creation Elders."

"I can't wait to see all that you create for Ra'ash," F'lorna said.

"What was yours?" Ralona asked.

F'lorna's smile faded, but she quickly tried to regain her composure. "I received these new foot coverings for dancing," she said looking down at her feet. Suddenly, she realized how awkward they looked.

"They look beautiful," Ralona said, genuinely. "You are such a beautiful dancer. I don't know how you do it. I can hardly keep up with making the *Holy Images of Jeyshen* with my body, and I am so little!"

F'lorna felt a sting in her eyes and she struggled with keeping her expression indifferent.

Ralona grabbed F'lorna's hand. "I didn't mean it as an insult, F'lorna. I see how hard you have worked to perfect your dancing, and you are quite amazing. When you chose dancing instead of singing, many of us were surprised. But you have really shown us that we can do whatever we want to honor Ra'ash if we believe and work towards it."

F'lorna tried to smile. "Thank you for your kinds words. I have worked hard to dance well. I better join my family now. I think we are starting soon."

"Oh, yes! You are right. I still have lots to do. I cannot wait to see your offering of Adoration on the village platform," Ralona said, walking off to greet more guests.

F'lorna looked down at her feet, willing them to move. But they looked too big to walk. How did she ever think she could dance?

Chapter 5

EXPRESSION OF CREATION

E xcitement seemed to bounce off the webbing of
green and white foliage decorating the Village
Achion cluster. When each table had not one
empty chair, Jaquarn walked up the large tree stump that
had been chopped into steps, leading up to the wooden
platform. Every family in Right River Hook was present,
in addition to many family visitors from other villages.
F'lorna looked across from her, where Eline was sitting
next to her mother. She was glad that her aunt had come.
She was understanding and sympathetic to her mother,
which would make the celebration much sweeter for her.

In her travels, Eline had met many Sand-shapers who
had left the coastal cities and mountains to live with the
River-dwellers, and she considered them Children of
Ra'ash even without the *Divine Oracle* in their Eternal
Memory, as long as they had the Indwelling.

F'lorna smiled at her aunt and mother chatting
like intimate friends. She tried to discern their words
above the noise of the crowd until she heard her father's
long hoot, signifying the beginning of Doublemoon
Ceremony. She looked toward the platform. Long
burning torches were planted all around the platform and
smaller ones at the ends of every table. The large village
fire blazed brightly from within the heart of the Village
Achion cluster. It was lined with stones to keep the ash
from pouring out. F'lorna could smell many scents of
foods wafting from behind the platform. All the food
would be cooked by her birth friends tonight, and she
was excited to see how the crowd would react to
Lemmeck's kill. Most of them had never eaten the meat
of the White Diamond Stag. This alone would make the
First Green Moon Children's Ceremony memorable.

The crowd hushed as Jaquarn looked around to
each face from the platform. His smile was genuine, and
F'lorna felt honored to have her father as the Spiritual
Elder of the celebration. She noticed a thick, dark
blanket of clouds in the distance of the northern horizon.
But the Violet Moon still shone bright in the Upper
Realm. The storm was a long way off and still might
dissipate before arriving in their section of the River.

Jaquarn cleared his throat. "I had the privilege of
blessing the First Green Moon Children and their
families today at each of their Achion clusters. I am

honored to serve as Spiritual Elder of this Doublemoon Ceremony. Let us open the ceremony with *Jeyshen's Holy Chant of Glory.*"

Jaquarn's voice was deep and clear, and his love for Ra'ash permeated the crowd. When F'lorna's father sang, most villagers said they could feel the Spirit of Ra'ash within them lift and dance. F'lorna looked at Zelara's father from the corner of her eye. He did not look at the platform while her father sang and Zelara followed her father's example. F'lorna wanted to point them out, but her distraction would have made the situation even worse. She looked ahead at her mother and aunt. They both had tears glistening in the firelight. Other villagers from the crowd also had shimmering eyes, and F'lorna saw many of them lift or bow their heads. F'lorna smiled inwardly and bowed her head. The Fishing Elder, Zelara's father, would dishonor himself and his family with his own lack of reverence.

Once the chant came to its fruition, Jaquarn blessed the First Green Moon Children collectively. F'lorna felt her heart begin to shudder within her. Her confidence in dance had been stripped away by Zelara's cruel words.

"I want to thank all the Elders who gave their time to mentor and train the First Green Moon Children in the Adorations they will be offering this evening. We had a large group, so the Elders were busy with as many as five students each. I want to commend each Elder who imparted their knowledge to the next generation of Novice Elders, so that our way of life can continue to serve and praise Ra'ash. The Adorations of Right River Hook include Cooking, Creation, Dancing and Fishing—

Fishing is a new one to our village and we are excited that Elder Trenton was able to take two pupils so quickly."

F'lorna looked toward where Zelara's father sat. He now looked fully at the platform. A moment ago, when her father was singing, he avoided looking at the village platform like it had the Heat Source on it.

Jaquarn continued. "Then we have Healing, Hunting, Planting, Singing and, finally, Tanning and Weaponry. Since I did not have a Healing pupil, I was able to assist the Dancing and Singing Elders with the spiritual aspects of their Adorations. I have grouped the Adorations into four main Expressions for the ceremony—Creation, Tanning and Weaponry, Sustenance and Music and Dance," Jaquarn announced formally. "You will find that every Adoration of the Doublemoon Ceremony blends with the next. We must have all the offerings of every member of our village in order to flourish as Rodeshians. We thank Ra'ash for His great design, and we ask His help to serve our portion during our brief walk on Rodesh."

Jaquarn looked to the Upper Realm. "The First Violet Moon is high, and now it is time to celebrate the newest Novice Elders of Right River Hook. But before I begin, I would like to thank the Help of Ra'ash for my sister and Healing Elder, Eline. She is Twofold on this First Violet Moon. She has lived under all of the Six Colored Moons two cycles each. Most of the Onefolds like myself remember her as Right River Hook's Healing Elder after my mother passed onto the Eternal Dwelling of Ra'ash. She further trained me as a Healing Elder when Ra'ash called her to leave Right River Hook in order to mentor Healing Elders in the villages surrounding the North and South River tributaries. We are honored that Eline would venture back to our village to watch my daughter and the First Green Moon Children offer their Adorations."

F'lorna looked toward her father's sister and smiled. She felt so much appreciation to have such an honored River-dweller in her family. Her mother may have lost her Eternal Memory and horns as a Sand-shaper, but the rest of her family were admired River-dwellers who worked hard to serve Ra'ash and the village with their offering of Adorations. She only hoped that she could maintain her family's lineage of offering, but her Adoration seemed so small compared to the greatness of her family.

Jaquarn continued, spreading his hands out to showcase the Village Achion cluster. "You have already seen some of the Creation offering as you walked into the Village Achion cluster. I must admit, the festive ornamentations are very well done. Will those who worked on the Doublemoon Ceremony beautifications please rise and be recognized?"

F'lorna watched several of her birth friends, including Ralona, stand up from their seats. She pounded the wooden table in front of her to applaud them. For a brief moment when she was young, she yearned to be able to create something beautiful like they do, but she quickly discovered that she was unable to produce the wonderful images she envisioned. She had little artistic talent.

"These four Novice Elders not only decorated the ceremony grounds with the green and white you see tonight, they also created the torches, the plates and bowls that the food will be served on. And as a special offering to us, they made each family a gift."

F'lorna watched as her four creation birth friends walked to the back of the platform and grabbed the stacks of woven baskets lining the wall. They were not noticeable at first because they hid in the dark, but each friend took a stack and brought it to the front of the platform. The seated villagers craned their necks to see the baskets, and a few of the younglings stood on their chairs.

"The creation children wove each family a basket. Inside each basket is green soap made of the Zulo vine. This soap enhances the peace and tranquility of the spirit. They made each family a tea pouch from the fibers of the waterbark plants. They made candies from the sap of the Achion tree spiced with the wild mint flowers that grow on the meadows surrounding the lower hills, which were harvested and donated by Dashion and Rashion in honor of their brother, Lemmeck and the other First Green Moon Children."

F'lorna looked for Lemmeck's family. They were close to the platform on the opposite side of the hearth fire. Lemmeck, the twins and their parents had the dark, handsome looks they were known for. F'lorna's eyes locked with Lemmeck's. She could sense his anticipation even though she sat a tree length away from him. She too couldn't wait for him to present his offering of Adoration before the villagers.

"And finally," Jaquarn said with obvious excitement. "Each basket has a carved image of Jeyshen's sphere. The sphere is dedicated to the fathers of each family as a reminder of Jeyshen's love and devotion. The First Green Moon Creation children ask that the fathers place this sphere in a pouch of the tunic belt, so the thought of Jeyshen and His Expansion will always be with you."

Jaquarn finished and motioned for the four birth friends to pass out their baskets to each family. F'lorna watched as her mother accepted hers from Ralona with great interest. Her mother loved teas, and the new fiber pouch would be a great addition to her cooking hearth. F'lorna was surprised when Ralona also honored her aunt with a basket. F'lorna realized how smart they were to make extra baskets in case of a special guest in attendance. F'lorna noticed that Lemmeck's twin brothers were also gifted a basket of their own in gratitude for their mint flower offering. F'lorna couldn't help but feel so proud of her birth friends, and the night had only begun. She dismissed the fear caught in the distant corners of her mind.

Chapter 6

EXPRESSION OF TANNING AND WEAPONRY

J aquarn waited for several moments, so each family could sift through their baskets before continuing, before continuing. "And since the Creation Adoration leads right into the Tanning and Weaponry, I would like to ask the First Green Moon Children of these two fine Adorations to Ra'ash to stand and come retrieve your offerings," Jaquarn said from the platform.

Several of F'lorna's birth friends stood up and made their way behind the village platform. F'lorna especially loved the Tanning Adoration. The mentors taught the most amazing methods of tanning and dyeing animal hides. She knew it would be too late for Lemmeck's White Diamond Stag's hide to be processed for the ceremony. It would probably be worked on by the Tanning Elder anyway. Beginners began their work on the hides of smaller, more abundant animals. F'lorna enjoyed her short introduction to tanning when she was younger, but she quickly discovered that she didn't have the patience for the process. There was a lot of repetitive movements and waiting involved. Still the work was worth it when beautiful and useful items were created.

F'lorna even heard that one of her birth friends made a waterproof leather basket to carry water from the River. The creator of the basket was gifted animal fat from a rare water fowl that lived near the Northeastern Mountains. F'lorna didn't know more, since the Adoration offerings were kept secret to ensure that the Doublemoon Ceremony would be filled with surprises.

F'lorna eyed Lemmeck. She knew he was anticipating the Weaponry Adoration. He had just harvested the great rack of ivory horns and the silver mane of the White Diamond Stag, so he now had something to barter with. She was sure that he would buy a new bow for his hunting. His bow was a secondhand from one of his brothers. He would be ready for a larger one as a Novice Elder of the village.

The tanning and weaponry birth friends lined themselves in front of the village platform. Many of them were holding several items. F'lorna observed one of her close friends, Vauntan. She was the second tallest of all the female birth friends next to F'lorna. She had flaxen hair like the dried grasses of the meadow, and her eyes were a light blue. Her Adoration was tanning, and F'lorna was surprised that she held a long, white leather tunic embroidered with colorful threads with the thin needle of a River Pine. Normally, Novice Elders were unable to make an entire tunic dress for their Doublemoon Ceremony with such detailed embroidery. F'lorna gazed at the tunic. She only owned fiber tunics because the leather tunics were too pricey for growing bodies. F'lorna noticed the length of the tunic. It would not fit many of her shorter friends. The tunic was made for Vauntan's height or taller. F'lorna couldn't help but feel better about her height. Vauntan embraced her long, willowy figure. F'lorna hoped that she had finally stopped growing. Maybe on a distant phase of a moon, she could have a leather tunic, like the one Vauntan made, but she had very little to offer in exchange.

Jaquarn stood next to the line of birth friends who were holding their creations. "Thank You, Ra'ash, for these offerings of tanning and weaponry. I have to admit that we have much to be grateful for," Jaquarn began. "If a piece interests you, you may come and inspect the offering of these First Green Moon Children, but I guarantee you that they have been working with excellent craftsmanship to create their Adorations. They have decided to gift the earnings of their Adoration for much needed maintenance of our Village. The Circle of Elders have also decided that if there are enough resources leftover from the Adoration offerings we will create a sanctuary around the Pillar. We want you to not only go to the Pillar to offer voiceless words to Ra'ash, we want your spirit to find peace and refreshment there."

Suddenly, a thread of light zig-zagged across the horizon in the distance. Several moments later, thunder rolled down the darkening Upper Realm. Jaquarn looked up for an instant, but he turned back quickly to the rapt attention of the villagers. "As you see, Ra'ash knows that you are ready to bid, and He wants me to hurry up," he said with a laugh.

The villagers smiled and laughed with him.

"Circle of Elders," Jaquarn continued. "Please stand behind these young Novice Elders to receive their bids."

Five elders got out of their seats and made their way behind the line of birth friends.

"If you see something you like, please inspect it and offer your bid to one of the Elders behind me. If your bid is accepted, the creator of your item will bring it to your table before our next offering of Adoration. I won't rush you, but I will say there is much more to celebrate. So please make your bid quickly. You may begin."

Lemmeck and several villagers got up at once to inspect the items. Lemmeck didn't stop to look at all the items. He knew what he wanted. He went straight to one of the Elders and whispered his price. F'lorna could see the Elder's eyebrows rise as he leaned in and repeated Lemmeck's words. F'lorna couldn't help but smile. She knew that Lemmeck was offering some of the ivory horns or mane from his White Diamond stag. She could see Lemmeck motioning to the broad bow that one of his closest birth friends was holding. Burdon came from a long line of weapon makers. His mother, his mother's father and his mother's two brothers developed new techniques in weaponry making.

"We'll be right back, F'lorna," she heard her mother saying. Eline and T'maya both got out of their seats to inspect the items. F'lorna watched her mother approach Nayran, her birth friend who was holding a large, oblong piece of leather. F'lorna realized it must be the waterproof leather basket that she had heard about. Apparently, Nayran was the tanner who created it.

F'lorna shook her head. She should have known. Nayran's distant cousins had visited from the north River near the Northeastern Mountains. They had brought several water fowl they harvested from the mountainside. She and her birth friends were still too young to choose their Adorations to Ra'ash then, but her parents must have saved the fat from the water fowl until her Doublemoon Ceremony. T'maya probably had known about it for some time, and F'lorna wondered what her mother would bid.

F'lorna quickly began to search for her father's sister, but by the time she spotted her, she was almost back to the table. Her aunt was tall, but now F'lorna realized that she had grown taller.

"That was exhilarating! Where did your mother go to?" she asked, searching the through the villagers still standing.

"She was inspecting the waterproof leather basket," F'lorna said. "I missed what you bid on."

"I think we will find out shortly if I received it or not!" Eline said, sitting down. "Oh! There is your mother."

T'maya walked back to the table with an animated smile. "I think I may have won the basket. How nice it will be to carry so much water! Nayran has devised a carrying system made up of sinews, so the weight of the basket can go on my back. How wonderful to not have to carry water on my hornless head."

F'lorna's smile faded. "Mother, I never knew it was so difficult for you," she said.

"I try not to complain, my dear daughter. Without horns, the basket presses down hard. I can only carry it for a few tree lengths at a time before I must take it down and rest." T'maya winked at her daughter. "Which is why I probably ask you more than I should to bring water in for me."

F'lorna smiled and reached over the table to squeeze her mother's hand. "Then I shall offer voiceless words that the leather basket is yours."

Another thread of light zig-zagged across the Upper Realm, producing loud booming sounds like two male Bastalion Goats fighting for territory.

"Villagers, it is time to take our seats. The bidding of these items has closed," Jaquarn said. He looked to the Elders behind the line of birth friends. "Circle of Elders, please let each First Green Moon child know the bids, so they may choose."

Jaquarn moved his attention to those holding their created items. "The offerings of the Tanning and Weaponry Adorations have been well received. When you accept a bid, bring your offering to each new owner. We will use your offerings to better our village and to create the sanctuary around our Pillar."

One by one, F'lorna watched her birth friends present their offerings of Adoration to the winning bidders. Burdon walked with pride over to Lemmeck's family's table. He handed the broad bow to Lemmeck. Lemmeck stood and put his left hand on Burdon's right shoulder. They exchanged words that F'lorna could not hear.

F'lorna wondered how good it would feel to create something that gave happiness to others. She knew that only a few villagers could afford to bid for the items created by the tanning and weaponry children, and she realized how wise her father was to have the Creation Adoration go first. The gifts that each village family received from the creation children were more than enough to honor each guest. F'lorna noticed Nayran coming to her table, carrying the waterproof leather basket. She walked straight to T'maya.

"I must confess, I am very happy this basket goes to you. I received another bid, but since my mother and I are not masterful cooks, we are delighted with your exchange. In order to keep your offer for ourselves, my father has volunteered to donate time to maintain the paths around the village. I offer you my fullest gratitude," Nayran said, as she handed the large leather basket to T'maya. "May the help of Ra'ash always be with you."

"You are a sweet Novice Elder. I look forward to serving you when the time comes. I will take care to make my menu offering particularly special for your joining," T'maya said, taking the basket.

T'maya watched as Nayran went back to her table. She lifted the leather basket. "It is much lighter than I expected and so supple. There is so much room. I'm so honored to have it," she said, as she spread the folds of leather to their full width.

"Mother, what did you offer for it?" F'lorna asked, curiously.

"I gave them an offer that Nayran and her mother could not refuse. I promised to prepare Nayran's wedding feast when the time comes."

F'lorna couldn't help but giggle under her breath. Nayran was one of her most creative birth friends, but she burned almost everything she cooked. She would get distracted with her thoughts, and the temperature would rise too quickly without constant supervision. F'lorna understood why her birth friend could be so good at the Tanning Adoration. She could do the repetitive movements required for the process while her mind wandered onto other thoughts.

"Mother, I am glad that Father and I eat so well from our cooking hearth. The villagers get to eat from your table once a week at the Shoam-sha, but Father and I get your offerings of Ra'ash almost every meal," F'lorna said.

T'maya smiled and nodded. "I appreciate your gratitude."

F'lorna was grateful for her mother. She was extremely detailed, which helped her be one of the best Cooking Elders in Right River Hook. She knew the amount of every ingredient that went into her food preparation and how hot the fire must be and for how long the food must cook. F'lorna understood that being so meticulous helped her mother to be a wonderful cook, but it also caused T'maya to be overly concerned with the details of her life. F'lorna knew the words of the prophets were correct—*Each Adoration comes with both strengths and weakness.*

"Eyes up, F'lorna. Someone is coming your way," F'lorna heard her aunt say.

When F'lorna looked up, she saw her birth friend, Vauntan, approaching her with the full-length leather tunic dyed white with colorfully stitched embellishments.

"I offer you this tunic and thank you for your aunt's donation on your behalf," Vauntan said. "There were very few villagers who could wear my tunic, but I made it purposely for those of us who stand like budding Achion trees," she said, standing tall. "My mother helped me embroider the markings. I wanted to create something new, so I embroidered the colors of the six moons into my own personal design. They really don't mean anything. They are more of a free flow of form and color from my imagination."

F'lorna covered her mouth and exhaled before standing up and embracing her birth friend. "Vauntan, this tunic makes the spirit in me sing," she whispered.

"You mean dance?" Vauntan asked.

"Yes, that is my Adoration, but I feel as if my spirit is both singing and dancing!" F'lorna exclaimed.

"Maybe you can wear it when you help your father at our village Shoam-sha," Vauntan said, pleased.

"I will wear this tunic to honor Ra-ash and you," F'lorna whispered into her friend's ear before releasing her embrace. She knew that there were still friends who cared for her. She would no longer neglect the other relationships that Ra'ash has given her.

Vauntan returned to her seat. As F'lorna watched her leave, she briefly noticed Zelara's scowl from the other end of the table. She had received a new tunic belt from the offerings, which didn't seem to please her.

F'lorna walked around the table and leaned down to embrace her father's sister. "Thank you, Eline. I never dreamed that this tunic would be mine."

Eline squeezed F'lorna's shoulder. "Don't tell anyone, but I sort of cheated. I was going to donate the medicines to Right River Hook anyway, but your father told me to wait for the offerings. When I saw this white tunic with such dramatic embroidery, I knew it had to be yours. It is my Doublemoon gift to you."

"But your presence here is more than enough. I know how busy you are," F'lorna said. "And I am honored that you came to celebrate with me."

"You are so dear to me. I remember when you were just a youngling, but now I believe you are taller than I. Ra'ash did not give me a husband or a child of my own. He knew I would be mentoring the Healing Elders along the River tributaries, but He honored me with a beautiful, talented niece who has a life of great purpose before her. I can't wait to watch your offering of Adoration. You make me so proud," Eline said, patting F'lorna's young hand with her aged palm.

F'lorna bowed slightly and walked back to her seat. She felt the supple leather in her fingers as she sat down carefully, ensuring the tunic did not touch the ground. She continued to smile pleasantly, but her heart felt heavy. She was about to disappoint her parents and now Eline. She didn't deserve the white leather tunic that now rested on her lap. Her offering of Adoration did not have the breath of Ra'ash within it.

Chapter 7

EXPRESSION OF SUSTENANCE

❝❝ Thank you, First Green Moon Children of Tanning and Weaponry. Your offering of Adoration honors our village. The Circle of Elders will dedicate the new sanctuary around the Pillar to you and your birth friends," Jaquarn said. "Let's begin our feast while the air is still dry!"

Jaquarn smiled intently and rubbed his hands together. F'lorna could see the delight in her father's eyes. He enjoyed the suspense of introducing the next Adorations. Her father told her that when he was younger, he was nervous to go on the village platform. However, he quickly grew more confident as he continued to offer his new Adoration to Ra'ash. Although F'lorna was his daughter, she knew that Jaquarn shined at being Spiritual Elder. He was patient, knowledgeable and congenial. He never laid blame without taking responsibility as well. Everyone respected him, except for Zelara's family.

"I know that you have been smelling the scents coming from Village Cooking Hearth," he continued. "And I'm not quite sure that the rumbling we've been hearing in the distance is not actually from the Upper Realm but really from the bellies of Right River Hook!"

A laughter rose up from the tables.

"We will be presenting the four Adorations of Sustenance, so will the Cooking, Planting, Fishing and Hunting Adorations stand up and retrieve the feast? I know that everyone will be pleased and surprised by the foods offered on each table during the Doublemoon Ceremony. My wife, T'maya, has filled my ears with praise for her cooking pupils. They have worked tirelessly on creating a diverse and delicious menu for tonight's feast. And we have a wonderful surprise that will truly mark this Doublemoon Ceremony as divinely honored."

F'lorna watched as many of her birth friends stood up, including Lemmeck. F'lorna couldn't wait until the villagers found out that they would be eating fresh White Diamond Stag. A few of the elders had eaten the dried stag meat, but no one to her knowledge ate the tender meat the day it was harvested.

"There go my young apprentices," T'maya whispered excitedly. "Three amazing pupils. I put Xartanian in charge of the meats. He is just as strong-willed and meticulous as I am. When he found out we had White Diamond Stag meat to serve, he insisted on creating a new recipe—with just a little help from me. I spent all afternoon with him, testing various flavors. Thanks to Ra'ash we discovered the perfect mixture of herbs to add to the stag meat without overpowering its flavor. I put Rosinlae in charge of the edible plants, and Lessel in charge of the grains. She has developed a sweet grain dish using a mixture of Achion sap and River Cane nectar. F'lorna, I know your love of sweets, so you may want to save room for this dish."

F'lorna felt the hunger in her stomach. "I will have to limit what I eat, so my Adoration is not affected tonight. I'll save room for Lemmeck's stag and for the sweet grain dish," F'lorna said. She hadn't thought that offering her Adoration last would cause her to miss out on the feast.

"Nonsense," Eline whispered. "Your mother and I will save you a dish and bring a taste of everything back to the hearth after the ceremony. You will be able to feast then."

F'lorna nodded. "Thank you," she said.

Jaquarn continued. "When the feast is in hand, will the selected First Green Moon Children bring your offerings of Adoration in front of the village platform and line up, so all the village can see? While they are bringing out the dishes, I want to feature our newest offering of Adoration to Ra'ash: Fishing! Elder Trenton has been training two First Green Moon Children not only how to fish, but how to cultivate the fish population, so it will continue to multiply and thrive in our tributary. Added to our feast this evening will be several fish species that are new to us. We thank Elder Trenton for his fishing expertise and offerings to Right River Hook. We ask the Help of Ra'ash to continue the prosperity of his work to our village."

F'lorna watched Zelara's father stand up briefly and nod to the other families. "I daresay that the fish you enjoy tonight will be the highlight of the ceremony," he said loudly. He nodded and smiled one last time and took his seat at the table.

F'lorna was surprised that Zelara's father spoke from his table to the villagers. Normally, only the one on the platform would speak to all the gathering of the village at such a special ceremony. His customs from up north were different she assumed. But she couldn't help but think that his words were spoken prematurely. Yes, the new fish would be a welcome delight to the feast, but F'lorna knew that Lemmeck's White Diamond Stag would be the highpoint.

Jaquarn said nothing about the interruption. Once all eyes were back on the platform, he continued with the ceremony. "Next the Planters have had quite the dilemma with Ra'ash withholding the rains. They worked tirelessly to bring water from the River to help the Charisse Bush berry for our drink tonight. By the Help of Ra'ash, they have been able to provide a pitcher of Charisse juice for each family. They allowed me to have a taste before the ceremony tonight, and I can assure you that it is as sweet as ever. Further, all of their root vegetables came out better than expected. They planted them near the River, so the soil was already rich and fertile. They also took several journeys to the valleys at the lower hills to gather wild plants, so you will see a variety of nuts, berries and a few other surprises that I'll let you discuss amongst your families."

F'lorna instantly looked for her planting birth friend, Le'ana. She spotted her already in line in front of the platform with her hands laden with platters covered in food. Le'ana's Achion cluster was only a dozen tree lengths away from her own, and F'lorna used to play with Le'ana and Raecli when they were younger. The three of them were always seen together. F'lorna realized that she had pushed Le'ana away too after Raecli moved to the north to become a Sand-shaper. She regretted shutting her out, and she suspected it was because Le'ana reminded her of their time together with Raecli. F'lorna looked at her birth friend, standing demurely on the platform. She had scarlet hair, like the scales of a Flamefish, and her green eyes matched the River tributary on cloudy days. She also had the speckles on her face and arms that bloom from the Heat Source's rays.

Le'ana was reserved and quiet, which may be why she never spoke up when F'lorna pushed her away. F'lorna decided that after the Doublemoon Ceremony tonight, she would have to make amends with many of her birth friends, starting with Le'ana.

F'lorna noticed her father pause for several moments on the platform. The Violet Moon was high in the Upper Realm, and the soft violet light from the moon discolored the yellow of the fire in the torches. The resulting light gave a mystical, dim glow across the faces of her birth friends lined up in front of the platform, holding large trays and platters of food. A hush fell over the families at each table.

Jaquarn let the expectation thicken before he began to speak. "For this Doublemoon Ceremony we only had one Hunting pupil," he motioned for Lemmeck and Xartanian, the Cooking pupil, to stand next to him. "As you know Lemmeck was mentored by his father and older brothers in the Adoration of Hunting. They taught him well, but truly Ra'ash Himself has guided this young Rodeshian into his offering for the Doublemoon Ceremony tonight."

The villagers moved in their seats to get a better view of Jaquarn and the two young men. "Xartanian was put in charge by my wife, T'maya, to develop new methods and recipes for the meat you will be served tonight, including the fish that our Fishing Elder has brought to our village," Jaquarn said, continuing to build the suspense.

F'lorna spied Zelara sitting toward the end of the table. Her eyes were pinned on Lemmeck.

Jaquarn continued. "We are grateful to the help of Ra'ash that our new Novice Elder harvested a White Diamond Stag this morning, so we will celebrate the First Green Moon Children's Doublemoon Ceremony with rare meat and a new recipe!"

F'lorna watched Lemmeck's face as he took in the whispers of the villagers. She could see the white of his teeth as his lips turned into a wide smiled. His emerald eyes shone brightly from the torch lights attached to the platform. She looked around at the different families, talking in disbelief under their breaths.

Jaquarn cleared his throat. "Lemmeck shot the White Diamond Stag as the Heat Source came into the morning horizon. I don't know why Ra'ash would withhold the rains but provide a White Diamond Stag, but His movements are always for our good. We will celebrate this great gift tonight, knowing that the First Green Moon Children have a certain honor from Ra'ash. I don't know about you, but I am already anticipating what the Help of Ra'ash will do next through these fine Novice Elders. So, before the rains fall on our feast—" Suddenly, Jaquarn's speech was interrupted.

F'lorna saw Zelara's father stand to his feet. "How could this youngling make such a kill? Did not his father or brothers make it for him? Who witnessed the kill?" Trenton asked, incredulously.

F'lorna and the rest of the villagers were stunned by the interjection. Jaquarn was not used to being interrupted and was unable to respond for several seconds. "Trenton, Lemmeck and his family would not lie about this kill. My daughter witnessed it this morning."

Trenton took several steps closer to the village platform. "How are we to trust two children who have only seen two cycles of the moons?"

Rashion and Dashion rose to their feet. "Sit down, my sons," their father insisted, as he stood up from his table. "May I speak, Jaquarn?" he asked.

"Yes, of course," Jaquarn said.

78

"I know that the feast is getting cold, so I will be brief. Trenton and his family are new to Right River Hook, so they do not know the families at our village very well. But the rest of you know my family and that we stand on truth. By the Help of Ra'ash, our son, Lemmeck, harvested this White Diamond Stag for his Doublemoon Ceremony to the benefit of our entire village. He is a fine hunter and an honest young man. F'lorna witnessed the kill this morning, but even without a witness, I know my son would not lie," he said and sat down.

F'lorna was too far away to see his full expression, but she could hear the tension in his speech. She had rarely seen Lemmeck's father angry. He was a patient, quiet man, and for him to speak in front of the village showed just how much Elder Trenton's words disturbed him. She looked back at Lemmeck, and she could see the emotion blazing in his expression, though, he tried to subdue it.

"I give you my apology of healing," Jaquarn said. "There is no need to defend your family and son. We all know that Lemmeck harvested the White Diamond Stag." He turned his attention to Trenton. "Fishing Elder, we understand that your customs are different than ours, and we trust that you will soon learn to embrace ours as your own. But we do not accuse others openly before we have come to them in private. We do not talk out of turn at village meetings, especially during the Doublemoon Ceremony. And we definitely do not offer words without being aware of their ability to create tension in our community. Lemmeck is a Novice Elder of our community, and not a youngling. Will you please be seated?"

Trenton looked around to the other tables and clumsily stepped back several paces. His expression appeared hurt at first, but he quickly replaced it with a rigid, blank stare. "I offer you my apology of healing," he said sternly. "Of course. this youngling was able to kill a White Diamond Stag all by himself just this morning. I don't know why I would question it."

F'lorna was horrified. She watched Zelara's father sit down next to his wife. Even in the dim night, she could see the embarrassment on Zelara's face.

Jaquarn tried to lighten the uncomfortable atmosphere that had descended onto the villagers. He stood next to Lemmeck who stared resolutely at the village fire. "Let us serve the feast!" Jaquarn announced. The birth children took their trays to their assigned table. Just before Lemmeck left, Jaquarn whispered something into his ear. Lemmeck nodded several times before taking his tray toward his own family's table.

Chapter 8

EXPRESSION OF MUSIC AND DANCE

Once the food was served, all the First Green Moon Children returned to their tables and sat down to eat. The families at each table took their time enjoying the flavors of foods. F'lorna noticed that Lemmeck was so upset by Elder Trenton's words that he had hardly eaten a bite of his White Diamond

Stag. F'lorna watched as Lemmeck's older twin brothers endeavored to distract his thoughts by pointing at his new bow and asking him questions. The bow was a lot bigger than the one F'lorna had seen Lemmeck carrying earlier that morning. Finally, Lemmeck seemed to relax, and he got out of his seat and tested the large bow, feeling the strength of the bowstring. F'lorna could see Lemmeck mouthing words to his brothers, and she figured he was already planning his next hunt.

Lemmeck's family supplied much of the meat for the weekly Shoam-sha, and they donated a portion of each kill to her father for being the Spiritual Elder of the village. The other villagers traded frequently with them to enjoy the meat they salted and dried. To insult such a family—or any family—at the Village Achion cluster was reckless and mean. F'lorna looked at Zelara's plate and noticed that she had only selected her father's fish as her main dish. Her entire family ignored the portion of White Diamond stag that sat on the platter in front of them.

"Who will be playing the Trinity of Instruments?" Eline asked, startling F'lorna out of her thoughts.

F'lorna looked up, relieved to distract her mind from the resentment building toward Zelara. "Lyisha is playing the leera, Marvine is playing the tingla, and both Marvine and Yarla are playing the poonga."

"Will the Trinity accompany the singers as well?" Eline asked.

"No. The singers asked the musicians not to play for them for their offering of Adoration." F'lorna knew that most of the time the instrumental Adorations generally played alongside the singers, but Zelara decided she and the others wanted to sing without accompaniment. She said that it wasn't fair sharing the platform with Trinity Instruments. She wanted their voices not to be overshadowed by the players. But F'lorna believed that the Trinity of Instruments enhanced the Adorations, especially of singing and dancing.

"That's interesting," Eline said. "I've been to many Doublemoon Ceremonies, and most villages don't have as many birth friends as Ra'ash has blessed you and your friends with. And the singers and dancers have to borrow Elders to play for them. The fact that you have an entire Trinity of Instruments is quite special."

"Yes, they play very well, and I believe Marvine and Yarla will be playing a poonga duet along with Lyisha's leera. They have created a special version of one of the *Sacred Songs*. I've had the honor of hearing a small piece, and it is quite mesmerizing."

"I adore all three instruments, but I especially love when the rhythmic, deep beat of the poonga mingles with the high, flittering whistle of the leera. Reminds me of Ra'ash. Sometimes He is so immense that I cannot comprehend Him, but other times He's so light that I could almost grasp Him," Eline said.

"Well said, Sister," Jaquarn said, wiping his lips on a small fabric cloth. "Excuse me for a moment as I introduce the next Adoration." He stood up and looked toward the Upper Realm. "It is getting dark and the Violet Moon is about to be hidden under the blanket of dark clouds coming in from the north. The wind smells of rain. Ra'ash may be sending His rains more quickly than I thought."

F'lorna watched as her father walked to the village platform. He would introduce the singers and she wouldn't be among them. It never bothered her until tonight. Suddenly, she felt like her dreams were sliding away like the music of the leera. Raecli was never coming back, and F'lorna was trapped in a voiceless destiny.

F'lorna saw her father making words with his mouth, but she couldn't concentrate on what he was saying. She felt her tightly woven heartbreak unraveling within her, and emotions were becoming harder to shield. She noticed movement around her as Shalane, Sage and Zelara got up from their seats and walked to the village platform. They were smiling with excitement. Where was her place in the chorus? She hadn't sung in the open since Raecli left. She merely recited the *Sacred Songs and Holy Chants* for her mother in their Achion cluster. She forgot how it felt to sing with passion. Her throat tightened as her feet bumped up against the leg of the table. *Too big. Too tall.* Why had she not noticed?

The voices of the trio floated from the village platform, winding around the seated villagers like a breeze. Their song glided sweetly, and the villagers smiled and nodded. *Too sweet*, F'lorna thought. *Where was the depth and angst? Where was the fight and compromise?* F'lorna knew the song well. It was a safe song for singers—the pitch moved not too high or too low. But the lyrics were beautiful and bubbly like a mist of water rising up from a small splash of a child in the River. It was the *Holy Chant of Gratitude to Jeyshen*, sung after the His limbs were ripped apart from being Expanded on the Sphere that continued to rise over the

Great Expanse into the Upper Realm. Did Zelara even believe what she sang? Or was this one of those *childish myths* that no longer counted?

F'lorna's thoughts returned to the world around her as the villagers pounded their table with approval. It was time for the Dancing Adoration. Her two dancing companions had suggested that they each offer a small solo instead of a longer collective dance for their Adorations. Did they suggest that because they were embarrassed to dance next to her? F'lorna had assumed they decided on solos to highlight the uniqueness of each dancer. Now she didn't know.

"Thank you, Singing Adoration. Your song has delighted us all," Jaquarn said after he walked back onto the platform. He looked at Sage, Shalane and Zelara as they took their seats. F'lorna noticed Zelara's father was praising his daughter so loudly that his voice interfered with her father's announcement from the village platform. Instead of raising his voice, Jaquarn waited patiently for Zelara's father to finish. Once his voice subsided, Jaquarn continued speaking. "Now all that is left is the Dancing Adoration. I saved it for last because I was hoping to plan a surprise celebration in honor of Ra'ash after the Doublemoon Ceremony had finished. Most of you now know that the River is sick. But instead of causing us fear, I wanted us to use this opportunity to offer our thanksgiving to Ra'ash and all that He has done for us. I hoped that we could join the First Green Moon Children in a dance to Ra'ash! We have the Trinity of Instruments, we have the singers and now we have the dancers."

The villagers pounded the wood tables with approval, but several of them looked toward the Upper Realm at the dark billows coming in from the north. F'lorna noticed that the wind had become cooler and faster.

Jaquarn cleared his throat and looked toward the northern horizon. "Although, I believe Ra'ash has already foreseen our celebration and is sending His rains ahead of time. I see dark, mountainous swells moving in quickly toward us." He replaced his look of apprehension with an overly confident smile and continued. "Just like the Singing Adoration, the Dancing Adoration will be a little different for this ceremony. But we support these small divergences because they promote the individuality of each Novice Elder in his or her chosen Adoration. We have three dancers tonight. Two of the dancers have chosen to share the village platform, while my daughter, F'lorna, will be dancing a solo."

F'lorna felt her limbs go cold. Her friends were dancing together. They didn't want her to dance with them after all. She couldn't believe it. Zelara was right. They were embarrassed by her.

"Will Layaton and Salyna please make their way to the village platform?" Jaquarn said and walked down the steps to sit with his family. F'lorna saw Layaton get up from the table next to hers. She tried to gain eye contact as she walked by, but Layaton wouldn't look her way. Salyna got to the platform first. She looked at each table besides F'lorna's. *They won't look at me*, she thought. She watched both dancers join hands on the platform. They each had a petite figure. F'lorna had to be at least two palm widths taller than both girls.

The Trinity of Instruments were already set up at the back of the platform. The dancers got into their first stance and waited for the music to begin. The cold in F'lorna's limbs began to move into the center of her body. Her dancing friends were dancing parts of a routine that she had suggested from the beginning. The combined parts were separated by solo parts that each dancer offered simultaneously with the other. They were weaving three routines into one. F'lorna didn't understand. She could have easily joined her two friends. She could have separated her solo into segments also, and learned the shared dance quickly. Why had they not asked her?

F'lorna noticed someone watching her from her peripheral view. She looked to see eyes the color of freshly turned soil staring at her. Zelara had a smirk on her face. When F'lorna's eyes were in view, her smirk grew wider and she mouthed a laugh before looking back at the platform. F'lorna instantly felt the cold that had seeped into the pit of her stomach disperse with raging heat. Had Zelara set all of this up?

"F'lorna, you told us that each dancer was doing her own solo," T'maya whispered when the dance ended and the villagers began pounding the wooden tables with applause.

"T'maya, the young River-dwellers are the authors of their Adoration. If they chose to dance together—even last minute—we must respect their choice."

F'lorna looked at her father. He knew that she had been betrayed. She felt the heat from her limbs shoot up to her cheeks. Even the chill in the wind couldn't hide her embarrassment.

"I've already announced all the dancers, F'lorna. You can go up on stage now," her father whispered encouragingly.

F'lorna realized that he had no idea how hurt she felt at that moment. She couldn't move. Suddenly, the villagers around her became quiet and they all looked her way. The torch light swirled with the heightened wind and the faces of the villagers appeared to sway with the flicker of the flames. She quickly found Lemmeck with her gaze. He was sitting at the table. His normally confident expression looked worried as he stared back at her. She scanned the villagers' faces once more before getting out of her seat. Had they all known, and agreed in secret, that she was a horrible dancer?

Jaquarn tapped the wood table in front of where F'lorna sat, and she flinched. "F'lorna, did you hear what I said?"

F'lorna looked at her father. "No, I offer you apology of healing. I didn't hear you."

F'lorna could see tension in her father's expression. "Ra'ash is sending a storm now. You need to offer your Adoration. I have to send the villagers to their Achion clusters soon. I underestimated how fast the storm is coming our way. The Violet Moon can no longer be seen in the Upper Realm," he said, looking worried.

F'lorna stared at the torches surrounding the village platform. The yellow light now brightened in the absence of the violet glow of the moon. She nodded. "Yes, I am going."

She got up out of her seat, feeling her knees weaken. She imagined her final dance move that was offered on her horns. She had achieved the move earlier that morning flawlessly, but this morning felt like an eternity ago. She walked onto the first step of the platform and looked at her foot. Too big. *"Ra'ash, I don't want to dance anymore!"* she exclaimed, giving up voiceless words to Ra'ash.

A large crack was heard in the distance. F'lorna looked up just in time to see the light split the Upper Realm. The wind came in faster, and she had to brace her feet as she walked up the rest of the stairs to the platform. She looked behind her to where the Trinity of Instruments were sitting. She knew each face from birth, but now they seemed like strangers. Had they laughed about her dancing as well? F'lorna nodded for them to start the music when she took position. She turned back to face the crowd. She had practiced looking at the faces of each villager seated at the tables, but now she stared into the darkness beyond the faces. Their expressions wobbled under her gaze in the firelight moving swiftly with the wind. Were they laughing?

She wouldn't allow herself to look directly at them. She waited for the music to start, but all she heard was the wind bellowing at her, trying to get her to leave the platform. She felt debris from the forest floor sweep across her body. A Zulo vine skittered across the wooden planks of the platform and wrapped around her feet. She tried to kick it off, but it wound up tighter. Was that music she heard?

She looked back toward the instruments. She saw her birth friends playing, but the melody could barely be heard above the wind. Another crack sounded above the forest, but this time it was louder. She looked up in time to see the Upper Realm bright with a zig-zag of light. The Violet Moon was covered by thick, dark plumes. F'lorna tried to move her feet into the beginning of her dance, but they wouldn't budge. She remembered the vine and bent down to wrench it off. She pulled so hard that she tripped herself, landing on her back and slamming her horns against the wood floor. She felt a sharp pain where her left horn was anchored to her forehead. She rested for a moment dazed, but a drop of water landed on her face, awakening her senses. Another drop landed on her arm. She heard the voices yelling and the shuffle of feet on the ground. She looked toward the villagers and saw her father running to the village platform. The water drops from the Upper Realm multiplied quickly, and F'lorna felt her entire body immersed in falling waves of rain.

"Everyone, grab all that you can and get to your Achion clusters! The storm is here!" she heard her father yell.

F'lorna tried to get up, but her feet were still wound in the vine that never broke. She closed her eyes. "Ra'ash! Help me!"

Isn't this what you wanted? A reason to not dance?

"No!" she felt an energy rise within her. "I will offer my Adoration!" she yelled to herself. She pressed her hands against the platform floor and pushed her body up. She slid her left foot up, and the Zulo vine slipped off.

"F'lorna, we need to go!" Lemmeck yelled.

She looked up and saw her father carrying her mother across the Village Achion cluster.

"What happened to my mother?" she yelled through the howl of the wind. Lemmeck was standing on the ground leaning against the platform facing her.

"I didn't see it. All I know is that after you fell, your aunt was on the ground, helping your mother. Your father told everyone to leave. They are taking your mom to the Village Achion trees. Come on! I told your father I would take you to your Achion tree!"

"Be my witness!" F'lorna yelled. "I need to offer my Adoration!" She tried to get into position as the wind blew across her body. "I want Ra'ash to be pleased!"

"F'lorna, you're hurt. You hit the platform hard. Your father can plan another ceremony for your Adoration later!" Lemmeck yelled, reaching for her.

"No! Please! Witness for me!" she yelled back. She didn't have time. She needed to begin her dance. She got into the first position and thrust her body against the gust. She continued to dance, adjusting to the pressure of the torrent pushing against her. At moments the wind lifted her into her next move, yet other moments the wind shoved her back. But she kept dancing, hoping that Lemmeck was still there, watching as her witness. She got onto her horns for her final move just as another crack sounded in the Upper Realm above them. The platform lit up as she spun her inverted body on her horns in the image of Jeyshen flying on His Swarve through the sphere. She felt another sharp pain in her forehead and a shift in her horn as she thrust her legs back to the platform. She landed on the platform hard, and suddenly the ground shuddered. She fell to her knees.

She looked up and saw only darkness. The torches were all out. "Lemmeck!" she cried.

"F'lorna, I'm here! I witnessed! Now let's go! The ground is shaking!" Lemmeck yelled.

F'lorna crawled to the edge of the platform and allowed Lemmeck to grab her and bring her to the ground. He wrapped his arm around her waist, and together they ran toward her family's Achion cluster. The wind brought the rain in torrential sprays. Her face was down and she tasted blood in the corner of her mouth. She wanted to reach up and feel her horn, but Lemmeck continued to pull her with him down the path.

The horizon rumbled and the cracks of thunder began to come one right after the other. The Upper Realm lit up with flashes of light. F'lorna couldn't help but think that Ra'ash was yelling at her. Was He angry with her Adoration? Did she cause this storm? The ground shook again, and she heard a thunderous sound coming up from the River. She and Lemmeck both fell onto the rocky, wet path.

"We're almost there!" she shouted to Lemmeck. "Follow me!" She crawled along the path until it opened up to the grassy floor that led to her Achion cluster. She continued to crawl until she passed her family's cooking hearth.

"Take our spare Achion tree. I'll go to mine!" she shouted over the wind.

"F'lorna! You are hurt. Let me help you!" Lemmeck yelled back.

"No, I'm fine! We need to get to our trees before the ground shudders again. The tree roots will keep us safe!"

She could see Lemmeck not wanting to listen to her, but he finally nodded and crawled to the spare tree.

She crawled to hers and forced her body to slide into the hole, trying to protect her horns as she stumbled in. Thankfully, the opening to her Achion tree was facing away from the wind, and her fabric mattress was fairly dry. She reached under her mattress and grabbed the hole covering made of thick hide. She placed it over the hole and secured the taut sinew from the anchor of the left side, across the covering, and to the anchor on the right side.

The noise outside muffled and she tucked her legs and torso under her fiber covers. She was wet, but she knew the thick fabric would warm her. She was grateful for the deep roots of her Achion tree. The ground trembled, but she felt safe curled up on her mattress, protected by her childhood resting place. Her mother must have fainted after she had tripped on stage and hit her horns. Only one other time had she seen her mother's eyes close and her body fall to the ground. That was when she found out that Raecli's mother had died.

F'lorna felt tiredness suddenly overwhelm her. She was grateful for the hole covering of her Achion tree. She rarely used it—only when the wind brought the rains in. But now it covered the flashes of light she knew

93

accompanied the claps of thunder outside. F'lorna had
never experienced ground shudders but her father had
spoken of them from when he was a youngling. She
heard the noise of the River. Never had it sounded so
close to her Achion cluster. Had the River come to
swallow her up?

F'lorna felt her eyes begin to close. The tightness
in her stomach dissipated. Even though the storm raged
outside, she felt a sudden peace engulf her. She didn't
have to dance anymore, and she didn't have to carry the
burden of Raecli's memory. She was no longer a
youngling, but a Novice Elder. She had a new start. The
villagers may have not seen her dance, but she had
offered her Adoration at her Doublemoon Ceremony.
Lemmeck witnessed it, and not even Zelara or her family
could take that moment away. She needed to find a new
Adoration, but she wanted to do more than simply dance
or sing. She yearned for an Adoration that impassioned
her, but nothing at Right River Hook gave her that. At
that moment, hidden in the palm of her Achion tree, she
felt a certainty that she would find it—or, at least, it
would find her. Ra'ash was leading her in the right
direction, and her path began on the other side of the
storm.

"Thank You, Ra'ash for saving me from myself.
Thank You for sending the storm before my Adoration.
Thank You. Thank You," she whispered, her eyes
closed. Slowly, she felt a warmth surround her, like
nectar collected on a hot, summer evening.

"Jeyshen, is that You? Did You send a storm on
my behalf? I don't want to offer dancing as my
Adoration anymore. Speak to me. Lead my life. I want

You to guide me in the right direction. Thank You for being Expanded on the Sphere, so I may know You."

F'lorna began to succumb to weariness before she heard voiceless words within her spirit that she didn't understand: *You will write symbols for Me.*

"Write symbols?" she murmured, before falling asleep.

Chapter 9

THE FLOODED RIVER

F'lorna heard the River rushing toward her, and she couldn't decide if she was dreaming or not. She opened her eyes, but the hole cover for her Achion tree was still on. There was no light, and she wondered if it was still dark outside. When she heard her father's voice, she knew it was probably morning.

She tried to move her head but winced in pain. Her matted hair was wrapped around her left horn and onto something that was preventing her from getting up. She couldn't move without the area above her left

96

temple throbbing. She reached over her head and tried to untangle her hair from whatever it was sticking to. It was her horn brace. It had slipped out from her horns and braids during the night and parts of it were wedged between the inner wall of her Achion tree and her mattress. She began to untie the brace and softly pull her tangled hair from it. After several moments of fingering the leather straps, she finally separated the brace from her head completely.

She slowly got up, her head continuing to throb. Her body wanted to stay in the safety of her Achion tree, but she couldn't stay tucked away forever. She needed to know why the River sounded so loud. She loosened the tight sinew of the hole covering and brought the cover into her tree, placing it at her feet. She would have to clean her Achion tree and wash and dry everything she knew would soil. She poked her head out of her hole and the light from the Heat Source blinded her. It was not morning. It was midday. She looked toward the cooking hearth and saw her mother and aunt sitting at the table, drinking a hot tea her mother made whenever she was worried. She looked toward the budding Achion trees that lined her family's property. They were gone. Instead, the River flowed only a few trees length away from where she slept.

"Father!" F'lorna yelled, regretting the sharp pain to her forehead where she had struck her horn.

Jaquarn, who had been standing at the River's new edge, looked back to his daughter. "Be soft, my daughter. You are badly hurt," he said as he walked toward her.

F'lorna carefully got out of her tree. "What happened to the River?" she asked, unable to look away. "Have all the waters from the Great Expanse come down into Right River Hook?"

Jaquarn looked at his daughter and scratched his chin. "We don't know yet. I met with the Circle of Elders this morning, and we will meet again when the Heat Source begins its decent into the evening horizon. All I know for sure is that our tributary has more than doubled its width."

F'lorna noticed that her father kept his gaze on her left horn. "Is it bad, Father?"

Jaquarn looked into her eyes. "It's definitely not good. Your left horn is now two-fingers widths lower than your right, and you have dried blood along your face." He stopped, and F'lorna knew he was holding back his full emotion. "Why, F'lorna? Why did you continue to dance?"

"My young brother, these are questions we can ask later. Let me look at her," Eline said, walking up to F'lorna and gently cupping her ears to bring her forehead down to her eye level.

"Can it be adjusted?" T'maya asked, coming up beside Eline.

"I fear if I move it too much, the root will come out. It will be best to clean and bind it. I've had to extract damaged horns, and F'lorna's has loosened more than I would like. It needs to heal as it rests," Eline looked into F'lorna's eyes. "It's not uncommon for them to pull back some toward their original position as they heal. I will offer voiceless words to Ra'ash that yours will do just that."

F'lorna didn't want to look up. She had her mother's disappointed face memorized, and she wasn't ready to see it. "Where is Lemmeck?" she asked as her aunt continued to move her head to get a better look of the wound.

"He left early this morning," Jaquarn said. "He was worried about his mother and his family's estate. The shallow pass across the River to his family's land is now completely immersed. He had to swim across. It looks like we will be building a bridge now."

"T'maya, can you bring me the water we boiled and the cleaning cloths? This wound has already been sitting all night. We need to clean and bind it now," Eline said. "F'lorna, I need you to sit and make yourself comfortable. It will take me a while to clean it thoroughly. Where is your horn binding?"

"It is in my Achion tree," she whispered. "It is dirty."

"I'll get it and wash it in the River," her father volunteered.

After her mother and father walked away for the moment, F'lorna turned toward her aunt. "What happened to my mother at the Doublemoon Ceremony?"

"After you struck your horn on the wooden floor, your mother stood up and fainted. I tended to her, and your father ran to you, but Lemmeck intercepted him. He told your father to help the villagers and that he would get you," Eline said. "Lemmeck carried much guilt this morning for being your witness for the dance because you caused further injury to your horn. He obviously didn't know your final move was on your horns or he wouldn't have agreed. Your mother told me this morning about it, but she couldn't remember what the move demonstrated."

"It was a demonstration of Jeyshen riding the Swarve through the sphere," F'lorna whispered. The move seemed silly to her now and did nothing to illustrate the Holy Image of Jeyshen.

Eline brought F'lorna's face toward her and stared into her eyes. "Why did you have to finish your offer of Adoration? We could have waited until after the storm and ground shudders were finished. Doublemoon Adorations have been delayed before, F'lorna. And a storm is a good reason to wait."

F'lorna felt tears well up in the corner of her grey eyes. "I wanted the storm to come, so I wouldn't have to offer my Adoration. I realized that I'm a horrible dancer, and I chose it for the wrong reasons. I didn't want to embarrass you and my family. But when it was time for me to quit, I couldn't. Giving up is not in me."

The tears streaked down the dried blood along F'lorna's rounded cheekbones, and Eline cupped her chin and brought her face close to hers. "The best offering to Ra'ash is not an Adoration, F'lorna. It is a life given up to His care and purpose. You can offer anything to Ra'ash—a song, a dance, a healing or a White Diamond Stag—but if your heart is not to please Him, the offering has no true value. I don't care that dancing was your Adoration. How was your heart when you offered it?"

F'lorna looked at the aged face of her aunt. The creases around her eyes and mouth were deep with many moon cycles, but her expression held youthfulness and vitality captive. "I wanted Ra'ash to be pleased with me.

I feel like I had been hiding from Him for so long. I just wanted to somehow offer Him my apology of healing—to make things right with Him again."

"Do you think Ra'ash was pleased?" Eline asked.

"I don't know," F'lorna admitted. "But I didn't feel any condemnation from Him. In fact—" she stopped.

"In fact, what?" Eline pressed.

"I felt His peace filling me when I crawled into my Achion tree during the storm," F'lorna said. "I was wet, hurt and tired, but I felt safe and loved."

Eline nodded. "The Indwelling."

"Is that what that was?" she asked.

"Of course. When Ra'ash fills you, He imparts all the goodness that He is."

"And He spoke to me," F'lorna said, hesitantly. "But I don't understand what He means."

"What did His Voiceless Words say?" Eline asked.

Suddenly, F'lorna heard footsteps along the grassy floor behind them. "He said my Adoration will be to *write*, but that doesn't make sense to me," she whispered. "I am not a Sand-shaper."

Eline said nothing and continue to stare for several moments. Then she looked toward the rustling in the distance. "I see your mother is returning. It's time for you to sit, so I can clean and bind your horn."

T'maya arrived as F'lorna sat on a thick, grassy patch of ground. "I have the boiling water, cleaning cloths and the herbs you set out," T'maya said, setting the tray of medicinal items on the ground next to F'lorna.

Eline kneeled in front of F'lorna and pinched some herbs into the water. Then she grabbed a cleaning cloth, dipped the edge into the liquid and began to clean F'lorna's wound and horns.

F'lorna finally looked toward her mother. Her normally braided hair was down, and there were no sticks masquerading as horns woven onto her head.

"Mother, why is your hair down?" F'lorna asked. The disappointed expression that F'lorna was expecting on her mother's face was not there. Instead, her face held a mixture of pain and love. She knelt down, took another cleaning cloth, dipped it in the liquid and began to clean F'lorna's face.

"Horns mean very little compared to the life of my daughter. When I saw you hit your head, I feared that I would lose you. And that fear was unbearable. When I awoke, and Eline told me that you were okay, I promised Ra'ash that I wouldn't worry anymore about what I don't have and who I am not. Nothing surprises Ra'ash. He knew that I would be born a Sand-shaper, and He knew I would find your father and come to the River. He honored me with you as a daughter on the First Green Moon. All your life, I've focused my attention on trying to fit it, but Ra'ash has created me to be me, not anyone else. And He has created you to be you, not anyone else. My spirit is weary from trying so hard to fit in and making sure that you do. Ra'ash has given me so much, and my life is full of joy."

As F'lorna listened to her mother's words, she felt her entire perspective change in an instant. "Your words, Mother, and my aunt's words are opening my mind to much I can't explain, but I feel this freedom in

Ra'ash that I have never felt before," F'lorna said. "It is like Ra'ash wants not what I can offer Him, but He wants who I am, and—" F'lorna thought. "He desires my love and adoration."

"Precisely," Eline said. "T'maya, do you know what your brave daughter just told me?"

T'maya thought and smiled. "She has the Indwelling? I can see it."

The trio heard a rustling coming from the River.

"I cleaned the binding off the best I could," Jaquarn yelled over the rumble of the River as he entered the Achion cluster. "F'lorna, you stained the leather with your bleeding, but it is clean." He handed it to Eline.

He walked up to three members of his small family, sitting on the forest floor. "I have a hunch that when I meet up with the Circle of Elders, we will discover that the River is completely healed."

"Does it taste different?" T'maya asked.

"In all my moon turns, I have never tasted the River so fresh, and there are hints of aromas I can't explain—qualities of minerals and organic materials that I have never tasted before. The ground shudders from the First Green Moon's Doublemoon Ceremony have not only changed the River's form, but its flavor."

T'maya stood. "And my daughter, F'lorna, danced those changes in with the storm. Lemmeck is a witness to it."

No one said anything and allowed the new insight to fully form in their minds. F'lorna remembered dancing with and against the wind and rain. At moments, the wind lifted her up. And other moments, the rain tempted her to slip again. All the while, though, she

103

continued to dance until the end, even damaging her left horn in the process.

"Okay." F'lorna smiled freely for the first time in a moon turn. "Tell me the truth. My dancing is not so bad, is it?"

Jaquarn chuckled. "F'lorna, you have seen me dance at the Shoam-sha, and I know you want to giggle. But it's not about how good I am, it's about my heart for Ra'ash and His family. I sing, I dance, I heal all for Him because pleasing Him brings me pleasure."

T'maya stroked her daughter's now clean cheek. "Don't worry, my daughter. You will find your way. The Indwelling of Ra'ash will guide you."

F'lorna looked at her aunt who had begun to bind her horns. She didn't want to mention what Ra'ash had told her about writing symbols. She still didn't know what that Adoration was, and she wanted to seek understanding before she told her parents.

"You are right, Mother. I just need to be me."

Chapter 10

THE STORM DANCER

❝ I have lost almost all of my land!" Trenton yelled. His feet were uncovered and his fabric pants were folded up to the knee. His dark hair was swept to the side with sweat, and he paced back and forth, pointing at the River. F'lorna watched him from the corner of her eye while she hung clothes and other hearth fabrics to dry on a strip of Zulo vine hung between the branches of two Achion trees. She carefully hung her new leather tunic. Her aunt made sure to secure all their items from the Doublemoon Ceremony, bringing them with her into the Village Achion tree she was hiding in. F'lorna was relieved that Elder Trenton did not bring Zelara with him.

"All of us with land near the River have lost large portions. I am now down to almost half my land, but what we got in return is nothing short of Ra'ash's blessing to us. The River is healthy and vibrant. You yourself have said you have seen at least three new species of fish that you have never seen before."

"I know these are good things, but the cost to me and my Achion cluster is the highest of all in the Village! My lands were along the Riverbanks, and now they are part of the River. Almost all of my fishing equipment was taken during the storm. Two of my storage Achion trees lost everything within them. I don't have the equipment or the tools to start all over again. I will need help from the Right River Hook, and maybe Left River Hook. You are part of the Circle of Elders. Tell them that I need their support!" Trenton yelled again, throwing up his hands.

"Trenton, no one was untouched by this storm. Some villagers lost entire Achion trees—aged ones that have been in their family for many moon folds. The Shoam-sha will be in two moon rises. I will talk to the villagers then, and we will come up with a plan for rebuilding our village," Jaquarn said, patiently. "Can I offer you a morning meal? I know you must be tired from surveying your land."

"My lack of land!" Trenton said, unmoved.

"I offer you my apology of healing for all your family has experienced from the storm. Ra'ash has His reasons, and I know that the transition has been difficult, especially since your family is new, but I believe that our Village is on the cusps of something truly special."

"What? Are you believing the whispers about your daughter's Storm Dance? That is nonsense! Her dance does not count because the Village had evacuated! Her dance does not qualify as an offering of Adoration, and she is not a Novice Elder in our community yet!"

"That is enough, Trenton! You must disengage in personal attacks on me and my family simply because we are having difficulty seeing through each other's eyes. Lemmeck was the witness for her offering to Ra'ash, and she is a Novice Elder of our Village and deserves respect as such," Jaquarn said.

F'lorna felt her palms tense together. She wanted to walk right up to Zelara's father and tell him exactly what she felt about it. But her father was right. Personal attacks did not help the situation, and they displeased Ra'ash.

"All I know is that if your daughter brought this storm with her dance, then she is responsible for the loss of my lands and fishing equipment! I hold her solely responsible," he said, disregarding that F'lorna was only a tree's length away from him.

"But, I thought you didn't believe in the stories about her Storm Dance." Jaquarn said calmly, folding his arms.

"I don't believe them! She is a silly dancer! Why would Ra'ash respond to her? In fact, He bent her horn from displeasure!" Trenton yelled.

F'lorna turned to face Trenton.

"My daughter," Jaquarn said, turning towards F'lorna and holding out his hand to stop her. "Don't let the Elder Trenton's insults have power over your actions."

"Yes, Father," she said, staring at Trenton.

"Trenton, as of now you have claimed two opposite opinions with the only anchoring point being my daughter is at fault. It seems to me that the truth doesn't matter to you as much as F'lorna being found guilty. I do not know why you have targeted my daughter with your anger, but you need to remember that Ra'ash is in control of everything and nothing goes on without His say so. You must halt these verbal attacks toward my daughter or I will have to bring your accusations to the Village for guidance."

Trenton's countenance faltered, and he tried to hide his anger. "I offer you my apology of healing. I am not attacking her. I am merely saying that the storm has taken my lands."

"And there is no one to blame," Jaquarn added. "Rodesh is a living planet, and she also gives birth to changes."

"The fact still remains," Trenton said in a controlled voice. "I have lost a lot, and I need more land. Can I have land on the other side of the River?"

Jaquarn shook his head. F'lorna knew that that land belonged to Lemmeck and his family.

"I didn't want to suggest this yet because we need to discuss it with the Village, and it will be a large undertaking," Jaquarn said. "I've seen these structures further south before the River disappears into the Desert Plains. They build piers along the River's edge in order to have more room. When we build the bridge, we can ask the Elders if we can also build a tree's lengths of pier on your land along the River. It would be small to start, but it can be expanded later when resources and time are not limiting us. We have several fallen trees now, and we might have enough wood to gain you extra space for your fishing and equipment."

Trenton rubbed his jaw with the knuckles of his right hand. "Yes, I have heard of those. That would give me workable space for my equipment and better access to the River." He stopped. "But how can I trade for such an undertaking?"

"We will have to stop our plans on the Village Pillar for now, and work on the bridge and the pier. The villagers have already donated their time, so I will have to talk to the Village and get approval. They will see the need of a bridge, and I think I can show them why we need the pier as well. The fish provided from the River is just as important to our village as the meat provided from the other side of the River."

F'lorna didn't like the thought of the village offering their time and resources to building a pier, but she knew the bridge was necessary if Lemmeck and his family would continue to be an essential part of Right River Hook. She turned back to pinning up the wet fabrics and continued listening to their conversation.

"I will speak to the villagers," Trenton demanded.

Jaquarn held up his hands. "It will be best if I speak to them first. If you are unhappy with the results, I welcome you to speak before the Elders."

Trenton stood quietly wrestling with his thoughts. "I will trust you, but make sure you get me the results I need." He exhaled and quickly muttered, "It's

109

best for the village." He marched off back towards his Achion cluster.

Jaquarn turned to face his daughter. "F'lorna, go to Le'ana's Achion cluster and tell her father that I need to speak with him at the Pillar." He took a step, then stopped. "And thank you for controlling your words. What Elder Trenton said was wrong, but we are accountable for our own actions, not the actions of others."

F'lorna nodded and watched her father walk away on his way to the Village Pillar.

F'lorna walked along the forest floor toward her birth friend's Achion cluster that opened into large meadow used for planting. She resisted the urge to scratch above her left temple. The wound around her horn had scabbed over and begun to itch. Her left horn was noticeably lower than her right, but her mother braided her hair in such a way that the difference lessened. She held out hope that the left horn would heal further up on her scalp.

Broken tree limbs and other organic debris scattered along her path. If she hadn't grown up walking to her friend's Achion cluster, she might have gotten off track. Le'ana's hearth was deeper in the forest and further from the River than hers, so she and her family hadn't lost any land. Le'ana's father was a planter, which was Le'ana's chosen Adoration. And her mother played the leera at the Shoam-sha and sung on occasion.

Her mother cared for Kytalia, a village widow, the same one who would come to F'lorna's Achion cluster to visit with her mother and recite parts of the *Divine Oracle* to her. F'lorna hadn't visited for many phases of the moon, and she looked forward to seeing them.

As she entered Le'ana's land, she saw her and her father in one of their planting fields. Le'ana had her tunic tied at her thighs and her father's pants were folded above the knee. They both walked through the dark, lined soil of their field. She noticed something she hadn't seen in the field before. There were long River Pine logs surrounding the rows of toiled soil. F'lorna could see that all the branches and needles had been stripped off the trees. She saw a pile of branches and several small, woven baskets, which she assumed held the pine needles.

"Ah, there is our little Storm Dancer! How are you today, F'lorna?" Rengor said, enthusiastically.

F'lorna didn't know how to respond to Le'ana's father's words. She hadn't seen anyone in two rises of the Heat Source since the storm until Trenton came to speak with her father earlier that morning. She tried to smile. "My father sent me to ask if you will meet him at the Village Pillar. He is there now," she said.

Rengor looked toward the direction of the River. "Yes, of course. We are all finished here," he said, returning his gaze back to F'lorna. "And because of our young Storm Dancer here, we have so much to thank Ra'ash for. The waters have saturated our fields. The soil smells like nothing I've ever known. The ground is rich with nutrients again. Thanks be to Ra'ash that we already harvested the previous season's growth, and now it is time to plant for the next season. I know that our next crop will be bountiful!"

F'lorna looked at the logs lining the field. "What are the logs for?" she asked.

Le'ana dusted off her tunic and walked to F'lorna. "Lemmeck came over yesterday and said that he had several fallen River Pines on his land washed up on the other side of the River. He and his twin brothers were hauling them to the Village Achion cluster. He asked if we could use a few, and that's when my father thought of his brilliant new plan for our fields!" Le'ana said unable to mask her excitement.

F'lorna noticed that Le'ana's speckles from the Heat Source were even more scattered around her face and arms from working in the open fields. Some of them even matched the scarlet color of her thick, unruly her hair that always swept across her forehead. She kept her hair shorter than most of her friends.

"With the great rains you brought in at the Doublemoon Ceremony, some of the field soil bled out. So, I thought to place the logs on the perimeter of our fields to hold the soil and rain in. Just give us fair warning before you offer your Adoration to Ra'ash again," Rengor said winking.

F'lorna felt her face blush and tried to cover her embarrassment by wiping off sweat from the side of her face. "I did not send the storm," she admitted. "Ra'ash did."

"Sage and her older sister saw you from the Village Achion tree they had hidden in for safety. They saw your dance coming in and out of the darkness as the flashes of white light illuminated all of Right River

Hook. Blaklin says you fought against the wind and rain to finish your dance, and as you did your final spin on your horns in honor of Jeyshen, the entire length of the Upper Realm lit up with delight!"

"Blaklin is saying that?" F'lorna asked. She knew Sage's sister was a storyteller visiting from Left River Hook. She didn't realize that she'd had witnesses other than Lemmeck.

Le'ana nodded, raising her hand to F'lorna's bound left horn. "And you risked your horn to make the River well again. I am offering voiceless words to Ra'ash that He saves your horn from being extracted and that it heals back in place."

F'lorna noticed tears gathering in Le'ana's eyes.

"I had better be going. I know your father is busy with the village needs," Rengor said. He looked at F'lorna. "I would squeeze your shoulder, but my hands are dirty with this rich soil and you are wearing a light-colored tunic. I wish I could have seen your Storm Dance, but I needed to get my family back to their hearth to safety. Thank you for your offering to Ra'ash. I believe you and your birth friends had a Doublemoon Ceremony that will be talked about for many moon folds to come," he said and looked to his daughter. "Le'ana, let F'lorna have a basket of River Pine Needles. I know creation is not her Adoration, but maybe she can trade them for something special."

"Yes, Father," Le'ana said, smiling.

F'lorna watched Rengor walk away before addressing her birth friend. "Le'ana, do you really believe I could cause this storm from our Doublemoon Ceremony? I was just trying to finish my dance."

113

Le'ana grabbed F'lorna's hand oblivious to the soil covering her palms. "You are always so modest, F'lorna, and always thinking of others first. But after what Zelara did to you at our Doublemoon Ceremony, I was so angry! But Ra'ash fought for you!"

"What?" F'lorna said, confused.

Le'ana leaned closer to F'lorna's face, even though no one was around to hear. "Zelara is the one who told Layaton and Salyna that they should do solos because you were too big and made them look silly. Zelara said that you would ruin their offering of Adoration. But Salyna is even quieter than I am, and as the Doublemoon Ceremony got closer, she was unable to sleep with worry. The rise before our ceremony, she finally begged Layaton to dance with her on the village platform, so she wouldn't be alone. I saw them practicing, and when I asked them about the change to their offering, they told me that you already knew. But when I saw your face after your father introduced them, I knew that they had lied to me. Can you believe it? Lies at our Doublemoon Ceremony. What were they thinking?"

F'lorna thought of Zelara's father making accusations about her. "It is not Layaton and Salyna's fault. Zelara has learned to be very deceptive."

"They both feel terrible now after hearing Blaklin's story about you. I don't doubt you will get apologies of healing from them both, especially Salyna. I spoke with her as the Violet Moon appeared in the Upper Realm yesterday. Did you know her family lost one of their oldest Achion trees?"

"But I don't want villagers to feel bad on my account, and I'm uncomfortable with Blaklin telling everyone that I did a Storm Dance," F'lorna said.

Le'ana let go of F'lorna's hands and grabbed both her shoulders. "I let you mourn the loss of Raecli because I know how much you loved her, but I loved her too. You are not accountable for Raecli's disappearance and you are not accountable for the stories others tell about you—good or bad. I understand you feel a pressure as the daughter of the Village Spiritual Elder, but you can't carry everyone's opinions of you. If Blaklin wants to talk about your Storm Dance, then that is what Blaklin will do. And if Zelara wants to try to ruin your Doublemoon Ceremony, then that is what Zelara will do. It is Ra'ash's job to bring both justice and honor to light, which is exactly what He did."

F'lorna looked at her normally shy birth friend. "You speak with so much confidence."

Le'ana brought F'lorna into an embrace. "I can't tell you how honored I felt to watch Ra'ash's love for you unfold before my very eyes. One moment you were on the village platform tripping on a Zulo vine, and I felt so embarrassed for you. But the next moment you were dancing against the storm, and Ra'ash lit up the Upper Realm and healed our tributaries and lands. Your struggle and triumph have given me so much confidence in Ra'ash. I am grateful to you."

F'lorna allowed herself to be hugged. When she looked into Le'ana's green eyes again, she couldn't help feeling thankful. "I have missed you, Le'ana. I am saddened that I pushed you away for so long, and I want to offer you my apology of healing."

"I believe I pushed you away too. I know I could have visited you more, but seeing you reminded me of the times we both spent with Raecli, and I wondered how she was doing. I used to fear for her, but after our Doublemoon Ceremony, I know Ra'ash is in complete control, and He loves her more than we both ever could."

It was F'lorna's turn to wipe her tear-filled eyes. "Thank you for your words. I know you are right."

Le'ana brought her hands to her hips and gave a knowing smile. "Now I believe it is time for you to pick out your basket of River Pine Needles. I tried to make sure they were each plucked out of the branch without breaking their root, so a hole could be made big enough for a string of fiber to go through, but some may be damaged. You'll have to throw out the bad ones and soak the good ones in water for the night. Don't forget to poke the hole at the root before you spread them out to let the Heat Source dry them, so they become dark brown and hard as rock."

"Thank you, Le'ana. I am glad my father sent me to you. I would be honored if I could help you and your father seed your fields tomorrow."

"He would like that," Le'ana said. "But don't be surprised if he asks you to offer your Adoration to Ra'ash."

F'lorna smiled and said nothing as she followed her birth friend to the baskets of River Pine needles. She wanted to tell Le'ana that Ra'ash had chosen a new Adoration for her, but that would have to wait until the village had been rebuilt.

Chapter 11

A RIVER MONSTER

❝ Mother, the Violet Moon is asleep again. I keep missing it every morning," F'lorna said, coming out of her Achion tree. "Did my aunt already leave?"

"Yes, there are many villagers who were hurt by the storm and ground shudders. She had to help out the other villages. She knows that you've been working hard these past several rises," T'maya said, handing F'lorna a bowl of mixed grains sweetened with sap from the Achion tree. "You have been helping Le'ana and her father deposit seeds into the soil. Kytalia came over earlier and recited the *Divine Oracle* to me as the Violet Moon said farewell to the Heat Source, and she told me of all your hard work. I am proud of you, my daughter."

F'lorna stared at her mother. She had changed, not only by letting her dark chestnut hair fall in waves around her face, but also something deep within her spirit was at peace. Somehow her mother looked younger and lighter than F'lorna could remember.

"Why are you staring at me?" T'maya asked.

F'lorna blinked and looked away embarrassed. "I don't know, Mother. You seem different somehow in a good way. I like your hair flowing down. It reminds me of the waterfalls along the mountainside that you used to describe to me."

T'maya thought. "Yes, they were beautiful. I would put my lips right above the rocks and drink straight from the mountain. I miss the mountain air. I would have never have left if my mother hadn't died."

"You never met my grandfather," F'lorna added, wanting to know more. The topic of T'maya's father had always caused her mother to become embarrassed and silent, but this time she continued to talk.

"My mother and father were never joined together in Ra'ash. She wouldn't tell me much except that he was a landowner of the farmlands south of the Northwestern Coast. His family's farms provided much of the edible plants that the Sand-shapers in the coastal cities consumed. I believe he was much older than my mother, and he might have had a family. He stopped visiting my mother when she learned that she was heavy with me," T'maya said, deep in thought.

"Grandmother never mentioned his name?" F'lorna asked.

"I walked in on her speaking words to Ra'ash. She didn't know the *Divine Oracle*, but River-dwellers would sometimes visit our village and show us how to offer voiceless words to Ra'ash. My mother didn't understand being voiceless, so she spoke her words aloud. I listened to her say his name, but I don't know if I heard her correctly. It sounded like Dextarnion or Deksarnian or something like that. I was never sure," T'maya said. "I miss my mother so. We were very close."

"As are we," F'lorna added.

T'maya came out of her reverie. "Yes, my dear daughter, as are we," she said. She got on her toes to get a look at F'lorna's horns. F'lorna bent down for her mother to see.

"Your left horn has healed much quicker than I anticipated. I will be able to take off the binding soon. It looks like it moved a little back in place. This is very good."

F'lorna nodded and took another bite of her sweetened grains. "Mother, did you ever want to try to find your father?"

T'maya leaned back and thought. She looked toward the River that had only receded an arm's length since the storm. "If he rejected my mother when she was heavy with me, he would reject me. The lands on the west of the River are vast with many landowners working the fields. It would be hard for me to find one Rodeshian out of many when I do not know what he

F'LORNA OF RODESH BY ALISA HOPE WAGNER

looks like," T'maya said, taking F'lorna's bowl after she took her last bite.

"Mother, did you look like my grandmother, your mother?" F'lorna asked.

T'maya moved quietly toward the cooking hearth and set F'lorna's bowl in the hollowed out Achion tree stump. She lingered for a moment and turned back to face F'lorna. "I looked nothing like my mother or the other villagers from the Northeastern Mountains. They are pale with light hair and eyes of the various green shades of the River or the blue shades of the Great Expanse beyond the Northwestern Coast. Many of them have speckles from the Heat Source like Le'ana."

F'lorna listened intently. Although, she looked more like her father, she did have her mother's grey eyes. "I always thought I got my grey eyes from your mother."

"No, they are the color of the Sand-shapers from the west of the River. There the farmland kinsfolks have tan skin and dark hair, like mine, but darker. Their eyes are shaped like mine as well, but more angular," T'maya said. "I gave voiceless words to Ra'ash that you would look like your father, and you do. But Ra'ash saw fit to give you my grey eyes. I'm glad He did."

"I like my grey eyes, Mother. You and I share them with no one else in Right or Left River Hook," F'lorna said.

Suddenly, they heard the piercing whistle of danger. F'lorna looked around. "Where is it coming from, Mother?"

"There," T'maya pointed. "It's Lemmeck."

F'lorna could see Lemmeck's dark braided hair. He was wet from swimming across the River, and he furiously waved his arms. She noted that he held his Tarnezion Crystal blade in his left hand. He whistled again.

"He sees something we don't!" F'lorna yelled. "Mother get up into your Achion tree!" F'lorna grabbed her mother's arm and pulled her to the small cutouts going up the back of the Achion tree that T'maya and Jaquarn shared. The steps made a ladder imprint to the tree's first set of thick branches.

"You get up first!" T'maya yelled at her daughter.

F'lorna knew her mother was as stubborn as she, so she began the climb up the tree, looking back to make sure her mother followed her. Again, F'lorna heard another piercing whistle, but this one came from another direction.

"That is your father's whistle," T'maya said when she joined her daughter on the first thick set of branches.

"Mother!" F'lorna cried. "A monster is coming out of the River!"

"Oh, Dear Ra'ash! Help us!" T'maya called out.

A large and broad snake-like beast with short, thick legs slinked out of the water toward their cooking hearth. Its body had large, pointy dark scales all over, and its jaws held rows of jagged teeth. It made powerful side-to-side movements quickened by the constant movement of its massive webbed feet. It left wide slither marks in the ground from its heavy weight and closeness to the ground. After only a short moment, the monster had its hard, ribbed nose sniffing the cooking bowl with the rest of that morning's grains. The monster grabbed the wooden bowl with his jaws and slammed down, shattering it into bits.

F'lorna held her scream tight within her throat. She looked back to the River and saw Lemmeck slowly coming into her family's land. Her father and Le'ana's father, Rengor, both had long wooden spears and were coming alongside Lemmeck. F'lorna saw two more flashes of black hair and dark skin on the other side of the River. It was Lemmeck's twin brothers, Dashion and Rashion. They were holding their bows and arrows over their heads and swimming swiftly toward her side of the River. F'lorna knew that they would need the strength of all five to take down the River Monster.

The River Monster heard a crack of a twig breaking under her father's foot, and it instantly turned around to face him. "No!" F'lorna shouted. "River Monster, come find me!"

"What are you doing?" T'maya said. "He hears you!"

"They need more time, Mother! The twins are still in the River. Get to the higher branches!"

T'maya listened to her daughter and reached up to grab the branches above her.

"Come here, River Monster. Come get me!" F'lorna took off one of her leather foot coverings and threw it at the monster. It turned back toward the cooking hearth and made its way to the tree. It put its front legs on the tree and began to scuttle up.

"Grab my hand!" T'maya yelled.

F'lorna reached her hand up and grabbed her mother's. Then she grasped the high branch with her other hand and helped her mother pull the weight of her body to the higher level. She pulled herself up just as the monster's jaws crashed down onto the lower branch F'lorna had just left. The River Monster lost its balance and fell to the ground with the branch still in its mouth.

The sharp point of a long, wooden spear bounced off the monster's thick skin. Rengor's hands were now empty. F'lorna watched as her father unleashed his spear. It sunk into one of the slits on the side of the monster's face. F'lorna could only imagine that the slits were ears. The monster turned toward Lemmeck, and the spear flew out of his ear slit. Finally, Dashion and Rashion came up beside Lemmeck and the three of them began unleashing an onslaught of arrows, one after another, from their bows. Several of the arrows landed in the monster's opened jaw. The monster lunged toward the twins and Lemmeck jumped onto the monster's back, driving his blade deep into one of the small, tender eyes on the front ledge of its face.

The monster roared in pain, shaking his body from side to side, throwing Lemmeck toward the Achion tree that now held F'lorna and her mother. F'lorna heard his body hit the base of the tree. The monster continued to roar in pain as it made its way back to the River, leaving a trail of orange blood on its path. She watched as the River Monster disappeared into the River and then looked down to see Lemmeck. He wasn't moving.

F'lorna leapt to the ground, rolling on the forest floor to disperse the weight of her fall. She placed her ear on Lemmeck's chest. He was still breathing. "Father! Please, Lemmeck needs you!"

Jaquarn ran to Lemmeck's body and knelt down. He stared for a moment, looking for bruising and then felt Lemmeck's head and neck for any broken bones. After a thorough examination, Jaquarn sat back on his heels and held Lemmeck's head up off the ground. "His horns took most of the impact. I see a little ripping on the front part of his right horn, but I believe the root is safe. However," Jaquarn said, holding out his hand, "he lost a piece of his left horn. F'lorna, take this piece and keep it safe for him. T'maya, will you get me a fabric filled cloth for his head? I don't want to lay his horns on the ground until we get a brace for him. Dashion, notify your parents. And Rashion, can you call the rest of the Circle of Elders here? We need to discuss the monster we just witnessed."

F'lorna stared at her birth friend. He had jumped on top of the River Monster and plunged his violet Tarnezion Crystal blade deep into the monster's eye. She allowed her mother to come with the fabric filled cloth and place it under Lemmeck's head. Jaquarn stood up to speak with Rengor, and T'maya followed him. F'lorna stayed down, gently stroking the side of his face with her finger. "Two times you have now saved my life," she whispered. "You hooted to make my feet stand firm and whistled to make my feet run. Thank you, Lemmeck."

124

Chapter 12

THE SHOAM-SHA FEAR

F'lorna sat next to Le'ana and watched her father sing the *Holy Chant of Jeyshen's Protection* from the platform at the Village Achion cluster. F'lorna was pleased that Le'ana's mother played the leera and noticed that her birth friend, Marvine, was playing the poonga. Normally, the poonga was played by another Elder, but F'lorna knew that many of the elders were gone into other villages, helping family members rebuild destroyed homes. The wind blew softly, which contradicted with the subject matter she knew her father would be discussing at the Shoam-sha. Storms, ground shudders and River Monsters were not appealing topics, but at least the Violet Moon was almost at its zenith in the Upper Realm, and no dark plumes halted its light from illuminating all of Right River Hook below.

When the song was over no one applauded by pounding the wooden tables. They had all heard the story of the River Monster, and they saw that Lemmeck's family was noticeably absent from their customary table. They wanted to know about this new predator that had never been seen before. F'lorna wondered how her father would commence his public statement as Spiritual Elder. Le'ana's mother made her way down the steps of the platform with her leera in her hand. Marvine rolled the large poonga to the back of the platform and exited the rear, coming around the side to sit with his family.

Her father stood still for several moments in the center of the village platform near the ledge. Finally, he looked towards his wife. "T'maya will you have the food brought out? I know the families have been working hard and need sustenance in their bodies. They can eat while I talk."

T'maya nodded and several Cooking Elders and three Novice Elders got up from their seats and walked around the platform to get the prepared food waiting on platters.

"My wife wanted to offer her apology of healing. Tonight's dinner will consist of a basic soup of grains and legumes. The storm took much of the villages' stored food, but they were able to prepare fresh bread and Charisse berry jam for each table. So please enjoy your food while I address the village," he said, waiting as the food was being dispersed.

A short time later, all the food was served and the drinking cups were filled with water from the River. The villagers waited for their Spiritual Elder to offer public words to Ra'ash. Jaquarn reached out both hands. "Ra'ash, thank You for the food prepared by Your servants. We will eat and be satisfied. Thank You for sending the rains and opening up the River—" he stopped. F'lorna saw her father concentrating over his next words.

"Guide and help us into this new transition and remind us that nothing is new to You. You know the beginning to the ending, so we trust in Your ways." He dropped his hands. "Please eat and enjoy."

The villagers began to eat, but F'lorna noticed that they continued to stare at the village platform, awaiting her father's words.

Jaquarn scratched his chin in thought. Finally, he began to speak. "As you have all noticed, the River is no longer sick. Take a sip from your water cup, and you will taste the health. However, there are also new flavors in the water that are unknown to us. I have met with the Circle of Elders from both Right and Left River Hook, and the only conclusion we can come up with is that the ground shudders have opened deep pools of water from within the ground itself, and they have fed into our River. We know that the Westland farmers use underground springs to water their fields, so we believe that somehow those springs entered into the River and its tributaries, healing it of the sickness coming from the Sand-shapers on the Northwestern Coast."

127

Jaquarn paused, looking at each table before resuming his speech. "Along with bringing us cleansing water, we have also received a few new plants that float along and grow their roots on the current. Rengor has collected the plants and is analyzing them for any beneficial uses. As of now, he has found one edible plant. I have given it to my wife for ideas on how to prepare it. Moreover, Trenton has discovered several new species of fish that have never been seen in the River. He is in the process of catching them, so he can analyze their benefits and uses, but he will need our help. To that end, the Circle of Elders have agreed to hold off on the sanctuary around the Pillar. Ra'ash knows we will honor Him with voiceless words at the Pillar without a sanctuary for a time. I ask that those of you who offered resources and services to the sanctuary will allow those offerings to be used to build a new bridge across the River and a pier along Trenton's land."

There were several nods of agreement from the villagers. "I am honored to serve Right River Hook. We have all pulled together during this time of change. Ra'ash's changes to Rodesh come with great benefit, but those changes can also cause fear. That is the one thing I desire for our village to not succumb to."

F'lorna noticed the villagers getting restless. They were waiting for news about the River Monster.

Jaquarn raised his hands. "Now I know most of you have heard about what came out of the River today and onto my family's land. We don't know exactly what it is, but it is clearly a predator since it bled orange."

"We are not at all ignorant of predators. Large cats and wolves have wandered into our village, and we have done what we can to protect ourselves and stay aware. But with the River widening and the new species of fish and plants, we now have a water predator to be cautious of. Lemmeck used the whistle alerting us to danger, and both my daughter and wife made it up our Achion tree. The predator is long and can reach to the first set of thick branches, so you will have to climb higher if one comes into our village."

The seated villagers began to whisper tensely, and Jaquarn waited for the noise to die down.

When Jaquarn had their attention again, he continued. "I plead with you not to carry the weight of fear. Ra'ash is in control. If you would like to know more about the predator, Rengor and I will be here when the Violet Moon disappears in the morning. Dashion and Rashion have also said they will try to be available to answer questions. They will survey the River before the Heat Source appears in the morning horizon and let us know what they find. Lemmeck was conscious when I left him at his family's Achion cluster earlier today. His right horn moved a little, but the root is still intact. He did lose a piece of his lower left horn, and the Tarnezion blade given to him as his Doublemoon gift was lost. He thrust the blade deep into the predator's eye."

Again, the villagers whispered amongst themselves. F'lorna felt for the piece of horn in her tunic belt. She wanted to keep it safe until Lemmeck was well enough to get it. She thought about taking it across the River to his Achion tree. She wondered if her father and mother would approve.

Jaquarn held up his hands once more. "I know there is a lot to discuss about the storm and the changes to the River but let us enjoy this night together. When the Violet Moon disappears tomorrow, we will begin work on plans for the bridge and fishing pier for the River. These two projects will be challenging undertakings, and we will need every villager to help."

With that said, Jaquarn walked to the edge of the village platform and down the wooden steps. F'lorna watched him make his way toward their table, attempting to cover his weary face with a smile.

"I can't believe Lemmeck jumped onto the River Monster's back," Le'ana whispered.

"My father doesn't want me to call it that," F'lorna whispered to her friend.

"It is too late. I heard my father telling the story to the elders, and that is the name he used. I wish I would have stayed in my Achion cluster with my father, but my mother asked me to come with her to Vauntan's hearth, so she could give her mother a basket of the River Pine needles," Le'ana complained.

F'lorna said nothing as her father sat down to join their table for the Shoam-sha dinner. He grabbed her mother's hand and squeezed it before picking up his bowl of soup and bringing it to his lips. When F'lorna was sure her father wasn't listening, she continued to whisper to Le'ana. "You should be glad you were gone. You would have been up an Achion tree like me."

"Yes, but you got to see the River Monster. And Lemmeck risked his life for you and your mother. He is the most handsome of all our birth friends, and he likes you, F'lorna," Le'ana whispered.

"We are good friends," F'lorna insisted.

"F'lorna, you may have grown taller than all of us, but you are still behind in your views of love. Lemmeck likes you. When you fell on the village platform, he was the first to get up. I don't care much for him, though," Le'ana whispered. "Dashion is so handsome and sweet. When my father and I bring crops to his family's Achion cluster in exchange for meat, he always comes to talk with me."

F'lorna couldn't help but laugh under her breath. Le'ana was always swooning over boys, but too shy to talk with them.

F'lorna looked at her father and mother to ensure they weren't listening and leaned closer to her friend. "I am thinking about going over there tomorrow," F'lorna said.

"Where?" Le'ana whispered. "To Lemmeck's family's land?"

F'lorna nodded. "I would ask my mother, but I think she is still upset by what happened. I know the River Monster is gone, but it would be good to have another pair of eyes. I could swim the River first while you watch. And when I get to the other side, I will watch you swim over. Do you think you can come with me?"

Le'ana thought for a moment. "Meet me before the Heat Source rises in the morning horizon. I have just a few more things to do in the field and then we can cross the River."

"I will. Now let us finish eating, so we can get sleep. We have an early start," F'lorna said, bringing the bowl to her mouth and taking a large sip.

Chapter 13

THE CROSSING OF FRIENDS

❦❦ Hurry, Le'ana. We need to get going. The Village
meeting for the bridge has already started," F'lorna
said, wiping her brow with the back of her arm. She
wore a cobalt tunic, so the fabric would not show stains
from working in the fields. But as the Heat Source
crawled up the Upper Realm, F'lorna's body became
hotter and hotter. She actually looked forward to
swimming across the River. "We don't need food.
Lemmeck's mother will provide for us once we arrive."

132

"But what if she is not there? You know, she's a hunter like the rest of the family. She may be out harvesting game with her husband," Le'ana said, filling the small leather pouch with food. "Besides, Lemmeck is sick. We are the ones who should be bringing him food. I know for certain Dashion loves the River Pine nuts, and I have plenty to share with him."

F'lorna placed her hands on her hips. "But they are the ones who gave you these River Pine Trees. I am sure that they have plenty nuts at their hearth."

"Yes, but mine have been shelled and roasted with specific herbs that only I have. Mine are better," Le'ana said, tying the leather bag with the sinew sewn to it. "Now we can go."

F'lorna exhaled and adjusted her tunic belt. She would have to carry it over her head when they swam across the River. She noticed Le'ana's outfit for the first time. "Why are you wearing an evening tunic, Le'ana? It will be very hot today with the Heat Source overhead."

"Not everyone has you and your mother's skin that tans under the Heat Source instead of burning like mine, F'lorna. We will be out of the forest, walking through Lemmeck's lands, and there are no trees for shade. My skin will be red from the Heat Source and my speckles will multiply," Le'ana said. "The extra fabric protects my skin."

"I forget how sensitive your skin is, "F'lorna said, remembering Le'ana's resistance to leaving the shade when they were younger.

"You forget many things," Le'ana said. "But now is the time to remember. Let us go. Both our families will be expecting us at our hearths later."

"Where are you two going?" a voice shouted from the other side of the field.

F'lorna looked up and saw Sage carrying something in her hands. The back half of Sage's burgundy hair fell in waves around her umber-colored arms, and the top half of her hair was braided around her horns. Her moss-colored eyes brightened against her umber skin. She wore a grey fabric tunic dress dyed from the inedible moss that grew along the muddy banks of the River.

"Must she shout so loudly?" Le'ana whispered. "My mother may not have left our Achion cluster yet."

F'lorna gave a hoot for Sage to stand still, then ran toward her with Le'ana following behind. Sage looked around like she was in trouble and stood very still. When F'lorna reached her, she leaned forward, placing her hands on her knees to catch her breath.

"Don't shout, Sage. Le'ana and I have an errand to run, and we don't want our parents to know that we will be missing for a time," she finally said through gasps of air.

"I don't think you have to worry about that. I just passed the Village Achion cluster, and the Elders are arguing about the bridge and the fishing pier. Zelara's father is demanding too much. He wants the pier built first, but everyone knows that bridge is more pressing. Almost everyone's parents are there. The rest of our birth friends know there will be work to be done starting tomorrow, but at least we have one more rise of the Heat Source to rest," Sage said. "It is almost unfair being a Novice Elder now. We are expected to work like the other Elders, yet we do not have full decision-making rights," Sage paused. "Where are you two going?"

F'lorna hesitated. "Nowhere important. There's just something we need to do," she said, eyeing Le'ana.

Sage laughed. "I doubt that, F'lorna. You are never off doing something unimportant. You are our Storm Dancer now. I think my sister has squeezed that story into her Eternal Memory by now."

Her face became serious again. "And about that. I want to offer my apology of healing. I have completely stopped being Zelara's friend. At first when we began singing together, I thought she was unique and fun to be with, but I soon realized that she and her family are mean and jealous. Zelara's father envies your father's power in the village, and she envies your confidence. I told her such, and she said I was ignorant and slow-minded. She and Shalane laughed and walked away."

"You think I'm confident?" F'lorna asked, stunned by the suggestion. She had always struggled with feelings of uncertainty.

Sage smiled again. "Of course you are. You have always walked in confidence, until—" Sage looked down embarrassed.

F'lorna reached her hand out to squeeze Sage's shoulder. "Don't be nervous to mention Raecli's name. I think it is good to remember her."

"I do miss her too," Sage said softly. "We used to sing duets together as we were being mentored. Her voice was deeper than mine, and I liked how we sounded together. Although—" Sage thought, looking at F'lorna. "I believe you and I sounded even better together. Do you remember when we were assigned to have our first singing lesson? I think the Indigo Moon was only on its third or fourth turn in the Upper Realm, and we hadn't chosen our Adorations yet. Your voice, F'lorna, was so strong even then. It was like your voice took hold of mine and propelled it up into the air with yours. I could simply weave my light, sweet voice through your intensity. I couldn't wait to sing with you again."

"I remember," F'lorna whispered and smiled in thought. "You have the voice of the Achion bird soaring through the trees."

Sage giggled. "And you have the voice of the mighty White Diamond Stag roaming the lower hills. And it's just as elusive as the stag too. I would love to sing with you again. If you ever offer your voice to your father at a Shoam-sha, please choose me to sing with you. It would be like a dream come true."

F'lorna looked at her friend, realizing for the first time how her actions over a moon turn ago had affected her as well. "I offer you my apology of healing, Sage. It seems I hurt a lot of River-dwellers after Raecli was taken."

Sage smiled and placed her left hand onto F'lorna's shoulder, squeezing it gently. "You were so hurt that you didn't notice the hurt of others, but now I think it is time for all of us to move on from our pain."

"Anyone else relieved that our Doublemoon Ceremony is over?" Le'ana asked, trying to dissipate the intensity of the moment. "I was stuck with my father and Gaspen every rise of the Heat Source for many phases of the Violet Moon. I like Gaspen well enough, but he is not my first choice of all our birth friend boys. I was so disappointed when he chose planting as his Adoration."

"I am glad it's over as well" F'lorna said. "I may have tripped and danced against the wind and rain, but at least I don't have to dance anymore. I wish to find another way to offer Adoration to Ra'ash."

"I have something for you that may help you on your quest," Sage said with a playful smile, holding out the fabric in her hands. "But first you must tell me where you and Le'ana are going."

F'lorna eyed the fabric and saw the lump hidden under it. She wondered what it was. "We will tell you, but you must not tell anyone. It is truly not a big deal. We are going to visit Lemmeck."

Sage gasped. "But, F'lorna, you were just attacked by the River Monster. You two don't know when it will be back. It is probably there right now lingering with Lemmeck's Tarnezion crystal blade sticking out of his eye!"

"Sage, you should have been a storyteller like your sister!" Le'ana said. "He may be a predator, but it is not like he's planning his revenge on Right River Hook."

"This is why we are not telling anyone. Lemmeck is hurt, and I want to visit him. He saved my mother's life and my life. Besides, did you hear my father's words at the Shoam-sha? He said we shouldn't carry the weight of fear. We have dealt with predators before."

"F'lorna don't talk like a Spiritual Elder to me. This is not about having fear; it's about common sense," Sage countered.

"We are taking extra precautions," Le'ana interjected. "I will watch F'lorna cross the River and she will watch me. If we see any movement, we will whistle and run to the nearest Achion tree—all the way to the top this time."

"Then I want to go too," Sage insisted.

"But why?" Le'ana asked. "It's dangerous."

"Didn't F'lorna just say that our Spiritual Elder told us not to carry fear? Besides, I want to go where F'lorna goes. Strange and awesome things happen when she's around, and I want to be a part of it," Sage said.

F'lorna looked at Le'ana and sighed. "Fine. You can go, but make sure that this is one story that you and your sister never tell."

Sage nodded. "Agreed. Now take this, so we can go." Sage stretched her arms, holding out the fabric cloth and hidden item on her palms. "I hope it does not offend you. I found it washed up on the edge of the River near my family's Achion cluster. When I picked up it, I felt the voiceless words of Ra'ash in my Spirit. But instead of actual words, an image of you came into my mind."

F'lorna softly handled the fabric, picking up the delicate object within. She opened the cloth and exhaled. "It is a Sand-shaper's cylinder!"

"It looks transparent, like looking at water under the Violet Moon," Le'ana said. "How do they do that?"

"They make the cylinders out of something they call *glass*—it's melted sand from the coast of the Great Expanse. They have to get their fires very hot to melt the sand into liquid, which is why they produce so much smoke. They must add dyes from different plants to tint the glass this color." F'lorna said, gently shaking the item within the glass.

"I knew instantly it was a Sand-shaper's object. It is too seamless and symmetrical to be from a River-dweller. What's that inside of it?" Sage asked in awe.

F'lorna brought the lavender cylinder up to the rays of the Heat Source to get a better look. "It's the parchment they use to put their symbols on. My mother has spoken of them before, but I have never seen the actual symbols. I asked her to make a few of the symbols in the dirt with a stick, but she wouldn't. They make the parchment out of the pulp from thick, hard grasses that they grow in their farms. They chop the grass, cook it to a pulp, dilute the pulp with water and spread the thinned pulp on sheets of hard glass. Then they place all of it in large cooking hearths made of stone."

"How do they put the symbols on pressed pulp?" Le'ana asked.

"My mother hasn't told me how they put the symbols on the parchment. I don't know if she knows or if she just didn't want me to know," F'lorna said, turning the cylinder with her fingers. "That is the seal they use to close the cylinder. It's some kind of hardened wax that must be melted off."

"I am surprised the River did not wash the wax away," Le'ana added. "It must be very waterproof and strong. We don't have anything in Right River Hook that could withstand a journey down the River to our little tributary."

"They use a special wax recipe that combines wax and melted sand to seal the translucent cylinder. You see this marking?" F'lorna asked, holding the cylinder up, so her friends could see the wax. "That symbol tells us who the maker is."

139

"Are you going to open it?" Sage asked.

F'lorna held the cylinder into her hands for a moment before quickly putting the tube into her leather tunic belt. "I will later but let us visit Lemmeck before we lose our opportunity."

Chapter 14

THE OTHER SIDE

The three friends stood on the banks of the River several tree lengths past F'lorna's family's land. This part of the River was deemed public land by the villagers. The land was more barren, and the shade of the Achion trees was limited. The tunics of the three young ladies bristled in the open breeze that blew, undeterred by any trees. The other side of the River was at least a dozen tree lengths in front of them.

"Why must we cross the River at the widest part?" Le'ana asked, holding the leather pouch with the River Pine nuts in her hands.

"Because the other part of the River is too close to my family's land, and if we went further north, we would be in Elder Trenton's land. This is the safest placed to cross," F'lorna said. "We are good swimmers and the current is slow here. It won't take us long."

"I want to go but I don't want to go." Sage struggled. "I feel like Jeyshen offering voiceless words to Ra'ash before His Expansion."

F'lorna looked at her birth friend. Her burgundy hair whipped around her face and horns with the wind. "Sage, this is nothing like Jeyshen's time in the sanctuary. You are being dramatic."

"Leave her alone, F'lorna. She might not be taking on the pains of Rodesh and our kinfolk, but she is overcoming her own fears. Not everyone is fearless like you," Le'ana said.

"I have fears and I lack confidence much of the time," F'lorna insisted.

"That you may," Le'ana noted. "But you overcome them. That is a trait you have always had. You are stubborn."

"I don't know if that qualifies as a compliment or an offense," F'lorna said, looking back toward the River.

"It is both," Le'ana said, thinking. "Can you imagine what the main body of the River looks like? If our tributaries have become this wide, the main River must look like the Great Expanse flowing down the center of Rodesh. I wonder if anyone from Left River

Hook has seen it. They are much closer to the main River than we are."

"Maybe Lemmeck knows," F'lorna said. "His uncle's family owns much land past Left River Hook, near the main River. They say the land around the main River is all rocky and nothing grows there, but they have hunted Bastalion Goats along its rocky shores."

"Blaklin has lived in Left River Hook since the Fourth Indigo Moon, and she's never visited the main River. There are other storytellers from her village who have explored the main River, and they describe it in detail. Blaklin would rather tell stories about villagers and their experiences rather than scenery. She says it is more interesting. After our Doublemoon Ceremony, she now has two very dramatic stories to tell—about the Great Storm that healed the River and F'lorna's Storm Dance. She couldn't wait to go back to Left River Hook and tell her stories."

"I thought dancing in the dark with all the villagers running from the village platform to their Achion clusters would allow me to offer my Adoration in secret. Lemmeck was supposed to be my only witness. Now both Right and Left River Hook know that I tripped on a Zulo vine and smashed my horn," F'lorna said, exasperated.

"Yes, but they also know that you fought the wind and rain and even the ground shudders to bring your offering of Adoration, and Ra'ash opened the River and healed its waters," Sage added, smiling slyly. "Every good storyteller knows that a good story must have setbacks to make the triumph more satisfying."

"Look, you two!" Le'ana said. "We need to cross. The village meeting is not going to last the entire time the Heat Source is in the Upper Realm. The Violet Moon will come too soon. Let's just go together. I don't see any River Monsters."

F'lorna quickly took off her leather tunic belt. "Follow me," she said.

The three friends began their slow walk into the River. The current was slow and they made their way almost to the middle of the River before they began to swim. F'lorna noticed that the River was cooler than normal, but it felt good under the Heat Source's constant stare.

"What was that?" Sage yelped.

"It is just a Rivertrout. Keep going," Le'ana said. "And stop splashing water. I'm trying to keep this pouch dry."

They finally made it to the other side of the River. F'lorna set her tunic belt on a stone and wrung out the edges of her tunic dress. "Our foot coverings will dry soon enough. Come on. I know the way from here," F'lorna said overconfidently. She had visited Lemmeck's Achion cluster on occasion with her father to pick up meat donated to her family or to the Shoam-sha, but as Lemmeck had gotten older, he began bringing the offerings to her family's land.

"That was underwhelming," Sage said. "I was expecting at least a little excitement. I thought we might at least see the corpse of the River Monster floating by. Didn't Lemmeck pierce him in his eye, and the twins pierce him with their many arrows? I wish I could have seen it. My sister would be asking me for every detail."

144

"You can ask Lemmeck when we see him," F'lorna said.

"I heard the River Monster almost bit off your legs," Sage added.

"He tried," F'lorna said. "Come. This way."

The three made their way into the forest on the other side of the River. F'lorna realized that some of the landscaping had changed since she had been there. The storm had shifted Lemmeck's family's land. Trails that once lead to his family's Achion cluster were now altered and erased. She smelled the air, hoping to smell scents from Lemmeck's cooking hearth. "I smell their cooking fire." F'lorna said, veering east.

"F'lorna, you have never been very good at storytelling. You lack detail. Or maybe you don't, but you keep everything tucked away in your thoughts. When Raecli was taken, you were there. But you wouldn't tell us anything about what happened. That's why I won't bother asking you about the River Monster. I know you won't describe the incident well," Sage said. "But maybe Lemmeck will."

F'lorna stopped, sniffed the air and continued her fast pace. "I know everything that happened. I see it all in my mind—every detail. And I analyze all the moments, including how I felt and what I thought. I just don't like speaking it aloud, like your sister. When I speak, the image I see is not captured by the listener, and I become frustrated. I would rather keep the story true in my mind. At least there it is safe. Lemmeck doesn't tell stories that well either."

"That is true, but he is better," Sage said, smiling.

145

"Thank Ra'ash for the shade," Le'ana said, changing the subject. "How could anyone remain in the heat during the Heat Source's journey from horizon to horizon?"

"My mother told me that the Sand-shapers in the west farmland have tan skin," F'lorna said, thinking of her grandfather but not mentioning him. "Their dark skin probably protects them from the Heat Source while they work the farms."

"My father says they wear large, woven coverings over their heads. I wish I could see the design. I would love to have one for when I work the fields," Le'ana said. "It would shield my face from the Heat Source."

"They don't have horns. Even if you found one of their head coverings, it wouldn't fit," F'lorna said.

"I can see why Sand-shapers extract their horns. Sometimes the fuss of them is not worth their benefit," Le'ana said, feeling the blonde braids along her horns to ensure they were still in place.

"My mother would give almost anything to have her horns back. She says that Ra'ash created us with them, so we should keep them. Lemmeck's horns protected his head from hitting the Achion tree. I think they are very beneficial," F'lorna said and stopped. "We are here. His land is at the edge of the tree line just ahead before the land opens to the meadows."

F'lorna faced her friends. "How do I look? Is there mud on my face? How are my braids? Does my left horn look too low?"

Sage and Le'ana stared a F'lorna.

"You really like him!" Sage exclaimed. "How did I not see this? You are terrible at showing your true feelings."

"F'lorna, your cheeks are turning red. Are you embarrassed?" Le'ana smiled and turned to Sage. "Now I see the reason why we came all the way over here. F'lorna doesn't care about adventures. She's in love."

"No, I am here to return something to Lemmeck," F'lorna said, flustered. "He left it at my Achion tree." F'lorna didn't want her friends to know she carried his broken piece of horn in her tunic belt.

"What could he possibly have left at your Achion tree as he was being thrown by the River Monster? F'lorna, you have too many secrets and you are too quiet about the details," Sage said, her expression lightening. "But that's what makes this adventure more interesting!"

"Here," Le'ana said, reaching toward F'lorna's horns. "Let me fix this braid. And you do have some mud on your chin. I'll wipe it for you." Le'ana took the edge of her tunic sleeve and wiped F'lorna's chin.

"And smooth out your tunic at the bottom. The fabric has bunched up," Sage added, swiping her hand down F'lorna's tunic dress.

F'lorna let her two friends fix her appearance, and she slipped the tunic belt that she had been carrying back around her waist. "Remember, we are simply here to return something to Lemmeck and nothing more."

"And don't forget that I have the roasted Pine nuts for Dashion," Le'ana said.

"Yes, and that too," F'lorna said, facing the path to Lemmeck's Achion cluster.

147

"And I want to ask Lemmeck about his victory over the River Monster," Sage added.

"Yes, I know," she said, fixing a nonchalant expression on her face. She began to stride to the smell of smoke from Lemmeck's cooking hearth. She would not let him know how she felt about him until she was sure about how he felt about her.

Chapter 15

HORN OF STRENGTH

F'lorna walked into Lemmeck's Achion cluster. Unlike her own hearth, his cluster had several large Achion trees—most being used for storage for their weapons, skins and dried meats. Normally, Lemmeck's hearth was full of noise from the twins, his mother and father and himself, but today the atmosphere felt desolate. If it hadn't been for a fire, F'lorna would have supposed no one was there. She walked toward Lemmeck's Achion tree and bent over to look inside. He wasn't there. She looked at his parents' Achion tree, and saw immense roots, like thick vines pulled out of the ground. The tree had fallen in the storm.

"Look at that Achion tree. It looks like the hand of Ra'ash pulled it right out of the ground of Rodesh," Le'ana said, standing in the shade of an Achion tree still standing. "It looks so sad lying there."

Sage pulled at burgundy strands that had wrapped around her neck. "Where are they? Do you think they may have gone hunting?"

"Someone has to be close. They would not leave a fire going with everyone gone," F'lorna said, eyeing the small fire in the cooking hearth. She turned her body slowly in a circle, scanning the trees. Lemmeck's Achion cluster was right on the edge of the forest before the meadow began.

Finally, they heard the sound of feet coming up from the other side of the Achion cluster.

"I am here," Lemmeck's voice rang out somewhere behind the fallen tree.

F'lorna turned and saw the dark braids of his hair and tawny shade of his skin. He walked slowly on the forest floor, stepping over sharp-edged branches of the aged Achion tree that had fallen.

He smiled when he came into view. He carried a giant meadow rabbit in his hand.

"I decided to check my traps, and Ra'ash has honored me with dinner tonight for my family. I will surprise them when they return," he said, dropping the rabbit into an oversized, grass-woven basket. He walked straight to F'lorna and pressed his hand against F'lorna's shoulder. "It is good to see you, F'lorna. Where is your

150

father?" he said, looking past the three friends into the forest.

"He did not join us," F'lorna said, trying to sound as nonchalant as possible.

Lemmeck dropped his arm and stepped back. "You mean you three came here without protection? You do realize that there is a monster in the River," he said.

Le'ana stepped in. "Actually, the River was very peaceful. We didn't see even a bird of prey in the air."

"Exactly," Sage added. "It was quite uneventful."

Lemmeck shook his head. "That is what makes this monster so cunning. It was a peaceful, uneventful morning when I was walking to F'lorna's Achion cluster. When I saw that thing crawl out of the River, the peace ended. You three should not be here. Does your father know that you are here alone?" Lemmeck asked, turning back to F'lorna.

F'lorna didn't want to tell the truth, but she couldn't deceive Lemmeck. "He knows that I am with my friends, but he is busy with the village meeting. I didn't want to bother him. Besides, we are Novice Elders now. Not everything we do must be common knowledge."

"I will take you all back to your Achion clusters," Lemmeck demanded, not wanting to relent from his frustration.

"I brought you something," F'lorna said, reaching into her tunic. She pulled out the broken pieces of horn, and the Sand-shaper's cylinder tub fell from her hand and onto the forest floor.

F'lorna reached down to pick it up, but Lemmeck was quicker. He grabbed the cylinder and held it up toward the sun. "This is Sand-shapers glass," he said.

It was F'lorna's turned to be shocked. "How do you know what it is?"

"Because I've already found three other tubes like it," he said. "They are washing up from the River. I guess the storm hit the Northeaster Coastlands too. I asked my father about them, and he told me they carry the Sand-shaper symbols."

"I found this one," Sage said. "I felt that F'lorna needed it."

"Yes." Lemmeck nodded and looked at F'lorna. "I was on my way to your Achion cluster to tell you about them when I saw the water monster. I thought maybe you could ask your mother to decipher the symbols for me."

"Can I see yours?" F'lorna asked. She wondered if her mother would talk about them. She had been so resistant to even speak about her time as a Sand-shaper before, but F'lorna saw that her mother was changing. She no longer wore her hair around the twigs with braids. Maybe she would tell her what instructions the symbols give.

Lemmeck walked back to his Achion tree and reach his arms and head inside. When he found what he was looking for, he drew out of his tree and walked back to where F'lorna stood.

"Here they are. I have one yellow and two green ones," he said, holding them up.

"I wonder if the colors mean anything?" Le'ana asked.

"Could they resemble the moons?" Sage asked. "Maybe the lavender one I found is really violet, like the moon. And there is the yellow moon and two green moons."

"Let me see the marking on the seals," F'lorna said.

Lemmeck moved the cylinders, so she could see the front of the wax seal. "The green ones have different seals, and they are different sizes as well. But the yellow seal matches the seal on the bigger green cylinder." She held up the lavender one. "None of them match mine. So we have three different seals and three different colors."

"What is in your other hand?" Lemmeck asked, looking at her fisted hand.

"Oh," F'lorna said, trying not to blush. "I saved this for you." She handed him the broken piece of horn. "I am saddened by all that you sacrificed to save us. I have so much gratitude for what you did for my mother and me."

Lemmeck stared at the broken piece of horn in her hand. "I haven't really looked at it yet. My mother was able to move my horn back in place, but there is nothing anyone can do about a missing piece. My father has a chip on the bottom of one of his horns, but he is closer to his Onefold than I am. I may be the youngest villager of both Right and Left River Hook with a piece of horn missing."

F'lorna balled her fist around the broken horn and brought her hand back to her body. "I offer you my apology of healing, Lemmeck. I should have not brought it to you so soon."

153

"I asked my mother if we could use wax to put the piece back," he said. "But she said the wax wouldn't hold in the River. There is no point in having it except to remind me that it is not where it should be."

F'lorna walked up to Lemmeck. She looked into emerald eyes, which seemed higher than they once were. He was still growing taller. "I've watched my mother all my life yearning for her horns. I don't know how you feel, but I know that it is a difficult change, especially since we are still only Novice Elders. But you are still strong and mighty, and you will always be my friend."

Lemmeck nodded, and his eyes lingered briefly on F'lorna's forehead where the horns sprouted. "I should not feel so much sorrow for just a small piece. You too have had to deal with changes to your horns."

"I did this to myself because I am stubborn. You fought the River Monster. And you lost your Doublemoon gift. I owe you so much." F'lorna felt the piece of horn in her right hand and the glass cylinder in her left. Suddenly, an idea came to her. She turned to the fire and walked up to it, sitting on one of the small stones set around the flames.

"What are you doing?" Le'ana asked.

"Everyone, sit around the fire with me. I do not know if this will work, but I ask Ra'ash in my audible voice to make it work."

Le'ana set her basket of River Pine nuts down and walked to the fire, sitting on F'lorna's left side. Lemmeck sat on her right. Sage walked around the fire and sat directly in front of F'lorna.

"What are you doing?" Lemmeck asked.

154

F'lorna turned to him. "Would you mind holding your piece of horn?" she asked, holding it out to him.

Lemmeck gently took the horn.

"Now, hold the broken part up, so I can see it," she said.

Lemmeck turned the piece and held the broken part up.

She turned to Sage. "Stand behind Lemmeck and make sure all his hair is away from his damaged horn."

Sage got up and walked behind Lemmeck. "Can I unbind your braids, so I can hold it to one side?"

"F'lorna, what is it that you're doing?" Lemmeck asked, tension in his voice.

"Trust me, Lemmeck. If this doesn't work, we have lost nothing. But if it does work, we have gained something," she said.

Lemmeck exhaled. "Okay, Sage. You can take down my hair."

Sage unbound the sinew around his dark braids. She then held his hair high away from his left horn.

"Le'ana hold this bottle, with the tip facing the fire," she said, getting up. "Sit here next to Lemmeck."

Le'ana moved to where F'lorna had been sitting and held the glass cylinder with the seal facing the fire.

"Don't do anything yet," F'lorna said to Le'ana. "Let me look." F'lorna got behind where Lemmeck was sitting and looked at his fragmented horn. The break was clean and neat. She then kneeled between Lemmeck and Le'ana. "Let me have the piece," she said to Lemmeck.

He handed her the horn fragment. She looked at it once more, flipping it to face the other way with the

155

break still facing up. "Le'ana bring the cylinder close to the fire, but not directly above it."

Le'ana reached her hand to the fire. "It is too hot, F'lorna."

F'lorna stood up and thought. She looked toward Sage holding Lemmeck's hair. "Where is the sinew that bound his hair?"

"I have it," Sage said, handing it to F'lorna.

F'lorna took it and looked around. She walked toward the fallen Achion tree and found a long, thin root that had broken off. She walked back to the fire and took the glass cylinder from Le'ana. "Let me see if this can work. The fire must be too hot for our fingers, but not too hot for a damp Achion root." She placed the lower portion of the cylinder against the tip of the root and tied the sinew around them both. She pulled the sinew tight and swung the root a few times to make sure the knot was secure.

"This should hold," F'lorna said, walking back to the fire and kneeling in between Le'ana and Lemmeck. She handed Le'ana the branch. "Now you can hold this over the fire and close to the flames, but not too close. I think the seal will melt quickly. Right when you see the wax about to drip, dangle it over the piece of horn and hold it still."

Le'ana nodded. She moved the root and brought the glass bottle just above the flames. "It is like browning a mushroom for a snack," she said, trying to lighten the tension.

All eyes were on the wax. The color of the wax was like that of stones that rimmed the River. After several moments, the seal marking melted and the first drip formed.

"Bring it to me slowly," F'lorna said.

Le'ana brought the root back toward F'lorna. F'lorna grabbed a portion of the root right above where the sinew was tied around the cylinder and brought the piece of broken horn just under the dripping wax, moving it back and forth across the melted seal.

"I think that is enough. Sage, make sure his horn is clear," F'lorna said, getting up quickly. She turned the broken part of the horn down and placed it on the bottom of Lemmeck's left horn, where the piece had been knocked off. She made sure the fit was perfect, then grasped her hands around the horn and the piece and held it tightly for several moments.

"Please, Ra'ash. Make this work," she whispered.

Le'ana got up and stood next to F'lorna. Sage held onto Lemmeck's hair, preventing the wind from blowing any of the thin braids from her hands.

F'lorna looked at both her friends before letting go of Lemmeck's horn. When she opened her hands, she saw that the piece had fixed almost perfectly back into place. F'lorna could only see one chip that couldn't be replaced.

"F'lorna, it looks perfect again!" Sage gasped.

"I can't believe it," Le'ana whispered. "Do you think it will hold?"

"Considering we found these bottles washed up from the River all the way from the Northwestern Coastlands with the seals still on them I think, as long as he stays away from fire, the piece will hold."

"Can Sage put my hair down now?" Lemmeck asked.

"Yes," F'lorna said, nodding to Sage. "You can put it down. The piece is dry."

Sage let go of Lemmeck's hair, and he stood up. He faced the girls and reached his left arm back, moving his hand across the bottom of his horn. He scratched his fingernails up and down the portion of horn that had been broken. The noise sounded seamless. He looked at F'lorna and smiled. "You fixed it."

F'lorna smiled back, as relief flooded her spirit. "I didn't know if it would work, but I thought I could at least try."

"Do you all know what this means?" Sage asked.

"What? It means his horn is fixed," F'lorna said, confused.

Sage shook her head, her burgundy waves moving in the breeze. "No, you used Sand-shaper methods to fix his horn. What are the villagers going to say?"

"Oh, no," Le'ana said. "They're going to know we found the cylinders. They're going to know we used fire to melt the seals."

F'lorna felt cold flood her body. "Lemmeck, I didn't think about that. I just wanted to heal your horn." F'lorna stared at Lemmeck. She knew that he was going to disown her as a friend. She may even be asked to leave Right River Hook for using Sand-shaper methods. What had she been thinking?

Lemmeck felt his horn one more time. He brought his arm back down and straightened his shoulders looking directly at F'lorna. "I don't care what the villagers think. You fixed my horn, and I owe you my gratitude. Ra'ash provided those Sand-shaper seals, so I could be whole again."

He reached out his hand. "Here, I want you to have the three I found. I agree with Sage. For some reason, Ra'ash wants you to have them."

Chapter 16

THE WEEP OF SORROW

F'lorna hesitated before coming into her Achion cluster. Lemmeck had brought them across the River safely, and she said goodbye to her friends before they parted ways. They each promised not to say anything about what they did for Lemmeck's horn until they were asked. Lemmeck's family as sure to be the first to discover that his horn had been mended. He had

160

swam completely submerged under the water in the River, and his broken piece of horn stayed intact. F'lorna felt the cylinders in her tunic belt. She had to carry the lavender one over her head as she swam across the tributary. She stuffed some moss into the inside tip of the cylinder to prevent the scroll from falling out. Now all four Sand-shaper tubes were together in her possession, each containing its own scroll of Sand-shaper symbols. She wanted to ask her mother about them, but she needed to see how the village meeting went first.

As her Achion cluster came into view, she heard crying and whispers of assurance. F'lorna stopped walking and shifted her right ear toward the voices. It was her mother crying. She hadn't heard those deep sobs from her mother since Raecli's mother died. The other voice wasn't her father's. F'lorna walked swiftly into her family's hearth. She saw her mother on the grass, leaning forward and covering her face with her hands. Kytalia, the aged widow living with Le'ana, was stroking her mother's long, chestnut hair.

"What has happened to my mother?" F'lorna demanded.

Kytalia looked up but continued to stroke her mother's hair. "It is that new villager! She has insulted your mother greatly before the Village Elders. I know that family was trouble the moment they asked for so much of our shared land on the River."

Instantly, F'lorna knew that Kytalia was speaking of Oslyn, Zelara's mother. "What has she said to my mother?"

Kytalia was about to say something when T'maya held up her hand.

161

"I will tell my daughter what happened." T'maya looked up to Kytalia. "Thank you for taking me to my cluster and speaking some of the *Divine Oracle* over me. I offer you my apology of healing for crying. Your words have helped me."

Kytalia patted T'maya on the shoulder. "You honor this old River-dweller with purpose. I am glad to have brought you out of the Village Achion cluster. The speech was becoming sicker than the Northwestern Coast waters. I'll head back to the meeting and see if your husband has talked some sense into the ears of Right River Hook. He is well-respected as a Healing and Spiritual Elder. I know that the villagers will listen to reason."

F'lorna watched as Kytalia got up from the forest floor and walked with haste toward the Village Achion cluster. Kytalia was more than Twofold, but whatever happened at the meeting had her feet moving like a meadow rabbit. T'maya stretched her torso and wiped back the strands of hair covering her face. She then wiped her tears with the palm of her hands and exhaled before looking back to F'lorna.

"What happened, Mother? I have not seen you like this since Raecli's mother died," F'lorna said. She didn't move as she watched her mother cry. She was ready to run to the Village Meeting and accuse Zelara and her mother for causing turmoil in the village.

T'maya tried to smile, but her face instantly fell into sorrow again. Fresh tears continued to pour down the sides of her face. F'lorna noticed how young her mother still was. Much younger than her father. Her tan skin shone against her white tunic top and her grey eyes glistened like the shallow parts of the River running over slate-colored rocks. F'lorna ran to her mother and fell to her knees where her mother sat. "Mother, what happened? Tell me. I am a Novice Elder. You were only a few moon turns older than I when you joined with father. I am strong. I will help you."

T'maya wiped her tears again, even as her eyes continued to water with sorrow. She stared at F'lorna and gave a sincere smile. "I know you are strong. You have had to navigate my brokenness all your life. But, finally, I realized that I am a daughter of Ra'ash like everyone else. None of us can earn the Indwelling. It is a gift from Ra'ash through Jeyshen's Expansion. I do not have my horns, but Jeyshen is my strength. He and Ra'ash are my right and left horns. But—" her mother stopped.

F'lorna had already guessed what had happened at the village and she deeply regretted not being there. "Are those the evil words Zelara's mother spoke over you? Did she say something about your missing horns?"

T'maya reached her hand and stroked the side of F'lorna's cheek. "You see, my daughter. Ra'ash has gifted you with great understanding. You see the outcome before your eyes," she said. Then she pulled her hair back with both hands at her forehead. "Oslyn says that she abhors seeing my hornless head. She said in front of all the elders that I cause her enough grief wearing braids that hold only twigs, but actually seeing my emptiness makes her sick. She insists that I don't wear my hair down anymore and is demanding that I wear braids when I'm in public, especially at the Shoam-sha."

F'lorna felt the skin on her body burn like flames from a torch. She stood up and paced their Achion cluster. "How dare she use those audible words against you! How could anyone ever say that you make them sick? She has no right! She and their family have been here for less than a full moon cycle. They have no right dictating to us what we can or cannot do!"

"F'lorna, calm down. Anger will not solve this. Kytalia just spoke one of the *Holy Chants of Jeyshen*, and He did not carry anger against those who Expanded Him. We must resist anger at all costs," T'maya insisted.

"What did Father say? He is the Spiritual Elder. What did he tell that horrible family?" F'lorna demanded.

"You know your father. He tried to make peace, but several villagers agreed with her," T'maya said. "And many of the other ones were quiet. They didn't know what to say. Only Kytalia, Le'ana's mother and Ralona's mother stood up for me. I'm sure if Lemmeck's family had been there, they would have stood up for me as well. But they must be caring for Lemmeck or hunting. We lost much of the village's dried meat during the storm."

F'lorna's mind went to Lemmeck and the Sand-shaper cylinders, but she quickly dismissed the subject. She would have to discuss the symbols with her mother at another time. Right now her mother's very existence had been demeaned, and her family with her.

"If my father's sister had been here, the subject of your braids would have been dismissed immediately. Eline has taught Sand-shapers who have found the Indwelling and now serve as Healing Elders of their

164

village. My aunt would have put a stop to the villagers' hateful words right away!" F'lorna yelled, not caring who heard her.

"F'lorna, keep your voice low," T'maya said. "Eline can be more forthcoming than your father because she does not live here, and she is not the Spiritual Elder. Your father must keep peace and consider the feelings of each villager of Right River Hook. His Adoration is the most respected because it is the most difficult to offer. He must have the eyes of Ra'ash and His love as well. I am saddened for your father and the horrible spot he is in."

"Mother, Oslyn has devalued you merely because your horns have been extracted, which was not your fault! She does not see your work at the village cooking hearth. She does not see how you care for Father. She has no idea how you help me and my friends' mothers. She is only concerned about appearances and control. She would have never caused you distress if she had Ra'ash's love within her spirit."

"But I do not have the *Divine Oracle* in my Eternal Memory. She is right to say I am not complete—even if she does focus on my horns. I can't think on the *Sacred Songs of the Prophets and the Holy Images and Chants of Jeyshen* without someone reciting them to me," T'maya said. "I have already come to peace with my lack, but Oslyn's words struck me and reopened my wounds."

F'lorna kneeled back before her mother. "That is not true, my mother. Just moments ago, I was angry, and you told me to not carry the anger because Jeyshen did not carry His."

165

T'maya looked into F'lorna's grey eyes that matched her own. "Yes, but I don't know the exact story. Once I've heard it and the speaker stops, I can't remember the details."

"But, Mother, you remember the heart of the songs and chants. You remember their purposes. The exact words of *Jeyshen's Chant of Forgiveness* may not be known to you, but you do know its influence in your spirit. Since I was a youngling, you have always told me the heart of Ra'ash's words. You would speak the belief over me, and I would guess what story you unearthed it from. The words of the *Divine Oracle* may not be in your Eternal Memory, but the presence of it is—no matter what anyone says," F'lorna grabbed her mother's hands and would not look away from her mother's eyes until she knew that her mother had heard her words.

"Good, F'lorna. I am glad you are back," Jaquarn said as he entered their Achion cluster. "This rise of the Heat Source has been like an invisible storm—you could feel the intensity on the inside. I could barely prevent the villagers from leaving in chaos. I don't understand it. The River is finally healed and now my village is sick. It's as if the voiceless attacks of the Adversary are upon us." Jaquarn walked straight to T'maya and sat behind her, wrapping his legs around hers and bringing her body into his arms.

F'lorna got up and went to sit on the cooking table. "The attacks are not voiceless, and they are not from the Adversary. They come from a single family in Right River Hook," F'lorna said, thinking of Zelara. "And the next time I see the daughter of that family, I will have audible words with her."

166

"You will not speak a single word about this, F'lorna," Jaquarn said. "The topic has ended, and I forbade the villagers from bringing it up again. This is the time we need to come together as one, not separate into factions. We will be starting construction on the bridge and the pier after the next Shoam-sha. We have to bury our difference and work together if we are going to rebuild our village."

"I will not build a pier for the elder who devalues my mother!" F'lorna shouted.

"F'lorna, come here and sit down before me," her father demanded in a hushed but firm voice.

F'lorna resisted the urge to walk away. Instead, she got up and sat on the grass in front of her parents.

"Where does your mother gain her value?" he asked simply.

F'lorna thought. "From Ra'ash."

He nodded. "Exactly. So how could someone else take that value away?"

F'lorna hesitated and looked down at the grassy floor. "They cannot."

"No one can take away value that they did not give in the first place. Your mother is a daughter of Ra'ash and valuable in His eyes. What someone else thinks will not change that truth. Do you understand me?"

"Yes," F'lorna whispered.

Jaquarn breathed deeply. "Come here," he said, holding out his right arm.

F'lorna crawled next to her father and allowed him to hold her and her mother together. "We are strong because we know the value we have—a value Jeyshen was Expanded to give us. We will not allow others to steal what is rightfully ours. We will walk in peace and truth—no matter the storms around us."

F'lorna sat quietly in her father's arms. Her mother's body felt relaxed next to her. Crying had worn out her muscles.

"What did the village decide?" T'maya finally asked.

Jaquarn breathed again. "They have decided that you must wear your hair in braids around the twigs when you are at the Village Achion cluster, but when you are here or on public land, you can wear it however you want."

"Father, everything is done at the Village Achion cluster. The Shoam-sha is where my mother offers her Adoration of cooking. All the village meetings are there, as well as the village ceremonies. This is like saying she must wear her braids always."

"Yes, I know my daughter. But this situation is new and many of the villagers were confused and scared. Change is difficult and can't be done in an instant. I had a chore just reminding the villagers that T'maya is a daughter of Ra'ash and her offering of Adoration is greatly valued and appreciated in our village."

T'maya moved Jaquarn's arm and pushed herself up from the grass. She looked down at her husband. "Then I will no longer go to the Village Achion cluster if I am not welcomed as I am," she said firmly as she walked to her Achion tree and began taking out her braids.

Chapter 17

BUILDING BRIDGES

F'lorna wiped the sweat off her brow with the back of her hand before looking up at the Upper Realm. The Heat Source was now directly above them, but she was thankful only a small portion of it could be seen between the large Achion trees where they had set up to work. She looked back at Lemmeck who was directing some younglings in his charge. She, Lemmeck and Sage had been assigned to make the cordage for the bridge out of the sinews he had brought back from his family storage Achion tree. The work was tedious and F'lorna's fingers tired from the constant winding of the tendons and ligaments of the animals. She looked about a tree's length next to her and saw Le'ana and Ralona working with younglings to make cordage made from three strands of braided roots from the waterbark plants they had pulled along the river. Their cordage would not be as waterproof and would be used for the upper sections of the bridge. F'lorna couldn't wait for the construction of the bridge and pier to be over with, but her father projected that it would take almost one phase of the moon.

"I am not happy that I couldn't be with my brothers cutting and moving the logs," Lemmeck said, as he returned to his position next to F'lorna. "This is work for younglings."

"That may be," F'lorna said frowning, "but these cords are the difference between the bridge collapsing or the bridge standing, and only you can make sure that they get done properly." F'lorna also wanted to be with the other Elders doing the real work, but she was at least happy to be working with Lemmeck.

Lemmeck saw her frown. "I am grateful that you were at least assigned to be on my team." He sat back on his heels. "We will not have near enough. The bridge is only two arm's lengths wide, but it is very long. They have positioned the rock platform in the middle of the River in order to connect the two sides of the bridge. The cordage we have now will not even make one side of the bridge."

F'lorna liked how some of Lemmeck's dark braids fell along the tawny pigment of his face. He had strong, masculine features for his age, and his emerald eyes brightened against his dark skin. "It is either find more sinews or swim across the River every time we want to get across."

"We can walk the distance to the end of Right River Hook," Lemmeck said. "I did it as the Heat Source rose in the morning horizon to see how long it took me, and the walk was not too long."

F'lorna giggled. "Yes, but not every villager walks as much as you do. My father would not enjoy spending so much energy simply to cross the water. He would need to eat two morning meals."

Lemmeck looked at the cord he was working on. "Yes, you are right. The bridge needs to be built, but I doubt the villagers will want to keep working to build the pier."

F'lorna leaned in, so she wouldn't be heard by the younglings near them. "My father had to tell Zelara's father that the pier would not be as massive as he would like. For now, we can only construct a smaller pier with the ability to be enlarged on a later moon phase."

Lemmeck raised his eyebrows. "I bet he wasn't too happy about that."

F'lorna shrugged. "No one is happy about any of this work. It is not about being happy. It is about doing what is best for the village."

"You sound like your father," Lemmeck said. "He spoke very well at the Shoam-sha last evening. You can see that Ra'ash is speaking through him. We needed his words of wisdom."

F'lorna nodded. "He has been reciting the *Sacred Songs of the Prophets* nonstop, especially the songs of rebuilding after *The Great Engulfing* that killed half of all Rodeshians when Ra'ash allowed the ground shudders to swallow up the Lake-keepers. The villages left standing on Rodeshian lands had to be rebuilt."

"It is interesting that your father is finding so many insights of encouragement from one of the most depressing songs in the *Divine Oracle,*" Lemmeck said. "I noticed that your mother did not attend the Shoam-sha."

F'lorna looked down at her hands and stretched her fingers, trying to prevent them from cramping. "It is difficult having a father who is Spiritual Elder, yet having a mother who won't go to the Shoam-sha."

"She can go if she wears her hair in braids. She has always worn her hair up. I don't know why she wants to wear it down now," Lemmeck said. "She does look strange without her braids. It makes the absence of horns more obvious."

F'lorna fisted both her hands. "Does she offend you too?"

Lemmeck's face did not move with emotion. "No, I am not offended. It's just I never really thought about her not having horns before because she always wore her hair in braids."

"Yes, but you could look behind her and see that she had no horns there," F'lorna insisted.

"I never looked behind her," Lemmeck said, simply. "I only look at her face. I am not saying that your mother is wrong for wearing her hair down. I am just saying that it is different, but I know that I could get used to it after a while."

"You'll never get the chance to get used to it because my mother cannot wear her hair down in public," F'lorna said.

"I disagree with that," Lemmeck said, "but some villagers embrace tradition more than anything— particularly to the ones that tradition comes easily."

"There is nothing traditional about my mother," F'lorna said. "But she is the daughter of Ra'ash, and she loves Him."

"I know, and I offer voiceless words that your mother's struggle leads to a new awareness in our village. But as you see with this bridge, everything new takes time and work." Lemmeck said and looked to several grass baskets next to him. "We are all out of sinew."

F'lorna looked at Sage, working with younglings. They were softening the raw tendons and ligaments in preparation to be wound into cords. "Sage, how much is left in your baskets?"

Sage looked up from the youngling she was helping. "All that is left is in the hands of these younglings, and we've worked only one rise of the Heat Source. We will not have enough for the bridge, let alone the pier."

"We must acquire more quickly, so they will not have to stop the work. We need to go to Left River Hook to ask if they have more," Lemmeck said.

"My father already inquired from the Circle of Elders. They do not have any to spare," F'lorna said, thinking. She watched Lemmeck reach back to stack the empty baskets. "Has no one said anything about your horn?"

Lemmeck looked back at her. "My mother noticed first. I told her you made a special adhesive out of wax and some other materials. She didn't say anything. I think she believes it will not hold, but it's been several rises of the Violet Moon and my horn is still intact. But now everyone is so distracted with the bridge work that no one has said anything. They have even forgotten about the River Monster."

"Yes, I have noticed, but it is best. The River Monster is just like any other predator that River-dwellers face every rise of the Heat Source, nothing more. We should not fear it more just because we have never seen it before."

"Where do you think it came from?" Lemmeck asked. "My father's family has been hunting these lands for many generations, and they have never seen it."

"I think the ground shudders opened up and it crawled out," F'lorna said.

"Yes, but it comes from both land and water. It couldn't have been underground all this time," Lemmeck countered.

"I don't know," F'lorna said. "My father has no answers either."

"Are you talking about me, my daughter?" Jaquarn's voice sounded above them.

F'lorna looked up to see her father's amber hair wet from the River. "I was saying that you have no answers for where the River Monster came from."

"Let's just hope that wherever it came from, there are no more of them. Or at least, they stay where they belong," Jaquarn said, sitting on the grass in between Lemmeck and F'lorna. "Ah, it feels good to rest my legs." He looked around. "Is this all the cordage we have left?"

"Yes, Spiritual Elder," Lemmeck said. "I have gathered from my hearth and from everyone in the village. This is all."

"It is as I feared. We will need more very soon. The building is already underway, and the cords will not last," Jaquarn said. Then he looked around to all the younglings. "Younglings, how would you like a little break to go play?"

The younglings nodded their heads enthusiastically.

"Well, get on with it. Go play!" Jaquarn said, smiling.

The younglings cheered and instantly ran off through the Achion trees.

"Sage, please join us over here," Jaquarn said, patting the grassy forest floor. Then he looked toward Le'ana and Ralona. "Join us you two. Send your younglings to play. They are done with their work."

F'lorna watched her two friends quickly send their little workers off into the forest and gather up their baskets of fiber cordage. They brought their baskets next to the ones that Lemmeck had stacked. The two girls sat down on either side of Sage. F'lorna looked at their little circle. She was part of a group again.

Jaquarn took a moment to look at each face around him. "Lemmeck, Le'ana, Sage, Ralona and my daughter, F'lorna—the Hunting, Planting, Singing, Creation and Dancing Adorations are represented in this circle."

As her father spoke, F'lorna remembered Ra'ash's words during the storm that she would write symbols. As of yet, she had not an inkling of what that Adoration was or even if it was an Adoration. Her aunt was the only other person who knew, but she had not given her any advice before she left.

Her father continued. "I have a job for you all to do. I have already discussed it with Rashion and Dashion, and they are more than willing to protect your little expedition."

F'lorna looked at Le'ana. She knew she liked Dashion. Her friend's pale skin was already red from working under the Heat Source during its course across the Upper Realm, but F'lorna was sure there was a blush there too.

"What sort of expedition?" Lemmeck asked, intrigued.

"One that you will be leading, Lemmeck. You have visited your distant family's land near the River, so you are the most qualified," he said.

Jaquarn looked at each face one more time before speaking further, creating anticipation to let them know that his words were serious. "I talked with the Elders of Left River Hook. They do not have any sinews to spare for our bridge cordage. However, they did say that many animals have washed up on the rocks of the main River. Dozens were spotted along the shore, and the meat is no longer good, but the ligaments and tendons can still be harvested. The predators have been feasting on these animals, so we must obtain these materials quickly. Rashion and Dashion say that it will take two rises of the Heat Source to get to the main River. With one afternoon to gather the materials, you all can be back at your Achion clusters within five or at most six rises. That will give us enough time to use the cordage you have already made and to prepare for the rest of the construction of the bridge and pier." Jaquarn stopped to read the faces of the Novice Elders around him.

"You would have to leave before the Heat Source rises in the morning horizon. You are all Novice Elders, so you must discuss this expedition with your mothers and fathers, but the choice is ultimately yours alone. I chose this group because I sense that you work well together, and I trust that you will get the job done. However, if you do not want to go, let me know now. I will find someone to take your place. You will all be expected to get to the main River quickly, harvest the tendons and ligaments and carry them back to the village," Jaquarn finished and leaned back on his hands stretching his torso. "Who wants to go?"

F'lorna had listened to her father's words with growing excitement. Never would she be allowed to go on a journey like this if the ground shudders hadn't changed the River and broken their bridge. She couldn't explain why, but she knew Ra'ash willed her to go.

"I will go!" F'lorna said, trying to sound nonchalant but failing.

"I am definitely in!" Lemmeck said almost at the same time.

F'lorna looked at Le'ana, Sage and Ralona. "What do you say? Will you come with me on this adventure?"

177

"I'm going wherever you go, F'lorna. You always find yourself in the storyteller's words," Sage said.

Le'ana and Ralona looked at each other from either side of Sage who was sitting in between them.

"What do you think, Ralona? You think the Creation Adoration wants to join the fun?" Le'ana said.

"Only if the Planting Adoration comes along!" Ralona said.

"Then it is agreed!" Jaquarn said. "Before the Violet Moon disappears in the morning, the five of you and the twins will begin your journey to the main River. I will be giving voiceless words that your adventure is uneventful yet highly productive. Please make your way back to your Achion clusters and pack everything you need. You will need a blade for cutting and leather sacks for carrying the sinews. Make sure to bring a bota bag filled with water and traveling food. Borrow whatever you do not have. And get plenty of sleep, so you will be strong for your journey. You are all released to leave."

F'lorna watched her friends gather their things.

"What about these baskets?" Lemmeck asked, looking at the ones he had stacked.

"I will take care of them. Just get back to your hearth," Jaquarn said.

Lemmeck nodded and turned to leave.

"Wait!" Jaquarn said, getting up. "Lemmeck, your horn is whole again!"

Jaquarn walked up to Lemmeck and stroked the edge of the horn that had broken. "I see it. The piece has been repaired. How did you do this?" he asked, amazed.

Lemmeck turned and looked at F'lorna. "It is an interesting story. I think your daughter will be the best Rodeshian to tell it."

Chapter 18

SAND-SHAPER SYMBOLS

❝ You can't let her leave on a journey like this, Jaquarn. She has only just become a Novice Elder of the village," T'maya said, as her long chestnut hair streamed along the sides of her high cheekbones. Her grey eyes shone dark with worry.

"My wife, you know I have no choice. The other Elders are questioning the rationality of the bridge. This bridge construction is on the verge of complete failure.

Villagers are murmuring. We don't have enough resources. I have to handle moment-to-moment complications through the Heat Source's entire journey across the Upper Realm. The Novice Elders must retrieve the sinews we need to finish the bridge and pier. Believe me, I've considered going myself, but I am needed here. There are no other options," Jaquarn said, rubbing the back of his neck and pacing their family's Achion cluster. "Eotham says he can continue preparing the wood, so when they get back, we will only need to fit everything together."

F'lorna wanted to interject, but she knew it was best to let her mother express her fears. Ralona took after her father. Eotham was a Creation Elder, and he had designed the previous bridge.

"Then why must you send our daughter? Can you not send someone else? Why not send Oslyn's daughter. Ra'ash knows that girl could use a little time away from the village with all the meddling she does," T'maya said, bitterly.

"T'maya, I will not send a young River-dweller on such a journey simply because we have difficulty with her family." He walked to T'maya and put his hands on each of her tan shoulders. "Besides, I chose F'lorna because she is the best choice, and I know she will accomplish what we have sent her to do. She is a leader, and she is creative in a way that I have never seen before in anyone. Plus, the group I have chosen—they work well together, and their strengths complement each other. I know Ra'ash has chosen them. You were not much older that they when you journeyed alone down the mountain along the River, were you?"

"But that is different. I had no other choice but to leave my village," T'maya said. "There are many forest nomads who hide in the trees and steal from sojourners. What if she runs into one of their bands?"

Jaquarn shook his head. "We haven't heard of any nomads in our area for quite some time. Most of them live on the west side of the River near the wetlands. Besides, I have no other choice. I must trust that Ra'ash will protect them."

T'maya wiped her eyes and shrugged Jaquarn's hands off her shoulders. "If she must go, I will help her pack."

Jaquarn helplessly watched T'maya walk away from him toward F'lorna's Achion tree. "I will go to the Pillar to give voiceless words to Ra'ash for a successful journey for F'lorna, Lemmeck and their friends," he said, turning toward the River and disappearing into the shadow of the trees.

The atmosphere of their Achion cluster illuminated with the violet glow of the moon. The fire near the cooking hearth and the torches attached to several trees gave enough light to see. F'lorna felt sad for her mother, yet she knew her father was right. She was the best choice to lead this expedition.

"Before I help you pack for your journey, please explain to me how you mended Lemmeck's horn with a Sand-shaper's cylinder. And why would you think to do such a thing?" T'maya asked, turning away from F'lorna's Achion tree to face her.

F'lorna adjusted her position on the table of the cooking hearth. "It wasn't like I was doing something new," she protested.

"Yes, you were. I have never met a River-dweller with a mended horn," T'maya said. "Where did you get the cylinder?"

"Sage found it for me. She told me that she felt Ra'ash wished for me to have it. After the storm, the cylinders have been washing up along the River. Lemmeck has already found three of them."

"Sage is a dreamer, like her sister. They both enjoy telling stories," T'maya said, placing her hands on her hips.

"But that is Blaklin's Adoration, not Sage's," F'lorna said.

"Do not speak out of turn, F'lorna. I know that Blaklin is a storyteller. I have heard her story about you and the Storm Dance repeated many times now. But she embellishes. And I guess that is what she was created to do, but you can't always take what they say literally."

"Sage gave it to me out of a pure heart, Mother," F'lorna asserted.

"That may be true, but River-dwellers consider the Sand-shaper's items to be evil," T'maya said flatly. "And you used one of them on Lemmeck's horn. F'lorna, the horn is very sacred to River-dwellers. What will the villagers say when they find out that Sand-shaper materials were used on it?"

F'lorna jumped off the table and stood up to face her mother. "Is not all material made by Ra'ash? How could something Ra'ash made be evil? What I did was not that difficult. I noticed the seal on the cylinder stayed intact during the storm and it was waterproof. I know that Sand-shapers use fire to make them, so I realized that fire would melt the wax. I simply put the melted wax on the piece of Lemmeck's broken horn and attached it. Once it dried, the broken piece stayed. There is nothing evil about the entire process. I did it because I care about Lemmeck, not because I wanted to hurt him."

T'maya said nothing for several moments and simply stared at her daughter. F'lorna looked into her mother's grey eyes and did not flinch. She wanted her mother to know that she was speaking truth. Finally, T'maya exhaled and walked up to her daughter, putting her hands on her shoulders. "Ra'ash knew what He was doing when He decided to give you to me and your father. You are a brilliant Rodeshian, and I am proud of you, although you do keep me offering voiceless words continually."

F'lorna's mouth dropped slightly in shock. "You are not angry?"

"Just answer me one question, F'lorna," T'maya said.

"Yes, mother."

"Did you feel Ra'ash's hand helping you mend Lemmeck's horn?"

F'lorna thought. "I don't know. The thought came to me suddenly, like the gift of a new colored moon. I wanted to help Lemmeck, and it was as if Ra'ash gave me what I needed."

T'maya smiled, pulling her daughter into an embrace. "My strong-willed, intelligent daughter. I fear your life will be marked by great tribulation and great triumphs."

"Like you, Mother. You lost your mother, but then you found Father," F'lorna said.

"Yes, like me. Thankfully, though, not all of you is like me," T'maya said, moving F'lorna to face her and patting her horn. "This horn looks almost as straight as the other. I doubt anyone will notice much now."

"Thank you for binding it back, Mother," F'lorna said.

"I've always worked hard to make your horns perfectly straight, but life has a way of making things a little crooked," T'maya said. "Now let me get you packed."

F'lorna thought while she watched her mother dig through her Achion tree. "Mother, will you tell me what the symbols mean—the ones on the parchment inside the cylinders?"

"They are symbols that represent the sounds we make. Each sound we make has a symbol," T'maya said, grabbing an extra tunic for F'lorna's traveling bag. "I've told you about the symbols before—even explaining how they make the parchment. Why are you so curious about the them still? You know how River-dwellers see them. They are foul in their sight."

"It is my heritage, Mother. I am just curious about them is all," F'lorna said, trying to sound casual "What else do they create the symbols for?" F'lorna asked.

"They mainly write down ingredients and instructions for various Sand-shaper methods. The scroll in the violet cylinder that Sage gave you is instructions on how to make a wood adhesive," T'maya said.

"I thought they only shaped sand," F'lorna said, confused.

"That is how it started countless moon folds ago, but now Sand-shapers use many materials to create their designs. They build structures to live in, beds to sleep on and windmills to irrigate their farmlands," T'maya said. "My mother had cylinders of recipes passed down to her."

"So they *write*," F'lorna said, pausing. "How many symbols are there?"

"How many sounds does the Rodeshian language have?" T'maya asked.

F'lorna thought. "Many. We have many sounds that we make to speak audible words."

T'maya smiled. "There are forty-four symbols in all."

"Have you created the symbols on parchment?" F'lorna asked.

T'maya folded F'lorna's tunic and stopped. "No, it is not customary for Rodeshians like me to create the symbols. We are only allowed to keep them and read them. My mother had dozens of glass cylinders that she kept safe. They are very valuable to Sand-shapers because they are difficult to reproduce."

"Why can't you create the symbols on new parchment?" F'lorna asked, confused.

T'maya looked at her daughter. "Sand-shaper customs are very different than ours here. In our village, each River-dweller has equal value. But that is not so on the Northwestern Coast or in the Northeastern Mountains. Up there only a small percentage of Sand-shapers are allowed to make parchment and to write the symbols. They are the ones who own everything, and the rest of us are the workers. We are only allowed to read

186

what has been written. I knew when I left my village on the mountain that River-dwellers looked at Sand-shaper symbols with fear, so I traded my mother's cylinders for everything I would need to travel down the mountain and to the River."

F'lorna was very quiet as she watched her mother pack for her. "Is Raecli's grandfather one of those powerful Sand-shapers?" F'lorna asked.

T'maya nodded slowly but did not look up. "Yes, he is very powerful. And he does many wrongs to keep his power and to take power from others. He must have a family heir who will maintain his lands and shaping mills. Sahara and her mother ran away from him when Sahara was still a youngling, hiding with friends in the coastal city until her mother was able to find passage to a small tributary where they lived isolated yet happy lives in a small village. A few moon turns later, Sahara joined with a River-dweller from this village who had been visiting distant family. They moved here, and that's when we became friends. We swelled with child together during the final Yellow Moon, and gave birth to you and Raecli during the First Green Moon. The changing of the moon color felt like a changing of our previous lives as Sand-shapers."

"That is why he took her, isn't it? He needed an heir?" F'lorna said.

T'maya closed the bag tightly with a long sinew before looking into her daughter's grey eyes. "Yes," she said simply. "Now, my daughter. It is late, and you must get some rest."

Chapter 19

THE JOURNEY BEGINS

F'lorna motioned for Lemmeck and his brothers to stay put on the other side of the River. There was no reason for them to swim across when she and the rest of the group were about to cross to join them. She looked at Sage and Le'ana who were both standing beside her. "I see the Heat Source awakening. If Ralona doesn't come soon, we will have to leave without her."

"I know she will be here," Le'ana said. "She told me that Ra'ash had given her a creation idea that would help us gather the sinews. I'm sure she will be here shortly."

"As I was leaving my Achion cluster, the villagers were already making their way to the bridge construction site. We better leave soon or they will think we are unable to handle the journey," Sage said. "My mother told me that many Elders were against us going. They do not believe we will be successful."

"I imagine that Zelara's parents were against us going," F'lorna said. F'lorna imagined Elder Trenton. He wore a frown every rise of the Heat Source. She tried to erase the frown and replace it with a smile, but the frown was permanently fixed. Not even in her imagination could Zelara's father be nice.

"Is that a surprise? Zelara's father has been against everyone and everything during this construction project," Sage said, leaning toward her friends. "My Achion cluster is close to theirs, and Elder Trenton's voice is always yelling mean words. His eyes only see the negative in his wife and Zelara. If he wasn't bringing the Fishing Adoration into our village, I don't think the Elders would have accepted him and his family."

F'lorna was stunned with the new insight. "Zelara does the same to me. Why would she offer malicious words when she knows how much they hurt?"

Sage shrugged, her deep, burgundy hair falling along her umber shoulders. "I don't know. We never really got close when we did our Adoration together. I would ask her to visit me at my Achion cluster, but she would always say she had to be with her family. I don't know why she would want to be with them. Her father yells all the time."

189

F'lorna said nothing. She realized that meanness begot meanness. She wondered if Zelara's Eternal Memory was shaped by it somehow.

"I see her!" Le'ana squealed. "Nayran is with her. They are carrying something.

F'lorna watched as Ralona and Nayran jogged along the River toward the Pillar where they waited. Ralona's dark, curly hair bounced in rhythm with every quick step she made. Nayran's straight, light brown hair streamed with the wind behind her. Both girls wore braids in the top half of their hair to cover their horns. F'lorna looked back to Lemmeck and his brothers waiting on the other side of the River. She waved, letting them know that they would be leaving shortly. When Ralona finally arrived with their tanning birth friend, they were both out of breath but smiling.

"I am so glad you didn't leave me," Ralona said. "Nayran and I worked the entire journey of the Violet Moon across the Upper Realm to finish these."

"What are they?" F'lorna asked. "They look like grass baskets that have been flattened."

"That's exactly right!" Nayran said enthusiastically. "Ralona came to my Achion cluster before the Heat Source left in the evening horizon and said that you all would be harvesting sinews from the animals washed up on the main River. She knew that you would need to gather a lot, so she wanted to make sure there was enough storage capacity to carry them back to Right River Hook."

"I know that Nayran made that large, leather pouch for your mother," Ralona said pointing to F'lorna. "So she could carry water on her back and not on her head, so I asked her if we could create something similar. But ours didn't have to be waterproof because we are carrying sinews."

"So," Nayran exclaimed, "we spent all night weaving these pliable baskets that you can easily fold and carry, but when it is time to harvest the sinews, they open up wide and you can carry them on your back with these straps!"

F'lorna started at the baskets in awe. The shades of yellow and green grasses woven together were simple yet beautiful.

"You made seven of them," Le'ana exclaimed, touching the fine weave of one of the baskets. "You used the thin grasses that we normally use for decoration along the thicker grasses. This truly must have taken you until the Heat Source awoke this morning. I didn't know you could weave grasses, Nayran."

"I usually work with animal skins, but weaving grass is similar to weaving strips of leather. I truly believe that the Help of Ra'ash guided me!"

"You did all this under the Violet Moon?" F'lorna asked, astonished.

The birth friends smiled and nodded. "We just finished," Ralona said. "And now we must leave immediately because many of the Elders saw us running through the village. I don't want them to think our journey has been delayed." She turned to Nayran. "I couldn't have done this without you. I owe you a moon phase of gratitude."

"I am honored to be of service to this journey," Nayran said. "It is much more interesting than sanding the logs under the full course of the Heat Source. That is what the Elders have chosen for me and Vauntan to do. It is so boring, but it is much like tanning hides for our Adoration. At least I will have plenty to talk about today with Vauntan. We will be offering voiceless words for your journey."

Nayran walked to F'lorna. "These are for Lemmeck and his brothers. Make sure to tell them that I made these ones special for them." Nayran handed the three flat baskets to F'lorna. "I wish I could go with you, but I need to finish sanding the logs for the bridge. We wouldn't want the younglings finding small splinters in their feet, now would we?"

F'lorna smiled. "No, we wouldn't." As she watched Nayran walk back to the village, F'lorna fully realized the honor her father had given her. She would not let him or the other villagers down.

"Oh no!" Ralona said. "How will we get these across the River without getting wet? Even a little water may damage them. They are not made to last."

"I have just the answer," F'lorna said, reaching to grab a large, oblong piece of leather within her traveling bag. "I have the leather water pouch Nayran made my mother. She said I could use it for this journey. I will carry the grass baskets on my back until we get to the main part of the River. That way I know they will be safe."

"Lemmeck and his brothers are waving to us," Le'ana interrupted. "We need to go."

F'lorna quickly opened the mouth of the large, leather pouch and gently placed the three baskets she held inside. Then she opened it wider, so Ralona could place the other four inside as well.

"There," Ralona said. "Four for the girls and three for the boys. Let's swim."

The girls left the Pillar and waded into the River. The tributary, though wide, was not deep until almost the center. They only had to swim for a few moments until the water became shallow again. F'lorna was still amazed at how much Right River Hook's tributaries had grown from the storm. She had never been to the main River, but she had heard many descriptions, and it was much bigger than even their swollen tributary. The current was rough—too rough to swim—and the edges of the River were steep and rocky. She hoped that the animals to be harvested were on their side of the River. Otherwise, there would be no way to get to them.

"What took you all so long?" Lemmeck asked, as the girls walked onto the marshy bank on the other side. "The Heat Source is almost completely above the horizon now. I see the Elders looking our way from the bridge construction site."

"Ralona and Nayran made us folding baskets that will allow us to carry more than enough sinews back to the village," F'lorna said. "I wouldn't have delayed unless it was important."

Lemmeck looked at Ralona. "You did that for us?"

She smiled and nodded.

"I was worried. I thought we might have to take a detour to Left River Hook for help. Are they in the leather pouch you carry?" he asked, looking at F'lorna. "Would you like me to carry them?"

F'lorna shook her head. "No, I have them. They are really light. Besides, you will be guiding us. That is enough work in itself."

Lemmeck nodded. "Here is the plan," he said, looking at the group. "We are all leaders on this expedition, but we each have different responsibilities. I will be guiding our group to the main part of the River. I've been there before with my father, but the storm has changed the landscape, so I will have to look closely at the land as we travel. Dashion and Rashion will keep a watch for any predators or strangers."

"Just think of us as Ra'ash's guards for our journey," Rashion said, pointing proudly to his chest. His hair and skin were the same shade as Lemmeck's, but instead of emerald eyes, his eyes were golden, like tree sap shining in the great Heat Source.

Dashion stood next to his twin, a serious demeanor on his face. "If you see anything threatening, like the forest nomads, give the whistle. If you think you heard something but are unsure, give the double hoot," Dashion said. "Rashion and I will be ready with our bows."

"My father says the forest nomads have moved on. We don't need to worry about them," F'lorna said. She was relieved that Dashion said his brother's name. She still had trouble distinguishing between the two. But now she knew that Dashion wore a tan tunic, and Rashion's was a mushroom color.

"That may be true, but they have two feet just like the rest of us. They can move back if they choose," Rashion said. "But my twin brother and I will protect all of us."

"Did everyone bring food?" Lemmeck asked. His hair was braided in many thin braids and pulled back. He wore a dark green tunic to blend into the forest.

The group nodded.

"Did you happen to bring more of your delicious roasted Pine Nuts?" Dashion asked, smiling widely at Le'ana.

Le'ana coughed and clear her throat. Her scarlet hair gleamed brightly as the Heat Source's rays rose over the horizon. She had to look up to speak to Dashion. "Yes, I did. And some dried nuts, berries and legumes."

"We will be traveling for at least five rises, so we will have to gather along the way. Le'ana if you see anything edible, let us know and we will refill our food pouches," Lemmeck said. "Let us all stay alert and send voiceless words to Ra'ash. Come. We begin our journey."

F'lorna fell in line behind Lemmeck. His twin brothers split directions—one going to the right and the other to the left. F'lorna knew that the twins would be weaving in and out from the forest to their group. They were skilled hunters and good at traveling the land. She looked next to her and was happy to see Ralona. "You look very tired," F'lorna said, suddenly realizing that her birth friend had gotten no sleep.

"I am tired, but being on this journey has awakened me," Ralona said.

"Thank you for creating the baskets. You have used your Adoration well. And I am honored that Nayran helped you. She is a gifted tanner. My mother greatly appreciates her water pouch," F'lorna said, moving her feet in a brisk walking pattern. "I haven't retrieved water since our Doublemoon Ceremony," F'lorna said, grinning. "My mother enjoys going to the River and using her pouch so much that she hasn't asked me to fetch water."

"Nayran will be pleased to hear that. She says that Vauntan's Adoration at our Doublemoon Ceremony was breathtaking. She thinks the white leather tunic with the moon-colored embroidery made her water pouch look drab," Le'ana said.

"Vauntan is a very good tanner as well; and I loved my new tunic," F'lorna said. "But Nayran's offering is useful."

"I noticed that you haven't worn the tunic yet. I thought you would have worn it to our last Shoam-sha," Ralona said.

F'lorna looked at Lemmeck walking a few paces in front of them. He was leading them west of his family's land, so she adjusted her direction. "I wanted to, but since my mother did not come, I decided to wait."

"I am sad about what happened to your mother. My parents did not decide either for or against her wearing her braids. They so tire of Elder Trenton's incessant words about the *Divine Oracle* that they didn't want to get involved. I offer you my apology of healing."

"I understand. My mother has always had difficulty fitting into our village. I guess it will take time—if ever," F'lorna said and looked at her birth friend. Her dark curly hair looked beautiful falling around her braided horns like coiling vines. She didn't want her birth friend to worry about her family. And she needed a break from the constant reminders that her mother was different. "You and Nayran have offered something that has never been created before. I already imagine many uses for the folding basket design. Lemmeck and his brothers could use them to gather small prey. And I know that Le'ana and her father could use them as they bring in the harvest of their fields."

Ralona smiled. "I am honored. I will create more and offer them for trade." She rubbed her eyes. "But now I must focus on staying awake until the Heat Source makes its decent."

Chapter 20

THE MARSH-LANDERS

66 Are we lost?" F'lorna asked, watching Lemmeck surveying the ground in front of them. They had just entered a densely wooded area, leaving the meadow of long grassy waves behind them. She tried to find the foot path he was looking for, but even she could see that the brush and debris hid everything like an organic covering.

"No and yes," he admitted. "I know where we are at this exact moment, but I don't know which way to go. Everything looks different."

F'lorna looked at the Heat Source above them through the dense canopy of the forest. "We are halfway done with our second rise of the Heat Source. We were supposed to arrive today. I want us to at least get to the main River before the Violet Moon awakens."

She watched Lemmeck squat down to the forest floor, looking for any sign of distant movement. She could see his almond-colored horns peeking out from under his braids on the back side of his neck. The broken piece that she had fastened was almost undistinguishable.

"I want that as well, but I need to be sure of where we are going," he said, as he ran his tawny colored hand across the mossy ground. He stood up. "When my brothers get back from checking the parameters of this land, we will decide," Lemmeck said, turning in a slow circle to look at the surrounding area. "Usually, I would see a Rodeshian trail of feet leading me to the River, but the storm has erased all the trampled paths. I can't even find tracks of animals looking for water. I'm sure we are close, but not close enough to hear the roaring current."

"It is difficult reading the land after a storm," F'lorna added. "I don't think the Elders considered it."

Lemmeck looked at F'lorna, and she stared into dark, emerald eyes. She could see his features frowning with worry. He looked to be much older than the fourteen turns of the moon he has seen. "We may not have rocky paths, but we have Ra'ash to guide us. I trust that He will show us the way," he stated with forced confidence.

"Yes, you are right. He will not let us fail," F'lorna agreed.

A screech howled above them. F'lorna looked up just as a large bird flew above the fingers of trees reaching for the Upper Realm. She saw glimpses of it through the foliage. "It's a bird of prey."

It screeched again. "It sounds like a Saber Falcon," Lemmeck announced. "They have beaks that can break open the shell of a Purzon River Tortoise, and talons that can crush the head of a large meadow rabbit with one squeeze."

"Will it bother us?" she asked, staring into Lemmeck's eyes looking for hints of fear.

He shook his head. "Rodeshian meat does not taste good to these falcons. They will only go after younglings if their food source is scarce."

"What do they eat?" she asked.

He looked back up into the trees. "Everything else but us. I think it is gone."

F'lorna stood next to Lemmeck and together they gazed up through the trees for several moments. She jumped when she heard the high-pitched voice of her birth friend.

"Look what we found!" Le'ana's voice sounded through the trees. F'lorna turned toward her friend's voice and squinted until she saw her image coming out of the undergrowth of the forest. Sage and Ralona were walking next to her. They were each holding several food pouches in their hands.

F'lorna craned her neck to see dark berries filling each pouch. "What are they?" F'lorna asked as they drew closer.

"Indigo berries!" Ralona said excitedly.

"Really?" F'lorna asked, happy for the diversion. She hoped her friends were so busy chatting that they didn't hear the screech.

"And they taste like drops of the Indigo Moon!" Sage said. Her lips were already blue from tasting them.

"I can't believe it! They haven't grown in many moon turns because the land has been too dry. When I saw them, I almost didn't believe my own eyes. My father tried to plant the seeds that he had been saving for when the Fifth Indigo Moon was in the Upper Realm," Le'ana said, facing Lemmeck. "That is when my cousin celebrated her Doublemoon Ceremony."

"I didn't realize that the Indigo berry could be planted," Lemmeck said. "I thought it only grew in the wild."

"He didn't mention it because the crop had failed. He donated another crop to the Doublemoon Ceremony, but he was very disappointed. I will save him a pouch, so he can try to plant another harvest. Maybe we can use the crop to celebrate the completion of the new village bridge!" Le'ana said enthusiastically.

Lemmeck frowned once more. "We must get to the main River or the bridge will never be finished." Lemmeck's neck suddenly became stiff. "Shhh! Be quiet!"

A piercing whistle had sounded.

F'lorna and the other girls froze. She listened, and a second whistle echoed through the quiet forest.

201

Then several rustling noises were heard from the forest floor deep within the forest. F'lorna looked at Lemmeck. He was staring past her. "It's one of my brothers' whistles of danger," he whispered.

F'lorna slowly moved her head in the direction Lemmeck was looking. Instantly, she saw a flash of a deep yellow, like sparkling honey, reflecting light from the Heat Source into the dark forest.

"Someone is coming," she whispered to Lemmeck.

He reached behind his back and pulled out his bow and several arrows. He quietly placed the forked back of the arrow along the long, tight sinew of his bow, and he pulled back his left arm.

She noticed something moving into view behind Lemmeck. It was Dashion, and he had his bow out and ready with an arrow. He noiselessly walked next to the group.

"Did you whistle?" Lemmeck asked, keeping his eyes on the movement in front of them.

"No, it must have been Rashion," Dashion whispered back.

A voice called out from within the forest. "You can put your bows away! We are the Marsh-landers from the south wetlands west of the River. We will not harm you! We are exploring and meeting new villagers!"

Lemmeck looked at F'lorna and she shook her head. "I've never heard of them," she whispered. "What if it's the forest nomads?" She felt her heart rapidly pulsing in her chest.

"We have never heard of the Marsh-landers!" Lemmeck yelled back.

"Well, if you don't trust us, we can go back the way we came, but let me ask you a question," the voice yelled.

Lemmeck thought for a brief moment. "What is it?" he asked loudly, holding his arm steady and prepared to let his arrow fly.

"We just came from Left River Hook. Do you know any villager there? I will verify that we stayed with them for several rises of the moon if you give me a name of someone you know!" the voice came back.

"Do you know Blaklin?" Sage yelled.

F'lorna looked at her friend. If the Marsh-landers were telling the truth, they would definitely know Sage's sister, the storyteller.

A laugh bounced off the trees of the forest. "Yes! The beautiful young storyteller with eyes the color of the forest floor. She tells the most imaginative stories! There is a young villager who has just asked to be joined with her."

"That's my sister," Sage whispered. "Jornan must have finally asked Blaklin to join in Ra'ash with him."

"Tell us one of her stories!" Lemmeck shouted.

The silence of the forest surrounded them until the voice came back. "My favorite is of the Storm Dancer! Supposedly, this dancer brought in the Great Storm after tripping over a Zulo Vine at something called the Doublemoon Ceremony. Very fascinating story, but one I have trouble believing. But all of Left River Hook seems to believe it!"

F'lorna felt her cheeks flame with embarrassment.

Lemmeck looked at F'lorna and smiled with relief. He slowly put his bow down, and Dashion followed suit. "Rashion! Is your arrow pointed at the Marsh-landers?" he yelled.

Quiet was heard again.

Finally, a voice came from another angle deep within forest. "Yes!"

"You can put it down now. These Rodeshians are friends of Left River Hook!"

"They are Sand-shapers!" the voice rang back. "They have no horns!"

Instantly, Lemmeck and Dashion brought their bows back up.

The voice from the Marshlands rang out. "Yes, we were Sand-shapers! Most of us worked the farms for powerful landowners. But our kin rebelled against their harsh treatment of us several moon turns ago, and we took our families and made our way south. We stayed away from the River for fear of dealings with the River-dwellers. We made our hearths in the harsh terrain of the marshlands, and we have established our village and found peace for our families. We are only just now exploring the River to introduce ourselves and to open trading routes and relations."

"By Ra'ash!" Lemmeck shouted. "Are you telling us the truth?"

"I have a son who was born in the final Indigo Moon, and I have allowed his horns to stay. We are trying to fit in and to make friends in our new land," the voice shouted. "But we can turn around if you still do not trust us!"

Lemmeck looked at F'lorna again. "We cannot let fear prevent us from showing kindness to other Rodeshians. We are all family of Ra'ash," she said firmly.

"Rashion! Come out and escort our new friends to us!" Lemmeck shouted, putting his bow back down.

A swishing of tree branches was heard and then a loud thud on the forest floor. F'lorna could hear voices in the distance. She noticed the flashing gold light became brighter. She inched closer to Lemmeck, and saw that Ralona, Sage and Le'ana came closer as well.

Finally, a Rodeshian who looked to be the age of a Triple moon walked into view, Rashion by his side. The Rodeshian wore a golden amulet around his neck. It was what flashed the rays of the Heat Source through the forest. A younger Rodeshian followed behind them. F'lorna noticed right away that they had no horns. More intriguing, though, was that they had angular eyes like her mother, but more pronounced. Instead of grey, their eyes were the color of dark soil. Their skin and hair were also a few shades darker.

The younger Rodeshian wore a thick, worn piece of leather around his left arm. He held his arm out in front of him and made a screeching sound, like the one she and Lemmeck heard over the forest canopy. A whooshing sound pierced through the dense forest air, and the Saber Falcon swooshed down and landed on the stranger's arm, grasping the heavy leather folds with his sharp talons.

F'lorna gaped speechless, as did the rest of her group. The Rodeshian reached his right hand into a tunic belt he wore around his waist and picked out a small animal. He threw the animal several inches towards the falcon's mighty beak, and the falcon gobbled it up with one bite. Then the falcon began to prune its silver and tan feathers, and the young Rodeshian stood grinning. He held his arm steady as the falcon continued to clean itself, oblivious to the audience gawking at him. F'lorna noticed the falcon had some sort of band around one of its legs.

"What a remarkable group you have here," the older Rodeshian said to Lemmeck. "My name is Merriton, and this is my younger brother, Weston. We represent our small village in the Marshlands of the Southwest. We have traveled north up the River to open relations and trade between my kin and yours."

Lemmeck stood still, not trusting the large falcon. "I hunt these lands, and I know this type of bird of prey. It is not natural for it to be on the arm of a Rodeshian."

Merriton nodded with understanding. "It does seem strange, does it not? But my brother here found this falcon thrown out of his nest by his own mother because he was too small. So he picked him up and cared for him. Now he is like family. And no longer very small. He is of no danger to you and your friends."

"As long as you keep him fed," Weston added, laughing. He reached into his tunic pouch and grabbed another small animal, throwing it toward the bird's powerful beak. The falcon ate the entire carcass again without chewing. "He loves the vermin that live in the Marshlands, but I have found these nice little field mice that he enjoys too."

F'lorna waited for Lemmeck to make the introductions, but he would not take his wary eyes away from the falcon. She realized that Lemmeck did not like the young Rodeshian's humor. She walked forward. "My name is F'lorna, and we are River-dwellers from Right River Hook," she said. She didn't want to tell them about their journey until she knew for sure their intentions.

Merriton reached out his left hand and squeezed her right shoulder. "The villagers at Left River Hook taught us your customary greeting. It is different than ours, but I rather enjoy the candor of the gesture." He instantly stopped and stared into F'lorna's eyes. "You have grey eyes," he said stunned.

F'lorna's curiosity overcame her embarrassment. "Yes, like my mother. Is that different in a way?" She knew that no one at Right or Left River Hook had grey eyes, as it was distinctly a Sand-shaper feature.

He moved in closer to her face, inspecting her eyes further. "Yes, they are grey, like the slate rocks that hem the River. They are culturally significant to my kin—both in a good and bad way," he said.

F'lorna could tell Merriton was struggling with his thoughts. He had a scar across his face. She wondered if had happened during the ground shudders.

Weston made a screech and jerked his left arm upward. The falcon leapt into the air with his strong wings. He brought his arm back down, moved beside his brother and stared into F'lorna's eyes before speaking. "What my brother means is that our culture—or the culture to which we once belonged—has a caste system. The wealthy landowners have the grey or violet eyes.

The rest of us farmhands or coastal workers usually have eyes the color of smokestone."

"My mother has spoken of smokestone," F'lorna said.

Weston looked at her. "It is a very dark grey—almost black. It is mined in the Northeastern Mountains. Sand-shapers use it to bake everything from bread to parchment. The River-dwellers we have spoken to are usually afraid of it."

Lemmeck squared his shoulders. "It is not fear the governs us. It is the health of the River. Smokestone sickens the Great Expanse."

Weston drew up both hands in surrender. "I mean no disrespect. I know the fear is rooted in a healthy stewardship of Rodesh. We are honored to be away from the farmlands, living further south among the River-dwellers."

Merriton smiled. "Which is why my brother and I have made our long journey—to introduce our kin to others, so we can live side-by-side with mutual respect and support. Our village saw many changes after the ground shudders during the storm, and we realized that we couldn't hide anymore if our village was going to thrive. Right River Hook was going to be our last stop. We have traveled as far north as we want and are missing our families."

"What is that around your neck?" Ralona asked timidly. "I've never seen anything shine like that before."

Merriton clutched the golden stone that hung on a fiber cord and then looked at his brother. "We prefer to talk to your Elders about what we have discovered," he said. "We have discussed what we have learned with the other villages we visited along our journey north. The Elders at Left River Hook were quite disturbed by our information."

"My brother and I are Elders of Right River Hook, although two of the younger ones," Dashion insisted.

Merriton shook his head. "No, we must talk to your entire village, and to your Spiritual Elder. The Elders at Left River Hook asked us to bring him the information and to see what his thoughts were. I have also found an item that belongs to one of your villagers, and I must return it. Will you take us?"

"My father is the Spiritual Elder of Right River Hook," F'lorna said. "We can bring you to him."

"We can't just yet," Lemmeck interrupted. "I am leading our group to the main River. We were told that many animals have washed up on the shores from the storm. Our village is in the midst of a building project, and we must harvest sinews to complete it."

"You are not too far from it," Merriton said, looking at his brother. "Do you mind if we delay going back to the wetlands a few more sun rises?"

Weston smiled. "You are the one with the wife and youngling. I am enjoying our journey along the River's tributaries, Brother."

Merriton nodded. "We have seen the animals on the shore. We will take you there. There are many predators, so we will make more torches tonight to scare them off." He looked up through the high trees. "The Heat Source is already descending. We will have to leave when the Violet Moon awakens in the morning.

209

We have just left a traveler's lodge that Left River Hook created between their village and the River. There is a cooking hearth and several of those large Achion trees you dwell in. We will have to stay there for the night."

Lemmeck nodded. He then walked in front of Merriton, raised his left hand and placed it on Merriton's right shoulder. "I offer you my apology of healing for distrusting you and your brother. I am grateful for your assistance. The landscape has changed much since I last traveled to the main River. I did not know which way to turn. I gave voiceless words to Ra'ash for help just before you arrived."

Merriton nodded his approval. "We have been learning a lot about your Ra'ash. Now, I will give you the Marshland greeting," he said, grasping Lemmeck's left hand into a ball and bowing down to gently place the center of his forehead on Lemmeck's fisted hand. "This is how we show friendship."

Lemmeck bowed slightly when Merriton finished the greeting. "I am indebted to you." He turned to his twin brothers. "Be on your guard for predators."

Merriton began to lead the way, and Dashion and Rashion went in opposing directions with bows in hand to watch for predators. F'lorna and Lemmeck fell behind Merriton, and Weston walked next to F'lorna. Weston was only a few turns of the moon older than she. Probably around the twins' age. His features were similar to her mother's—tan skin, high cheekbones and angular eyes—though more pronounced. She felt comfortable next to him. F'lorna could hear Sage, Ralona and Le'ana whispering behind her. She knew they were fascinated by their new friends. A few moments later, Le'ana came up to Weston.

"Would you like some Indigo berries?" she asked.

He looked at the leather pouch she was carrying. "My brother and I walked past berries like those, but we did not know if they were poisonous or not. We have never seen berries the color of the Indigo moon before."

Le'ana popped a berry into her mouth. "Believe me, you will not want to miss tasting one of these. They are sweet like nectar yet tart like a citrus tree fruit."

Weston reached over and gently grabbed a few of the berries, and cautiously placed them in his mouth. He slowly chewed and instantly smiled. "They are delicious!"

"And quite a prize too. They haven't been able to grow for many turns of the moon," Le'ana said. "Here," she said, handing the pouch to F'lorna. "Why don't you three eat these? We have more. I'm saving a pouch for Dashion and Rashion."

F'lorna gave a knowing smile to Le'ana, then took the pouch and allowed Lemmeck and Weston to take turns grabbing handfuls of berries. She was able to snatch a few for herself as well.

"Brother, come here and taste these Indigo berries," Weston said with blue stained lips.

Merriton turned around and looked at F'lorna's hands. "I thought they may be edible, but I didn't want to risk getting sick so far from our village." He reached his hand in and grabbed several, cupping them in the palm of his hand and placing them one by one into his mouth. "These berries are lifting my mood and my feet," he said.

Sage and Ralona joined the group with more berries.

"Here is another pouch for you," Sage said, handing a smaller pouch to Merriton.

"I am grateful," Merriton said. "I can plainly see that you are the storyteller's sister. You look very much like her. We enjoyed her stories, especially, as I shouted through the forest, the one of the Storm Dancer."

Sage smiled, mischievously. "Did you know that the renowned Storm Dancer is here with us?"

Weston stopped and turned to face the group. "Which one of you is the Storm Dancer?" he asked, curiously.

"F'lorna is," Sage said, pointing to her. "And everything my sister said is true. I watched F'lorna bring in the storm with my own eyes. The Upper Realm lit up with white threads of the Heat Source splitting the darkness. And there F'lorna danced on stage through flickers of dark and light—even after slamming her horns on the platform because a Zulo vine had imprisoned her legs. She fought against the rain and wind with only Lemmeck, my sister and me as her witnesses."

F'lorna dropped the pouch she was carrying, and a few of the berries rolled onto the ground. She quickly retrieved it and turned to her friend. She felt heat rising in her cheeks. "Sage, we are not here to trade stories."

"On the contrary," Weston said, smiling at F'lorna with a new appreciation. "That is exactly why we are here—to trade resources, friendships, customs and—" he smiled, "stories."

Chapter 21

THE FIRELIGHT DANCE

F'lorna sat in the hole of one of the traveler's Achion trees. There were five sleeping trees, so she, Le'ana, Ralona and Sage each got her own. The last was used to safeguard more Indigo berries that Le'ana had found on their walk to the traveler's lodge. Merriton and the others said they would prefer to sleep directly under the Violet Moon. They made several

214

torches using bark and dried brush and saved them in a pile for when they made it to the River the following moonrise. Finally, they built a fire in the cooking hearth and sat on large stones encircling it.

F'lorna heard a controlled flap of wings. She looked toward the storage Achion tree just as Banthem, Weston's falcon, landed on the thick leather arm covering that he had wrapped around a lower branch. The falcon looked at the group of Rodeshians around the fire for a moment. Then he bowed his head and slept. F'lorna watched him sleep, surprised at how quickly he slumbered. Then she listened back on the conversation around the fire. Lemmeck had just finished telling his story about his Doublemoon Ceremony hunt.

"A White Diamond stag—we saw one of those in the lower hills before arriving at Left River Hook. They are quite amazing animals," Merriton said, obviously impressed with Lemmeck's story. "And that is your—what is it?—Adoration to your Ra'ash?"

"Yes, our village offers Adorations to Ra'ash that demonstrate our appreciation for how He has gifted each of us, and these offerings support the village in various but vital ways," Lemmeck said confidently.

F'lorna knew that Lemmeck's family was one of the village's most respected because they valued the village and its shared system of support, created around serving Ra'ash and other villagers. Although his family's land was the furthest from the Village Achion cluster, they attended almost every Shoam-sha and provided meat for each one when possible. She felt proud that Lemmeck spoke assured, audible words about their village and customs.

Merriton leaned back, placing the palms of his hands on the forest floor behind him, his appearance illuminated by the upward light of the fire. "Now I see why your Village Elders allowed you to lead this expedition. When I discovered you were only starting the first turn of your third moon, I was surprised. But you are a true warrior."

"I am no warrior," Lemmeck said. "The Lake-keepers were warriors. I am a hunter. The real warriors all died in *The Great Engulfing*. The story of them is found in several of the *Sacred Songs of the Prophets*."

Merriton nodded. "Yes, all your River-dwellers have your *Divine Oracle* stored in what we call our youngling memories. You River-dwellers call it your Eternal Memory. The farmland we worked before moving to the Marshlands was isolated from the River, so I never heard any of the songs or chants—only a whisper or two from someone who had heard a story as a youngling about flying animals called Swarves that once reigned the Upper Realm or a holy Rodeshian who was strapped to a rising sphere and killed, but nothing more. We were taught the Sand-shaper symbols, so we could read instructions on parchment. I can tell you how to turn soil, plant seed, harvest grain and even bake bread. But I know very little about who we Rodeshians are or how we came to Rodesh."

"Did Left River Hook not sing you any of the *Sacred Songs or Holy Chants of Jeyshen*? F'lorna asked.

"We asked them to, but they didn't know if it was right to share their *Divine Oracle* with foreigners," Weston said, seriously. "They wanted us to ask your Spiritual Elder," he smiled in thought. "But the

216

storytellers did tell us many stories. They have them memorized, but the newer ones they must recite often, so they are not forgotten."

The group became quiet. Only the snapping and popping of the flames devouring the wood could be heard. The Violet Moon's subtle waves of light streamed in through the trees.

F'lorna finally broke the silence. "My mother was a Sand-shaper. She had her horns extracted at a young age, but she met my father when she left the Northeastern Mountains, and they were joined in Ra'ash. Ever since I was a youngling, I remember my father always reciting the *Divine Oracle* to her. When I would memorize a song or chant, I would then recite to her as well   to lift his burden."

"Why is it that the storytellers can repeat new stories, but your mother can't repeat the *Divine Oracle*?" Merriton asked. "It sounds like she hears it every day."

F'lorna got up from the Achion hole. "I must stand. My legs are going numb from sitting." She began to pace just inside the dimming light of the fire. "I wondered that as a youngling and asked my father. He said that as a Rodeshian ages, only memories that are experienced at the moment—with the eyes and ears and with mouth and skin—can be kept if they are repeated often. However, the *Divine Oracle* happened many moon folds ago—each experience being added to a sacred chronicle of events with each turn of a moon. Ra'ash wanted to store those events in the minds of Rodeshians, so we could remember Him and the Liberator He sent to us. He gave us an Eternal Memory as a gift, so we could store His sacred words, and we would know who we are and where we came from. The Eternal Memory stays opened for only about two moon cycles in each youngling, and at an unforeseen moment before we see our fourteenth moon turn, the memory closes, like putting an Achion hole cover on permanently. Whatever is inside stays, and nothing else can be added."

"So only the *Divine Oracle* is in your Eternal Memory?" Merriton asked.

"No," Sage said, getting out of the Achion tree where she had been sitting. She walked to the cooking hearth and sat on an empty rock next to Lemmeck. "We usually have other things from our time as younglings. I have many stories that my sister learned from Rodeshian history. During her training at Left River Hook, she would come back to our Achion cluster and visit. We'd sit under the Indigo Moon, and I would listen to her stories. My Adoration is singing, so I didn't have much to learn other than the *Divine Oracle*."

"Are there no other songs that you can memorize?" Weston asked. "Songs that Rodeshians sing for fun?"

"Singing is only used for the *Divine Oracle*," Dashion said. He was sitting in front of the fire with his twin to his right and Merriton to his left. "My brothers and I sing very well, but our village limits our songs to only the *Divine Oracle*, which is one reason why we chose not to offer singing as our Adoration. It was better for us to spend more time with our father and mother and learn as much about hunting and traversing the landscape around us."

"It is limiting," Sage agreed. "Which is why I am grateful to Blaklin. I learned the *Divine Oracle* and many of her stories before my Eternal Memory shut," she turned to look at F'lorna. "Come sit with us. You are the only one not in our circle."

F'lorna walked deeper into the light and sat next to Ralona. "My father is Spiritual Elder of Right River Hook, but he's also the Healing Elder," she smiled. "He absorbed much information as a youngling from many moon turns of listening to his elder sister talk about healing plants and procedures."

"Is that your Adoration?" Weston asked, staring at F'lorna from the other side of the fire. "Healing?"

F'lorna was glad the warm atmosphere camouflaged the heat rising in her cheeks. "No, I chose dance," she said. "But I know a lot about both my parents' Adorations. My mother offers cooking."

"So, you learned Sand-shaper recipes," Merriton said.

"Yes, but my mother was able to alter those recipes with what grows in the River tributaries and by watching the other offerings of the villagers," F'lorna said.

Suddenly, Weston got up and walked to the traveling bags hanging from the storage Achion tree. He reached into one of the leather pouches and pulled out a small wooden instrument with a handle and a long stick that looked like a bow.

"Why are you getting that out, Brother?" Merriton asked.

"Because we have a dancer here. Play for us, so we can dance," Weston said.

219

F'lorna looked at the strange instrument. "I cannot dance to that."

"Why not?" Weston asked, handing the instrument and bow to his brother.

"I have never seen an instrument like that before," F'lorna said.

"It is just like your instrument called the tingla, but we do not strum this one with our fingers. We use the bow to rub up and down against the tightened sinews," Weston said. "Come. Let us dance."

F'lorna scooted back on her rock. "I only offer dance to Ra'ash. In our village we only sing or dance the *Divine Oracle* to honor Him," she said.

"Does not your Ra'ash like to see you happy?" Weston asked.

"Yes," F'lorna answered hesitantly.

"On the farmlands, we worked every rise of the Heat Source except one. On that rise, the landowners allowed the workers to rest. But we did not rest. We celebrated! My brother may have memorized how to bake bread, but he has also memorized how to bow the cords. And I have memorized the songs and dances of my kin—the workers of the farmlands. Come, and I will teach you one."

"I must ask my father first," F'lorna said, unsure.

"Why do the River-dwellers keep saying that?" Weston Pressed. "You are just as capable of deciding as anyone. You have the *Divine Oracle*. What does it say about dancing?"

"They are the *Holy Images of Jeyshen*," F'lorna said. "They are what I dance."

"But you change them a little, right? That's what the storyteller told us—you made them into something new, like your mother and her recipes," Weston said.

"Yes, but cooking is different than dancing," F'lorna said.

"No, it is just like storytelling and all the other Adorations. Why would Ra'ash give you dancing only for use in your Eternal Memory, but not your everyday life? It feels good to move the body to music just for the fun of it," Weston said, holding out his hand to F'lorna.

F'lorna looked at Sage. "What do you think?"

"My sister experiences new stories to tell, and she loves it. Dancing could be the same," Sage offered. Her moss-colored eyes sparkled in the flickering fire and her burgundy hair seemed to glow against the umber hue of her face. "It's a new experience with our new friends!"

F'lorna knew that many in her village disagreed with storytelling as an Adoration, which led to Blaklin going to Left River Hook. F'lorna had never agreed with her village's resistance to it. Ralona must have known her thoughts because she pressed further.

"Nayran made that water carrying pouch that your mother received. Nothing like that had ever been done before, but she created it. She inspired me to make our folding baskets for when we gather the sinews," Ralona said. "Those are new creations too—just like a new experience."

F'lorna looked Ralona. Her dark curly hair bounced as she nodded her approval, and her pale blue eyes gleamed with enthusiasm. Next F'lorna looked to Le'ana. The speckles across her nose had become more plentiful from being out of the shade and under the Heat Source. Her scarlet braids bobbed enthusiastically as she too nodded her head in approval.

"My father and I put the logs around our fields, so they would be better at holding in the rains," Le'ana said. "That had never been done before in our village. How is offering a new dance any different from offering a new method of planting?"

F'lorna looked towards Lemmeck. He was not smiling.

"Come," Weston said again, walking up to F'lorna and grasping her hands. "Let me show you one of the dances of my kin." He turned to his brother. "Play my favorite dancing song, the Flight of the Raptors!"

Weston held both F'lorna's hands, his fingertips rough, like dried earth warmed under the rays of the Heat Source. She looked eye-level to him. His eyes stared playfully into hers.

"You are very tall," he said smiling. "I like that."

F'lorna gave an awkward smile. She had never been complimented by a male about her height.

Merriton stood and fitted the instrument onto the side of his waist. He then held the bow over the instrument and waited for a moment until all eyes were on him. The quiet atmosphere was instantly pushed to the side by the quick rhythm of the stringed instrument. F'lorna listened intently for only a moment before Weston pulled her into the first step. She stared down at his feet, so she could keep the pace and follow his lead. There seemed to be no structure to his steps, and she whirled on the forest floor around the cooking hearth. Her eyes opened wide, and a smile sprung to her lips.

At first, Weston had to guide F'lorna to stay in step with the fast rhythm, but she quickly learned how to anticipate his movements by the shift of his body and the repetition of the steps. She began to dance in time with him and the music. She lifted her eyes from the ground and looked at him with a mischievous smile.

"See, you've got it!" he shouted. "Now, let's try this." He let go of one of her hands and spun her twice before bringing her back to him. She instinctively went into the next move. "Impressive!" he shouted.

The music climaxed and came to a sudden stop, and F'lorna faced Weston breathless. "That was very enjoyable!" she said breathlessly.

"Thank you," he said, bowing slightly. "I chose one of the more difficult songs to test your skills. I did not think you would be able to keep up. Did you want to try a slower one? It is for beginners."

F'lorna stared into Weston's dark eyes and felt embarrassment rise up again. "Ah, why don't you teach Le'ana?" She looked at her birth friend whose silken scarlet hair gleamed in the firelight. "Her mother plays the leera, so I know she knows much about music, though she chose her father's Adoration of planting."

"I would love to!" Le'ana said jumping up.

Weston frowned briefly, but quickly covered up his disappointment. "And after Le'ana, I will dance with Ralona and Sage."

Chapter 22

THE MOUNTAIN TERROR

F'lorna could hear the crashing current of the River, though they hadn't yet cleared the dense foliage of the forest. She walked with Sage, behind Le'ana and Ralona, who were walking on either side of Weston. He had sent his falcon on ahead to survey the rocky landscape surrounding the River. F'lorna could hear the three of them talking about their dance under the Violet Moon. Two of her friends danced twice with Weston. Sage, who never fully caught on to the spontaneous

224

dance, decided once was enough with her. Merriton finally put his stringed instrument back into its bag and said they should all get some rest before the Heat Source rose in the morning horizon. They had a lot of work ahead of them. F'lorna could not see Lemmeck, but she knew he was leading the group with Merriton. Dashion and Rashion were walking with them.

F'lorna noticed that the trees in the forest were thinning out, and the mossy forest floor was becoming rocky and more uneven. The Heat Source was fully above the horizon, and F'lorna appreciated its fullness in the Upper Realm. The wooded area close to the main River was cooler than their village tributary, and the breeze flowing off the cold current made her wish she had brought a thicker tunic. F'lorna noticed that there were few Achion trees growing on the rocky landscape, but Sea Pines—whose roots did not burrow so deep—were plentiful.

"I'm worried about Merriton and Weston," Sage whispered.

F'lorna looked at her birth friend. She noticed her umber skin was also cold and covered with chills. "Why?"

"When my sister chose storytelling as her Adoration, many of the villagers did not want to accept her offering at the Doublemoon Ceremony. They said that her Adoration did not benefit the village," Sage began.

"But they like her stories now," F'lorna said.

Sage nodded. "Yes, I am glad. Because of you, they finally listen to her stories. But—" she hesitated. "Look what they are doing to your mother. They won't allow her to attend the Shoam-sha without her hair braided. If they are so unyielding to the wife of the Spiritual and Healing Elder of our village, how more unyielding will they be to our new friends?" Sage asked.

F'lorna thought of her mother. She had endured unspoken exclusion since she could remember—never accepted, only tolerated. It was only of late that she realized that this quiet discrimination had become her normal way of life. She had always felt the need to please others—even when she disagreed with them. She wondered if that was the real reason she shut her birth friends out after Raecli was taken. She felt lost without her birth friend who was half Sand-shaper like she was. "Many of our kinfolk are resistant to change. I believe that Zelara and her family are giving voice to the resistance our village has against anything different."

Sage nodded. "Zelara's father has said many times that Sand-shapers are the reason their north tributary became sick and they had to move. He has so much aversion towards them—like they are undeserving of our friendship. I know he will give audible words against accepting them. Will the villagers even let Merriton and Weston speak at the Village Achion cluster?"

"Left River Hook let them speak," F'lorna said.

"Yes, but they are closer to the main River. They have had more foreigners on their lands. Our village has much fewer visitors. The last Sand-shaper to enter our village was Raecli's grandfather, and he did not leave a pleasing image behind," Sage said.

F'lorna thought. "But they are not Sand-shapers. They are Marsh-landers from the south wetlands. No one has to know that they were field workers from the farmlands."

Sage's moss-colored eyes lightened with understanding. "Yes, I see your point. We will not mention that they were Sand-shapers at all. Merriton and Weston do not have their horns, but Merriton himself said that his youngling has his horns. Eventually, all the Marsh-landers will have horns like us."

"And my father is very good with his words. I know he will use just the right ones to introduce them onto the platform to speak to the village. I wonder what they are going to say. I will ask them to tell my father first. He likes to be informed, so he can be prepared for the possible reactions of the villagers."

"I want us to hurry up and get this harvesting done, so we can be back at our village on the sixth rise of the Heat Source," Sage said.

F'lorna nodded. "So do I."

The roaring sound of flooding torrents surrounded the friends as they walked onto the ground that was now made completely of stone. The clearing of trees allowed the full shine of the Heat Source to warm F'lorna's body, and her grey eyes blinked from the glare of the rays reflecting off the bare surface. F'lorna looked in the distance and her mouth fell open in awe. Gaping stone cliffs lined either side of the River, and mighty waves crashed against the shores with sprays reaching a tree's length high. "Look at it, Sage! I've never seen water look so threatening, not even when the storm poured waves of water from the Upper Realm."

"My sister will not be happy when I tell her what she's missing by refusing to visit the main River. Ra'ash has scraped the center of Rodesh with His mighty finger, stripping off everything green and leaving only this impenetrable stone ground," Sage said.

A falcon's screech penetrated the grumble of the River, and F'lorna saw Weston's falcon soaring the airstream that glided above the current. F'lorna watched the falcon land on a dark spot on the River's shore. She focused her sight on the spot and realized it was one of the animals that washed up after the storm. She stared further along the rocky ledge and saw more darks spots. Many animals littered the shores of the River. She saw more movement and looked back toward the rocky cliff above the River. It was Merriton waving at them. The others were already standing with him.

"Sage, we better hurry," F'lorna said. "They are waiting for us."

F'lorna hiked quickly up the gradual incline of the rugged land toward the cliff. As she drew nearer to the group, her heart began to sprint within her. Something was wrong. She felt fear that she couldn't explain. She watched as Le'ana peered over the ledge of the cliff. The sharp decline toward the River was over two tree lengths down. "Le'ana!" F'lorna screamed, reaching out her hand. "Don't get so close to the ledge!"

"Are you okay?" Sage asked, staring at F'lorna with concern.

"Look at that drop!" F'lorna said. Her feet began to slow, and her knees felt wobbly, like they were pushing against the current. Just before F'lorna reached the group, she felt her body come down to the knees. Her palms flattened themselves against the stone floor. "I can't move!" Her chest was rapidly taking in air, and she began to feel dizzy. "The ground is spinning!"

"What is wrong with her?" Lemmeck demanded, falling to his knees beside F'lorna.

"I don't know," Sage said, worried. "She saw Le'ana look over the ledge, and she began to scream."

"We need to help her!" Le'ana said anxiously.

"Take her back toward the forest!" Merriton yelled.

Instantly, Lemmeck scooped up F'lorna's body and brought her into his arms. He stood up and began running carefully away from the River's edge. F'lorna's head began to shake. "Her breathing is rapid, like a mother giving birth!" Lemmeck yelled.

Weston came up beside Lemmeck. "Do you need help?"

"Do you have something I can lay her head on? She still wears her horn binding," he said, looking straight ahead.

Weston hurriedly took off the leather covering from his arm. "I have this. It is very thick."

Merriton ran ahead of them toward the Forest. When the incline of the land leveled out, he waved Lemmeck over. "Here! Set her down."

Weston laid the leather covering on the ground, and Lemmeck came down one knee and gently placed F'lorna's head on the leather, stretching her body in front of her. Le'ana, Sage and Ralona came and knelt on the other side of her.

"Gently hold her head and keep it from moving off the leather," Lemmeck told Le'ana. He leaned over her face. "F'lorna, you are near the forest. No one is hurt. The River is far away from us."

Le'ana grabbed F'lorna's left hand. "I am alright. Nothing is wrong. We are no longer near the main River," she whispered.

F'lorna opened her eyes and tried to focus on her friends. "Le'ana was too close to the edge. The cliff—it is too far down. Too many jagged rocks." She looked to Le'ana and squeezed her hand. "You must be careful! The land is not kind here!" she yelled, tears streaming down her face.

Lemmeck looked at Merriton who had his arms crossed, watching the situation unfold. "What is wrong with her?" he asked.

Merriton squatted down and watched as F'lorna continued to weep. "She has the Mountain Terror," he answered.

F'lorna wiped her amber hair away from her face with the back of her arm. She squatted over the small Wood Deer, cutting the tendons and ligament away from the bone and muscle with the sharpened stone blade Lemmeck had given her to use. She looked toward the River from a safe distance and watched Ralona hiking up the ledge of the cliff. She wasn't afraid—none of them were. They were all making their way up and down the stone ledge carefully without fear of being swallowed up by the rocky mouth of the River.

F'lorna wiped her blade on the small patch of river grass next to her. Then she placed the sinews she had harvested into the folding basket that Ralona had made. *"What in the name of Ra'ash happened to me?"* she whispered to herself.

"It was not your fault."

She jumped when she heard the deep voice behind her. A shadow fell across where she was looking. She looked up behind her and squinted. The Heat Source was descending to the evening horizon. Merriton held two folding baskets in his arms that were now swollen with sinews.

She looked away. "I am so humiliated," she whispered.

He squatted down next to her, setting the baskets next to him. "Why because you have a weakness?"

She looked at Merriton's face without squinting. She could see his features now that he was out of the Heat Source's rays. He was about a moon cycle older than she. Probably her father's age when he joined with her mother. His eyes were the dark color of the soil wet with the spring rain. His dark hair was long and pulled back at the nape of his neck. The light creases around his eyes showed wisdom, and he reminded her so much of her own mother.

"It is difficult to experience something that you have no control over," she said.

"Your body was giving birth to fear. That is what happens when you have the Mountain Terror and you come close to rocky ledges. I have never seen it, but a foreigner passed through our farmland village many moon turns ago. He had just come from the Northeastern

231

Mountains to visit family. He had the same reaction seeing the mountains as you did when you saw the River's edge, but his was much worse. He slept through three rises of the Heat Source before he woke up again. They thought he had died," Merriton said.

F'lorna looked back at the ground. "It looks like I will not be visiting the mountains any time soon." She looked toward the River. "Or the main River."

"You shouldn't feel too bad about it," Merriton said. "Nothing can really live out here. The water is fresh, but the current is too difficult to navigate."

"How did you get on this side?" she asked. She wondered if they had found a part of the main River that could be crossed.

Merriton looked toward the River. "There are only two ways to go from west to east on Rodesh. The Sand-shapers have built a massive bridge on the north River just before it splinters into the Four Horns. The bridge tethers the Northwestern Coastal cities to the Northeastern Mountains."

"My mother has told me about the Four Horns. They are the mighty coastal tributaries that feed into the Great Expanse," F'lorna said. "She did not tell me about the bridge."

"They had smaller bridges that would disappear under the high moon tide. Those structures would not last long. I believe they began this bridge over a moon cycle ago. It took four moon turns in all to finish it. It is the biggest structure made by Rodeshian hands in all of Rodesh," Merriton said. "It allows for bigger shipments of smokestone to cross from the mountains to the coastal cities."

"I wonder how many parchments of symbols they had to create to plan the bridge," F'lorna said in awe.

Merriton laughed. "They have to use scrolls. Those are the long parchments that roll."

F'lorna thought. "And what is the other way across?"

"That is the way my brother and I came. Our marshlands are located just north of the Desert Plains where the River disappears under the endless sands. There is a natural bridge made of stone where the River and the Desert Plains merge. We crossed over that bridge."

F'lorna stared at him confused. "I have never heard of a stone bridge there."

Merriton looked at the ground for a moment, thinking. "That discussion will have to wait for when we get back to your village," he said, looking back toward the River. "The Heat Source is getting low. We will need to make our way back to the traveling Achion tree cluster before the land becomes dark."

F'lorna wondered if something happened to the lands because of the storm and ground shudders, but she knew now was not the time to discuss it. They needed to get the sinews back to the village. Her father counted on her. The entire village did. "I need to wash off the blade that Lemmeck lent me," she said, holding up the grey stone blade.

Merriton nodded. "I'll wash the one I used. He reached into a fold of his tunic belt and pulled out a violet crystal blade.

F'lorna gasped. "That is Lemmeck's Tarnezion crystal blade!"

Merriton held up the blade. "Are you telling me that Lemmeck was the one who plunged this blade into the eye of the monster we found?"

F'lorna stared at the blade and nodded. "Yes, that is it. He saved my mother and me from the teeth of the River Monster."

Merriton shot up to his feet and scanned the horizon. "I must speak with him!"

Chapter 23

THE SONG OF THE WOUNDED

F'lorna adjusted the oblong leather pouch she held on her back. It was filled with sinews they had harvested for the bridge. She had given her folding grass basket to Weston, and he carried the sinew-stuffed pouch on his back next to her. His falcon, Banthem, rested on his arm. F'lorna looked at the bird of prey. She was becoming accustomed to his presence. His head turned side to side stealthily, his vision piercing through the darkness. Merriton led the group and held two lit torches, as did Lemmeck and the twins. The River had been clear of predators, so they were able to save the torches for their journey back to the traveler's Achion cluster. The Violet Moon could not be seen overhead. The canopy of the forest was too thick. Le'ana, Ralona and Sage walked closely behind Merriton and the torch light. They took turns whispering stories about their time at the River. Sage was especially descriptive with her words.

F'lorna laughed under her breath. Her friends looked like brook turtles slowly wobbling the forest. Their bulging baskets of sinews were comfortably fastened to their backs.

"I have great respect for Lemmeck," Weston whispered. F'lorna had been quietly walking next to him, each deep in thought. "When my brother and I found the dead River Monster, I thought that another beast had beaten him. But we saw the blade in his eye and there was a trail of darkened orange blood behind him. I remember remarking that the Rodeshian who plunged his blade into this monster's eye was the bravest Rodeshian I will ever know. My brother retrieved the blade and vowed that he would find its owner," Weston said pondering. "Then we went to Left River Hook, and they told us a story of the River-dweller from Right River Hook who bested the River Monster. I couldn't believe it. My brother could return the blade, and I could meet the brave Rodeshian face-to-face."

F'lorna smiled. "And so you have."

Weston shook his head. "I envisioned a mighty warrior."

"As Lemmeck said earlier, the warriors died with the Lake-keepers," F'lorna said seriously. "Lemmeck is a hunter and a friend."

"But how could he take on the River Monster like that?" Weston asked pressing. "The monster was as big as three predator cats that roam the desert plains. I tried to cut through its skin, but the scales covering it were like stones. It was impenetrable."

"He was not thinking of the monster's size. He was only thinking of saving us. He was not the only one there. My father, Le'ana's father and the twins were all there, throwing their spheres and arrows," F'lorna said.

"Yes, but it was he who jumped onto the monster's back. Did he not consider the outcome of his actions?" Merriton asked.

F'lorna sensed that Weston needed a deeper explanation for Lemmeck's actions. "Do you remember how we talked about our Adorations to Ra'ash?"

He nodded.

"Lemmeck's offering of Adoration is hunting. He is not only trained in hunting, but he feels the pleasure of Ra'ash when he hunts. He knows that he is supporting his family and the village with the animals he harvests. It is hard to explain," she said thinking. Suddenly, she thought of something. "You know how you worked the fields for the landowners?"

"Yes," Weston said nodding.

"Did you want to do the work?" she asked.

"No. I hated picking the rows of grain with my hands from the time the Heat Source awoke to the time the Heat Source slept. I wanted to leave, but my hands and feet were bound by custom," he said heatedly. "They use force to keep those custom, which is why my brother now has a scar across his face."

F'lorna saw the anger rise on Weston's face. She had noticed Merriton's scar when they first met the Marsh-landers. Now was not the time to ask about it. "I offer you my apology of healing bringing audible words to your pain, but it will help me explain."

"Go on," Weston said, adjusting the arm that Banthem held.

F'lorna looked at Banthem who had now bowed his head to sleep. She nodded to the falcon. "You have held Banthem on your arm since we began our journey in the woods. Is your arm not tired?"

Weston looked at his falcon and smiled. "He is heavy, but I do not mind the burden."

"Why?" she asked.

"Because he is like family," he answered looking back at her.

"Yes. Working for family is much different from working for landowners, is it not?" F'lorna asked.

Weston looked at the falcon and then back at F'lorna. "I think I understand what you are telling me. Lemmeck fought the River Monster because he cares about you. He wants to court you."

F'lorna felt her cheeks heat with embarrassment. "No. It isn't that," she whispered, looking ahead to see if anyone had heard. "He is not allowed to court another until he is sixteen turns of the moon."

"That is a River-dwelling custom?" Weston asked, raising his eyebrows.

"Yes," she nodded. "But that is not what I am trying to explain. My friends tell me that I do not give enough details in my words. Maybe someone else should explain."

"No. I am grateful for your explanation. Please continue," he said.

"If it were Sage or Le'ana or Ralona in the tree, Lemmeck would have still jumped onto the River Monster's back," F'lorna said. "He is a hunter and his mind and heart respond as one. And the work of hunting is not burdensome to him—even though it is a very difficult Adoration to offer. The burden feels light because it gives his actions purpose and his life meaning. He adds value to himself and others when he hunts. Does that make sense?"

Weston stared ahead of him and stretched his left arm where the falcon slept. The falcon did not awaken from his sleep. "The work I did as a farmhand felt burdensome because my work was demanded by those who did not care. But really all I did was pick heads of grain, which is not very dangerous, though tiresome. Now my brother and I are respected leaders of the Marshland Village. Much is expected of us—even traveling through distant lands to open relations with the River-dwellers. But this work feels light. I believe I understand your words."

"Yes," F'lorna nodded. "But even more, as River-dwellers, we believe Ra'ash created us as His family. We feel not only our pleasure but His pleasure when we offer our Adorations to Him. When Lemmeck shoots an animal with his arrow, he offers silent words to Ra'ash, thanking Him for His assistance."

"You think this Ra'ash helps you?" Weston asked. "But you cannot touch or see Him."

"We believe the Help of Ra'ash is inside of us, guiding, protecting and helping us. We call this the Indwelling. When Lemmeck jumped onto the monster's back, he was not alone. The Help of Ra'ash was with him," F'lorna finished.

"These are difficult words to understand," Weston said, shaking his head.

"You are not expected to understand them in a single moment. I have the *Divine Oracle* in my Eternal Memory, and I still do not understand much," F'lorna said.

"I doubt if I will ever understand," Weston added.

"I think no one will fully understand everything, but I do sense the presence of Ra'ash. I feel His love and guidance. I may not understand it, but I feel it," she said.

The two walked in the lingering light of the torches in silence. Banthem awoke and looked around. He wiggled his wings and pushed off Weston's arm with his talons. His wings beat against the soft wooded air, and he soared though the trees toward the Violet Moon.

"I think he senses that we are almost there," Weston said. "I am tired. I believe I could sleep until the Heat Source reaches its highest point in the Upper Realm."

"So could I, but we have to leave before it awakens. It will take us two more rises to get back to my village. The bridge is underway, and they are waiting for the sinews. I believe we have more than enough."

"We are here! Thank Ra'ash," Le'ana whispered, looking back to F'lorna. "I see Dashion securing one of his torches on my Achion tree. And Merriton is starting the fire in the cooking hearth!"

"My arms are so tired," Ralona added. "Cutting ligaments and tendons is hard work. I am very happy I did not choose tanning as my Adoration. I thought about it once."

"My hands are blistered," Sage said, staring down at her palms. "They didn't hurt much when we left, but now each cut stings."

"When you get settled, meet me at the cooking fire. I want to see them with as much light as possible," F'lorna said. She walked into the traveler's Achion cluster and brought her bags to the storage tree. She handed the folding basket to Lemmeck who was stacking them. "How are your hands?" she asked.

"Mine are fine. I am used to harvesting animals. Why? Is someone hurt?" he asked, concerned.

"Yes, Sage says her hands are hurt. I will have to look at Ralona's and Le'ana's too, but I doubt they blistered as badly as Sage's. Le'ana is a planter and Ralona creates, so they always work with their hands," F'lorna said.

"How about your hands?" Lemmeck asked.

"No, mine are fine. I help my mother cook and look for plants with my father. They are strong. Plus," F'lorna said, ashamed. "I could not go to the River, so I had to wait for animals to be brought to me. I did more waiting than cutting."

Lemmeck squeezed F'lorna's right shoulder. "You did not know you had the Mountain Terror. Do not

241

be embarrassed. You did nothing wrong," he said. His smile was genuine and his emerald eyes shone with care.

"I am glad you received your blade back," she added.

His smiled lengthened. "So am I. Merriton explained where he found the River Monster. It crawled quite a distance after leaving the River. Let me know if you need any help with Sage. I'm almost done here."

F'lorna nodded and turned to the cooking hearth. Le'ana and Ralona were already inspecting Sage's hands, and they looked worried. F'lorna quickly walked to Sage and gently grabbed both of her wrists and moved her palms to eye level. "Sage! Why did you not say anything?"

Sage shrugged her shoulders. "Le'ana found berries and the other edible plants for us. Ralona made those folding baskets. You even danced," Sage said, tears streaming down her umber cheeks. "I wanted to offer something, but all I can do is sing. I was not going to complain when I could actually offer work that was useful."

F'lorna shook her head. "You should have stopped when the first blister formed. Your hands are very angry at you. If we do not apply medicine and bind your hands now, they may become infected. Sage, you were cutting sinews with wounds on your hands! Do you realize how dangerous that is?"

Sage's moss-colored eyes glistened with tears against the light of the flames. "No, I've never done it before."

"What is going on?" Merriton asked when he came into the light of the fire.

"Look," F'lorna said. "Her palms are completely torn. I must find the medicine she needs."

"Do you know where it is?" he asked.

"Yes, it is the clotting vine. They are very abundant in the forest. I am sure I can find one. They crawl along the forest floor. I will need light, though," F'lorna said.

"I will help her," Weston said, coming up to his brother.

"No, I need to talk with you," Merriton said to his brother. He glanced around the Achion cluster. "Dashion and Rashion, grab two torches each and help F'lorna find the clotting vine."

The twins quickly grabbed the torches they had pinned to the trees and came up to F'lorna.

"I think I saw some of that vine. I remember your father using it on Lemmeck when they brought him to our hearth after he fought the monster," Dashion said. "The leaves fade from yellow to orange."

"Yes," F'lorna said. "That's it."

"He just pointed them out," Rashion added. "It is not far."

"I am glad the vine is close," she said. She looked to Le'ana and Ralona. "Find me clean fiber fabric. I will need a lot to bind both of her hands. I also need some hot water."

"I have a tunic that I washed in the River. I will take off the sleeves for you," Le'ana said and walked off to her Achion tree.

"And I will set the cooking stones in the fire. It won't take long to heat them," Ralona said.

F'lorna nodded and looked back to Sage. "Did you wash your hands in the River before we left?"

"Yes," she answered.

"Good. Now wait here until I get back. We will hurry," F'lorna said. She turned to Dashion and Rashion. "Let us go."

F'lorna sat on her stone around the fire. The stories were beginning to dissipate, but no one yet wanted to leave the warmth. The group of nine sat in silence, each caught up in their own thoughts of the River and their harvest of sinews. Weston's falcon had recently landed on his leather covering that Weston had wrapped around a sturdy branch of the storage Achion tree. The falcon had bowed his head to slumber, and now sleep called out to each of them.

F'lorna looked next to her where Sage was staring into the flames. She had covered her palms with the salve and bandaged both of her hands. F'lorna was satisfied, knowing that they would not become infected. But she would have her father look at them just in case. "Do they feel better?" F'lorna asked quietly. "I wish I could have given you something to help you sleep, but it is too dark to find the herb."

Sage smiled. "It does not hurt as much now that I know they are cared for. Thank you, F'lorna."

F'lorna thought. "I did not like being unprepared. Next time I travel I will take an herb pouch with me, like my father and aunt wear on their tunic belts."

"You are gifted in so many ways," Sage said, smiling at F'lorna.

F'lorna looked at her friend. They had become closer now than they ever were. "I don't feel very talented. Your hands are wounded because you offered them up for the sinew harvest. I fell into a Mountain Terror and was of no use to anyone."

"You helped me," Sage said.

"I feel like it is my fault that your hands were wounded. Mending something you tore is not helping—it is making it right," F'lorna said.

"I disagree. We have done a great thing for our village. We are bringing back enough sinew to build a bridge and the pier and maybe more. We all did it together," Sage said. "And we have met new friends and learned new things. This journey feels like our first step as Novice Elders."

F'lorna nodded. "It does."

"I wish my sister were here," Sage said, staring into the fire once more. "I know she would create a beautiful story to commemorate our victory."

"She would," F'lorna said smiling. She thought of Lemmeck. Every time he shot an animal with his bow, he offered voiceless words to Ra'ash. She knew her friend needed some way to offer thanks for their successful journey. "Would you like to sing with me?"

Sage abruptly looked at F'lorna. "Would you do that? I would be honored to offer a song to Ra'ash of thanks."

"Which song would you like to sing?" F'lorna asked. "And don't forget, I haven't sung in over a moon turn except for my mother at our own Achion cluster. Do not expect too much from me."

Sage thought. "Let us sing Prophet's Lean'za's song."

"Which one?" F'lorna asked, hesitantly.

"*The Song of the Great Rescue*," Sage said, smiling mischievously.

"You know that is one of the most difficult *Sacred Songs of the Prophets* to sing," F'lorna said.

"I know, but we have our new friends to impress. I want to offer them Right River Hook's best. Wouldn't your mother prepare her finest meal for guests?" Sage implored.

F'lorna looked discreetly at the others. Weston and Merriton were whispering to each other, but everyone else stared into the flames. "Our visitors seem to be occupied," F'lorna noted.

"Let us unoccupy them. You have the stronger voice, so I will follow your lead," Sage said, straightening her shoulders and softly clearing her throat.

F'lorna looked back at Weston again. Maybe he would not notice. She closed her eyes and opened her mind to the *Divine Oracle* tucked into her Eternal Memory. She found the ancient song, allowing the sounds of each word to fill her mind and heart. She sat up straight and offered silent words to Ra'ash to help her voice flow flawlessly. She began the eerie first words, knowing that the feel of the song would transform from defeat to victory at the end. Sage's honeyed voice came in softly, but quickly rose up to surround F'lorna's rich, melodic voice that grew with intensity. Sage echoed the prophet's words like the flow of the inner tributaries, but

F'lorna's voice rolled out like the thundering waves of the main River. Together their voices encompassed both the robustness and tenderness of the water. Finally, the song ended, and the rhythm of their two voices ebbed slowly away, like the vanishing of morning dew.

F'lorna opened her eyes and looked at her friend. She could see her moss-colored eyes glistening. Sage nodded gently.

F'lorna looked back to her circle of friends. Ralona and Le'ana smiled knowingly. She glanced briefly at Lemmeck, and she felt his stare unmoving on her. She tried to smile at him, but he continued looking at her with his emerald eyes unblinking in the firelight. He kept his expression blank, like he was hiding a secret. She felt embarrassed by his response, but she didn't know why. She looked at Weston, and his mouth was agape. When he saw her looking at him, a wide smile spread across his face.

"F'lorna! Sage! You both have been hiding your talent from us!" Merriton said, standing up. "Was that a song from your *Divine Oracle*?"

"Yes," Sage answered with satisfaction. "F'lorna and I wanted to dedicate a song from the prophets to our new friends and to our successful journey. We have worked hard to accomplish this offering for our village. We are honored to serve with you all."

"Well done!" Merriton said. "Your song is the highlight of our journey to the River-dwellers. Thank you for sharing it with us."

"I have not sung publicly for over a turn of a moon. I am honored to have sung with my birth friend before people I care about," F'lorna said, looking at

247

Lemmeck. He finally smiled and bowed his head slightly. She watched his face in the dim light of the fire and saw him mouth two voiceless word: *"Thank you."*

Chapter 24

DRAWING ON PARCHMENT

F'lorna took the large leather pouch off of her back and set it on the grassy forest floor. She stretched her arms, feeling the tightness of her shoulder muscles release some. Although the design of the water pouch did a wonderful job of dispersing the weight of the sinews, carrying it for so long began to take its toll on her body. Her friends carried the folding grass baskets that Ralona had made, and they were much lighter than the leather one she carried. Merriton had given their group a moment to rest. F'lorna left her friends and took that moment to think quietly. She enjoyed everyone's company immensely, but she missed her time alone at her Achion cluster. The landscape around her was becoming familiar. Lemmeck said that they would make it to the village before the following rise just as the Heat Source makes its way to the Zenith of the Upper Realm. They would sleep under the Violet Moon one more time.

F'lorna looked up. The Heat Source was headed to the evening horizon. They would continue walking until they reached the Achion cluster where they had slept the first evening of their journey. Six moon rises were all they needed to finish their journey. But she knew her father and mother would be waiting for her now, hoping the journey would only take five rises.

F'lorna heard an unfamiliar clanking noise. She looked in the direction from which it came and listened. The sound stopped and was replaced with a raspy sound similar to when two wood plates slide against each other but softer. She saw something that looked like stiffened fabric floating with the wind along the forest ground. It flattened against the base of a tree and the wind pinned it still. F'lorna looked at it and walked toward the tree. *"What is that?"* she whispered aloud. She walked up to it and leaned down, bringing her fingers to the mysterious fabric and pinched either side. She picked it up, and it flapped in the wind. It felt thin like fabric but stiffer. It was the color of her skin, but slightly darker— closer almost to the color of her horns.

"It looks like parchment," she exhaled. "But bigger." The parchment she found in the cylinders they found on the shores of the tributaries were smaller. She wondered if this was a scroll that Merriton had described, and if so, why it would be so far away from the River and out of a cylinder.

The wind blew across the parchment and flipped it over, exposing the other side. She gasped. She saw her river reflection marked on the parchment.

"That is mine," a voice said from behind her.

She looked and saw Weston. He was holding a long cylinder, but this one was dyed black. "I dropped my cylinder and my parchments fell out. I am sorry," he said, reaching out his hand.

F'lorna brought her fingertips toward him, pinching the parchment tightly. "I didn't know what it was. I did not mean to pry into your belongings."

"That is all right," he said uneasily. "It was an accident." He took the parchment from F'lorna's hand and looked at the image that he had drawn on it. "Oh no. I had hoped it was not that one."

F'lorna looked at Weston. She could see that he was embarrassed. "How is my reflection on that parchment?" she asked.

He looked at her. "I drew it," he answered.

"But how? I thought you are not supposed to make symbols," she said.

"I am not a Sand-shaper anymore," he said, resolutely. "I can draw and write if I want to."

F'lorna's eyes opened wide. "You write?" she asked intently.

He looked around uneasily. "I told my brother I would not tell you. He thinks your village will not accept us if they find out what I do."

"What are those markings on the bottom of my reflection?" she asked, looking back at the parchment. "They look like Sand-shaper symbols."

"I don't want to get you in trouble," Weston said, nervously looking around.

"My mother is a Sand-shaper. I am not ashamed of her or the markings you have made. I want to know how you did it and why," she said firmly. She stared into Weston's eyes, the color of smokestone.

"Okay, but follow me," he said. He placed the parchment F'lorna found onto the others he was holding and rolled them up. He placed them into the black cylinder and grasped her hand, leading her further away from the opening. "It is safer over here where the trees are denser."

F'lorna allowed him to lead her. She remembered feeling the same hands when they danced under the Violet Moon.

"This is good," he said, letting go of her hand. He lifted the cylinder and placed the opening down, shaking it downward, so the parchments could come out. He grabbed the stack of parchments with his fingers and slid them out of the tube. "Since you already saw the very one that I didn't want you to see, you might as well see them all," he whispered, handing them to her.

She took the thick stack of parchments and unrolled them. She yelped. "The River Monster!"

Weston laughed slightly. "It is not going to hurt you. It is a drawing."

F'lorna stroked her finger across the black image. "How did you do this?

"I use slivers of smokestone. It allows me to draw anything I see. Someday, I will learn to add color to it," he said. "You see the blade coming out of his eye? I would want to color it. It was strange seeing this giant monster dead on the ground with a violet crystal stuck in his eye."

"What are the symbols on the bottom?" she asked.

"That one is the written word for Blade Beast. That is what I named it when I saw it. But you see this long mark like a thread? I crossed the name out when we went to Left River Hook and the Story-teller told us about the River Monster. There," he said pointing. "These are the symbols for River Monster."

"You captured it exactly," she whispered in awe.

Weston smiled. "That is indeed a compliment. Here, look at the next one." He took the top parchment off, revealing an image of a youngling who had just sprouted his horns.

"This youngling looks like you," she said.

He nodded. "It is my brother's son. When he sprouted his horns, I wanted to capture an image of him. This is his name, Ruvarren," Weston said, pointing to the symbols. "It was our father's name," he said. "He is the first youngling with horns. My brother insisted on keeping them, so hopefully our kin will do the same. We want to be like the River-dwellers, but change, even good change, is hard for others."

F'lorna nodded. "I have seen this in our own village with my mother." She moved the parchment with the youngling under the stack, revealing the next one. "These are the Northeastern Mountains," she said.

253

"Where my mother is from. I did not know that you've been there."

"I haven't," he said.

"But how did you make its reflection?" she asked, feeling her heart begin to flutter from the image. She quickly moved the parchment to the bottom.

"I simply listened to the description of the mountains from others and drew what I imagined with my mind," he said.

"I see," she said, looking at the next one. She saw a great waterfall with a rocky path floating above it. The waterfall continued down a path surrounded by smooth hills. "What is this? It looks just as fearful as the mountains." She closed her eyes, but the image stayed.

Weston took the parchments from F'lorna's hands. "My brother will be angry with me. That is the one he told me never to show. I am sorry."

"Is that the stone bridge you crossed to get to the other side of the River?" she asked.

Weston stopped. "How did you know about it?"

"Your brother told me about a pass near the Desert Plains, but I have never heard of a stone bridge dividing the River's descent into the Desert Plains," she said. "What has happened? Is this the reason why the River has been healed and new animals are coming into our tributaries? Was it because of the ground shudders?"

Weston shook his head. "I promised my brother. He is the one who does the talking. I am not good at building relations with the River-dwellers. He will explain everything when we get to your village. But my brother is worried we won't be accepted. He talks to Lemmeck about your village, and my brother sees how resistant your people are to Sand-shapers and our culture. This is why he does not want me to show my drawings. I did not show them to Left River Hook either. They are very resistant to our symbols."

"Yes, you are right," F'lorna said, thinking. "Our village views the symbols as the counterfeit to Ra'ash's *Divine Oracle*. They are evil to many people. So is the smokestone you use." She looked at Weston. "Will you teach me how to make the symbols? I know there are forty-four of them. That is not too many. I want to learn how to write."

Weston looked at her with surprise. "Why would you want to learn?"

"You won't understand," she said. "It is about what Ra'ash told me the night I received the Indwelling."

"He can speak to you?" Weston asked doubtfully.

"Not with audible words—only voiceless ones down in here," she said pointing to her chest. "He said that He wanted me to write."

Weston kept his eyes locked on F'lorna's. "That is what I do," he whispered. "I am a writer."

"You write the names of the reflections you draw," she said, wondering what else he would write. "Do you write Sand-shaper methods?"

"No," he said. "I write something more valuable. I write conversations that cannot be spoken aloud. That is how my people were able to leave the landowners without being caught. We secretly planned our escape with the written symbols."

"Teach me how. I want to learn how to write your symbols too," F'lorna said again. She couldn't explain it, but something in her needed to learn. She felt the Help of Ra'ash urging her.

Weston shook his head. "I can't."

"Why?" she asked. "I am a good pupil. I will learn quickly. You can teach me in secret when we get to my village before you return to the Marshlands."

"If your mother cannot learn the *Divine Oracle*, what makes you think you can learn our symbols?" he asked.

"There are only forty-four of them," she said thinking.

"Yes, but learning symbols is not like learning about plants or cooking or hunting. Remember what you told me? You can't experience the symbols or taste or smell or feel them. They are merely markings that represent sounds. I think it is too late for you if your Eternal Memory is shut," he said.

"There has to be a way. I feel it in my spirit. I must learn. I don't know why, but I know that I must write," she insisted.

"But what if we get caught?" he asked seriously. "What if the villagers see you write Sand-shaper symbols with smokestone onto parchment? Tell me the truth. What would they do to you?"

"My father is the Spiritual and Healing Elder. They will not force us to leave Right River Hook. My family has been part of that village for many folds of the moon. Besides," she continued, "you planned an entire escape for your entire village without getting caught. What makes you think we will get caught?"

Weston grinned. "It would mean that I get to spend more time with you," he said. He looked overhead. "The Heat Source has descended further. We'd better split up and return to our group."

F'lorna grabbed his hand. "Promise me first. You will teach me how to write those symbols."

"Yes, I will try," he said, squeezing her hand. "But I doubt if the symbols will take root in your imagination. Their life in your mind may be too stagnant for you to memorize."

Chapter 25

FAMILIAR ACHION CLUSTER

❝ Can you believe we are almost to our village?" Sage asked excitedly. "I am so tired of carrying this basket of sinews. I appreciate my Adoration more now. I don't have to carry heavy things to sing."

F'lorna looked at her birth friend. Her usual tidy appearance was somewhat disheveled. Her burgundy braids were unraveling around her horns. F'lorna knew that she too looked unkempt. They all did. There wasn't time to wash up and re-braid each other's hair. They

258

wanted to get back to their Achion clusters before the Heat Source found its zenith in the Upper Realm.

"How are your hands?" F'lorna asked. She adjusted the heavy leather pouch on her back. She would have to clean the leather right away, so the water her mother fetched with it would not taste like animal parts.

Sage lifted her bare hands and stared at her palms. "I'm glad the bindings are off. It feels good to let the breeze roll over them. But sometimes I forget they are tender, and I try to grab something. It is difficult not using them."

"Give them a few more moon rises before you use them. I'll tell my father to let you rest until they are healed," F'lorna said.

"I think we all deserve a few rises to rest," Sage said. "This journey has been successful, but it has been difficult. I am glad Merriton and Weston found us. Ra'ash sent them to help us."

"I think you are right," F'lorna said.

Lemmeck came up on the other side of F'lorna. "I am ready to sleep in my own tree," he said. He had taken off his horn binding and all of his braids. His thick, black hair fell into tight waves around his tawny cheeks. Many hunters wore their hair braided to prevent the distraction of strands blowing in the wind. But F'lorna liked his hair down. It softened his masculine features.

"You took off your horn binding," she said.

"Yes, I gave it to Merriton and showed him how to bind his son's horns when it is time. I don't need it anymore," Lemmeck said. "I am honored it will now be used to help the Marsh-landers."

F'lorna sensed concern in his voice. "Is something wrong?" she asked.

He looked at Sage. "I offer you my apology of healing, Sage. Would you mind if I speak to F'lorna alone?" he asked. A slight awkwardness could be heard in his words.

Sage nodded. "I see that Le'ana and Ralona have opened another pouch of Indigo berries. I should try to get some before Dashion eats them all." Sage smiled and walked quickly to her other birth friends a few tree lengths away.

F'lorna and Lemmeck walked several steps in silence. F'lorna finally decided to help her birth friend verbalize his worries. "I see your face is heavy with concern," she began.

He nodded. "I am worried about our village and how they will react to our new friends. I have given voiceless words that some of the Circle of Elders from Left River Hook have already contacted your father with the news of them, but I doubt they have had the time. Our village is very peaceful and not much has changed in many moon turns, but I sense Merriton has news of change."

The image of the stone bridge that Weston drew came into her mind. She knew something had happened to the base of the River when it disappeared at the Desert Plains. This information would cause fear at first, but the villagers needed to adjust with the changes of Rodesh. "You are right, but there is nothing we can do if Ra'ash decides to change the landscape of Rodesh. Just like with *The Great Engulfing*, Rodeshians have to adapt."

"No, that is not what I mean," Lemmeck said, shaking his head. "No one can blame Rodesh for changing. The villagers know that they have to accept those changes. But I do not think they will be so accepting of our friends. They were Sand-shapers, but now they are Marsh-landers. They are a blend of old and new traditions, which makes them very different. Weston carries his falcon, and that alone will cause much talk. I fear that our village will not accept them or their words."

"You do not accept them?" F'lorna asked.

"I have become close to Merriton. I have given him much of my leadership of our group and this journey because I trust him. I am watching him and learning a great deal from his actions. He is like your father when he guides the village, but he's different in a way that I identify with. He led his kinsman away from the control of the landowners, and he has established a healthy village in the Marshlands. Now he is establishing relationships with the villages on the other side of the River. He takes risks to better the lives of his family and friends. I have great respect for him, but I do not believe our village will be receptive. We are too closed off from others, and many of the villagers are scared of change. Your mother let down her hair, and the village Elders argued about it for too long."

F'lorna looked ahead as she walked and listened. She knew Lemmeck was right, but she needed Weston to teach her the symbols. "I will take them straight to my father. Merriton will tell him about the golden stone he wears around the neck and what happened to the River after the ground shudders. My father will decide if they

261

can speak at the Village Achion cluster. He knows what it best for the village. We need to know what has happened to Rodesh and the River."

"That is my concern," Lemmeck continued. "Your father thinks very highly of the villagers. Too highly. He believes Ra'ash will have the ultimate say in each villager's words, but that is not so for many of them. Many of our Elders let fear have more power in their lives than Ra'ash. Your father's weakness is that he believes everyone sees through the eyes of Ra'ash, like he does. But they do not." Lemmeck waited for F'lorna to look at him. His emerald eyes were filled with sincerity. "That is the difference between Merriton and your father. Merriton sees the evil hidden in others, and your father only sees the good. Merriton knows that they will not be accepted, and I have to agree with him."

Lemmeck's words hurt her because they revealed what she had always thought secretly of her father. He cared deeply, and the villagers took advantage of it on occasion. Her father saw no wrong unless it was right in front of him—but even then, he kept hope that the wrong would become right again. "My father loves like Ra'ash. He chose to be joined with my mother even though she was a Sand-shaper. He has an open heart and spirit toward others and it exposes him. But isn't that just like Ra'ash? Doesn't the *Divine* Oracle say that Ra'ash loved us with an unending love that held no account of wrong?"

"Yes, it does. But—" he stopped and looked around at the others. They all continued to walk ahead of them. He grabbed both of F'lorna's hands into his.

262

F'lorna felt the heat in her face rise as he held her hands. Strands from her amber hair blew across her face, but she did not wipe them away. She had never joined hands with Lemmeck and his touch was surprisingly soft for being a hunter. She looked down at their hands. His tawny, strong fingers intertwined with her taupe, slender ones. Their hands looked different yet comfortable together. She couldn't distinguish between his touch and hers—it all felt like one combined hand.

She looked back up and he continued looking intently into her grey eyes, his emerald eyes reflecting the Heat Source's rays like crystal. "I know I am not allowed to court you until we are sixteen turns of the moon, but I want you to know that is exactly what I am planning to do. I will be patient and not go against the traditions of our village, but I want you to be aware my intentions. I care about you, and I know what happens to your father affects you. I don't want the villagers to speak against your family. Merriton understands that. He will bring the information to your father, but I have asked him to leave when the Heat Source awakens in the morning horizon. Our village will not be open to them."

F'lorna could not speak, and she felt her heartbeat race like the current of the river. She wanted to look away from Lemmeck's gaze from embarrassment, but his eyes' intensity kept her locked. She finally found her voice. "I understand," she whispered.

For the first time in many rises of the moon, Lemmeck smiled, his expression filled with relief. "Good," he said. "I will lead you all to the Pillar. It is closest to your Achion cluster. My brothers and I must see our parents right away. It is very difficult to have all three sons gone from the hearth."

  F'lorna did not mind the coolness of the water dripping from her skin and tunic. After so many rises without washing, the water revived her. She felt clean again. She looked on the other side of the River. Lemmeck waved before walking with his brothers to their family's land. She looked at her birth friends. They smiled as they wrung out their tunics. They piled the baskets of sinews by the Pillar. Weston and Merriton volunteered to carry Lemmeck's and his brothers' baskets across with their own. Seeing all the baskets of sinews piled together filled F'lorna with a profound sense of accomplishment. They had done what the village needed them to do. They would have enough cordage to build the bridge and pier.

  F'lorna heard a screech and looked toward Weston just as he jerked his arm up. Banthem flapped his mighty wings and soared into the Upper Realm. "Where is he going?" she asked.

  "He will look for a nice, shady tree to take a nap," Weston said smiling. "He knows to look for me when I call him. He comes back to my leather arm covering."

  "You can wrap it around one of our spare Achion trees. That is where my father will let you rest until the Violet Moon rises in the morning horizon tomorrow," she said.

Weston looked around and walked up to her. Merriton was still wringing out his belongings that had spilled open while he swam across the River. "How will I teach you the symbols if we must leave so soon?" he whispered.

"We will meet here when the Violet Moon reaches its zenith. There are fewer trees, so hopefully the light of the moon will be enough," she whispered. "My Achion cluster is not far from here."

Weston nodded and backed away when he heard his brother's voice.

"I am glad I am at least clean before I meet the Spiritual Leader of your village," Merriton said, smiling. "Although I did lose a leather pouch down your tributary."

"We have extra pouches we can give you. My father will be indebted to you both. He will make sure you are prepared for your journey back to the Marshlands. He will give you food and whatever else you may need," F'lorna said. She turned to her friends. Le'ana, Ralona and Sage had wrung out their tunics and were now getting their travel bags ready to return to their Achion clusters. "I know you three are anxious to get back to your hearths."

"I just found out my sister is going to be joined! My mother will want to know right away," Sage said excitedly.

"And I need to get out of the intensity of this Heat Source," Le'ana said, wiping her scarlet hair to the side. F'lorna noticed that the appearance of speckles on her face had multiplied like the crops she planted and harvested in the fields. "I just want to go into my Achion

265

hole, put a covering over me and sleep in the sweet, cool darkness of my tree."

Ralona pointed to the stack of folding baskets that she had made. "I must go tell Nayran that our baskets worked! She will be so pleased that she helped our journey. I will ask my father to come get the baskets and bring them to the Village Achion cluster. He helped design the bridge, so he will be most thrilled."

"Don't forget to let us know what happens with Merriton, Weston and your father. We have decided to not say anything about our new friends until we know what your father plans to do," Sage said.

"My birth friends," F'lorna said, tears stinging her eyes. "I am privileged to have journeyed with you for these six moon rises. I feel that I know you more than ever, and I am grateful to Ra'ash for allowing us this time together."

"We feel the same," Le'ana said, coming up to F'lorna and squeezing her right shoulder with her left hand. "May the Help of Ra'ash be with you."

"And with you all," F'lorna said, bowing her head slightly. She watched her birth friends make their way back to their families. They disappeared into the shade of the forest just before they came into the land surrounding her family's Achion cluster.

"We are ready to meet your father," Merriton said, trying to sound light-hearted.

"Follow me," F'lorna said. "It is not far down the River."

They began to walk briskly along the River's shore. F'lorna thought of the main River. It was nothing like the safe waters of her hearth. The land of her village

was the color of growth and tranquility. The land around
the main River was the color of her eyes but lacked life
and warmth. Suddenly, she saw the color of amber hair
appear onto the edge of the River in front of her Achion
cluster. It was her father. She knew he was giving
voiceless words to Ra'ash. She felt her feet begin to run.
She swung her arms to match their pace. "Father!" she
yelled. He turned to her and instantly began to run to
meet her.

Quickly, she was in his arms. He had picked her
up and was swinging her in a circle. "My daughter! My
daughter! You are safe!" he yelled.

She heard the voice of her mother calling her
name. Her father slowed his circling and when her feet
touched the ground, she felt her mother's embrace as
well. Both her parents held her and cried joyful tears.

"Ra'ash answered my voiceless request," T'maya
said. "I begged Him to have you return before the Heat
Source reached its zenith, and He answered me!"

F'lorna allowed her parents to hold her for a few
moments longer, basking in their parental love. The
journey away from them had helped her see how much
she valued their love for her. She heard footsteps in the
grass coming up behind them. She knew Merriton and
Weston were patiently waiting to be introduced.

She came out of her parents' embrace and faced
her mother and father. She had not seen them look so
happy in many moons. "Mother, Father, I would like you
to meet our new friends. Without their help, we would
not have successfully found and harvested the vast
amount of sinews we carried back with us. They are
from a village located on the Marshlands just above the

Desert Plains. This is Merriton and his younger brother, Weston," F'lorna said, as she looked toward her new friends.

Her parents' gaze followed hers. "You are Sand-shapers from the farmlands," T'maya exclaimed.

Merriton walked up to T'maya and gently cupped her hand into a ball. He placed the center of his forehead onto her closed fist. "No, we are Marsh-landers from the Southwest, and we come bearing news and an offer of friendship."

Weston came up next to his brother. "I am touched by the tenderness you have shown your daughter and to each other. I am glad that our paths have crossed."

Jaquarn reach out his hand and placed it onto Weston's right shoulder and squeezed. "Thank you for bringing our daughter back to us safely. I was worried that the forest nomads had come back to our lands, but I am honored that the Marsh-landers have."

"We have not intercepted any of the forest nomads on our travels, but we will be careful on our journey back to the Marshlands," Weston said. "We intercepted Lemmeck and his brothers in the forest, and they each had their arrows pointing at us. I know if they had met the forest nomads, they would have protected your daughter and the others bravely."

"Thank you," Jaquarn said. "Lemmeck and the twins are fine hunters, and I trust their family and their aim. I am glad I chose them for this journey."

"We were leaving Left River Hook to come visit your village. This was our last stop before returning back to our own village in the Marshlands. We delayed our return to help our new friends. We were honored to take this journey with them. We brought back more than enough sinew to build just about any structure your village needs," Merriton said.

Jaquarn moved to Merriton and placed his left hand onto his right shoulder. Suddenly, he stopped. "What is that stone around your neck? It looks like honey that has hardened, but it shines like light reflecting off of the water."

Merriton cupped the stone with his palm and looked at Jaquarn. "That is what I've come to discuss with you."

Chapter 26

RIVERS IN DESERT PLACES

F'lorna sat in her Achion hole, content to lean her head against the face of the tree she had known since her birth. Her father sat around the cooking hearth. The parents of Lemmeck, Sage and Le'ana had been summoned. The three couples sat on stones around the fire, while her mother served a meal of mixed edible plants that Le'ana's father brought and strips of salted meat that Lemmeck's mother brought. Merriton and Weston were also nearby.

None of her birth friends had come. F'lorna realized that they must be sleeping in their Achion tree, exhausted from their long journey. She was tired too, but she had too many questions that needed to be answered. She listened to the conversation. She knew they were talking about Ralona's father.

"Eotham asked me to go over the details with him when the Violet Moon rises this evening, so I will stop by later. When his daughter told him about the sinews they left by the Pillar, he instantly went to retrieve them. They have been waiting to wrap key parts of the bridge since two moon rises ago, so he was anxious to get the work caught up. He sends his apology of healing to miss this meeting," Le'ana's father said.

"That is quite understandable," her father said. "I know the work has been halted. I think now that we have the cordage, we will finish the bridge quicker than anticipated."

Unexpectedly, a screech sounded from above F'lorna's tree. She looked up. Banthem, Weston's falcon, had returned. Weston asked if he could wrap his arm covering around the sturdy branch of her Achion tree. She couldn't help but smile. He no longer frightened her. In fact, he felt like a friend and somewhat of a protector."

"And you say that this bird of prey is your friend?" Lemmeck's mother asked skeptically. She looked a lot like Lemmeck. She had his tawny skin color, but her eyes matched the honey color of the twins' eyes— almost the same as the golden stone Merriton wore around his neck.

Weston was standing near F'lorna's tree. "Yes, I found him as a hatchling before we moved to the Marshlands. I have trained him well. Plus," Weston said, grinning. "I keep his belly full, which makes him stay close to me." He threw a small animal at the falcon just above where F'lorna was sitting. Banthem snatched the animal and gulped it down.

"Astonishing," Lemmeck's father said. "I have watched the Saber Falcon hunt. They are one of the stealthiest hunters of all Ra'ash's animals on Rodesh."

Weston looked up, smiling with pride. "Banthem is that. When he catches a kill too big for one gulp, he will bring it to me. He wants me to cut his food for him like a youngling. But he will share."

"What is that around his leg?" Sage's father asked, pointing to the falcon.

Weston quickly eyed his brother. "Ah, that is just a way I can distinguish him from the other falcons," he said.

"Well, I know that our Marshland friends are fascinating, but they leave when the Heat Source rises in the morning horizon. They have much to tell us, so we should let Merriton have the platform," Jaquarn said. "I have talked with Merriton, and we both agree that a Village meeting would not be the right choice for us. We will hear what he has to say and inform the Elders."

"Come help me," T'maya whispered to F'lorna.

"Yes, Mother." F'lorna pushed up from her Achion tree hole and walked to their cooking table. She grabbed two of the wooden platters and walked to Weston. "This is for you," she said.

He smiled and took the platter. "It will be nice to taste some of your mother's cooking."

"She's honored to serve you," F'lorna said. Then she walked to Merriton and handed him his platter. She went back to the cooking table and grabbed two more platters, giving them to Sage's parents. Her mother had already handed out the rest of the food. She got her platter and walked back to her Achion hole and sat down. She pinched a grouping of the herb and vegetables and placed it in her mouth. She had missed her mother's flavorful cooking.

Merriton reached to the back of his neck and untied the fiber cord that held the golden stone. He handed it to Le'ana's father. "Please inspect this and then pass it around."

Le'ana's father felt the stone and turned it in his hand. He reached it up toward the dimming light of the Heat Source that was now heading to the evening horizon. "I've never seen such a stone," he whispered and passed it along.

Merriton waited while each Elder handled the stone. When Jaquarn was done, he handed it to Weston. Weston walked to F'lorna and handed it to her. She placed her platter on her lap and held the stone. It had a natural shape with no particular structure. It was heavy, even though it wasn't very big. Merriton had wound a thin, strong piece of fiber around one of the oblong pieces of the golden stone, which allowed the rest of it to dangle freely. She could tell someone had smoothed it and polished it. She held it up toward the Heat Source. The stone shined brightly in her hands. She decided it

273

was almost as beautiful as the crystals harvested in the Northeastern Mountains.

"What is it?" Jaquarn asked when it had been passed around.

"That is what Sand-shapers call auraium. They have found some in the Northeastern Mountains, and it is very rare and sought after."

"Why does this concern us?" Sage's mother asked. "Is it worse than smokestone? Will it hurt the Great Expanse even more?"

Merriton paced, thinking. "No, it does not hurt the water, but it is strong. It is not as strong as crystal, but it is more pliable when heated. Wealthy Landowners began to wear this material before we left to the Marshlands. It is now a symbol of status among the Sand-shaper elite. They crave this material above all else."

Jaquarn stood. "Merriton, have you and your people found this material in the lower Marshlands?" he asked with concern.

Merriton looked at F'lorna's father for several moments and then nodded. "Yes, we have found it."

"What does that mean?" Le'ana's mother asked, fear filling her voice.

Jaquarn looked at her and then to all the Elders seated around the fire. "It means that Sand-shapers will want to travel south."

"But this is our territory!" Sage's mother exclaimed, getting up.

Merriton raised his hands. "There is more. This is the main reason Left River Hook wanted me to come

bring you the news. The Elders are struggling to make
sense of it."

F'lorna thought of the stone bridge drawing that
Weston created on parchment with a thin sliver of
smokestone. She looked at him. He had finished his food
and was now working on a large, thick section of leather
that her father had given him. He was rubbing fat into
the porous skin to make it more durable for Banthem's
talons. The fat came from a stone jar that her mother
kept under the cooking table. He was making a new arm
covering for his falcon to rest on when they traveled.

"You all know about the storm and the ground
shudders. We have already discussed it with Left River
Hook. Their storyteller told us the intriguing story of the
Storm Dancer," he said, giving a small smile to F'lorna.

F'lorna wouldn't let herself become embarrassed
from the story anymore. She had to accept it as part of
her history. She looked at Sage's parents. Their daughter
Blaklin would be joining with Jornan in Ra'ash soon.
She wondered if the celebration would be altered by the
news they were about to hear.

The group of Elders nodded, so he continued.
"What you don't know is that the ground shudders were
much more intense further south. We have talked to
villages on our way to Right River Hook, and they
became less strong the further north we went. The
damage the villages experienced in Left and Right River
Hook are minimal compared to the southern villages."

"The north may have not received the ground
shudders, but they did have a rain storm or at least
swelling in the north part of the River," Jaquarn stated.
"We have had several of their cylinders floating down

our tributaries and washing up onto our shores. What about your village in the Marshlands? Did it receive great damage?"

Merriton looked down at his hands. "Our ground shudders were mighty. It felt as if all of Rodesh was falling inward. But we lived in small structures and our village is very new. Plus, our land may be harsh to live in, but it is very soft to fall on. We did lose three villagers to drowning and one was struck by a falling tree."

"I lost my best friend," Weston said, rising. The leather he had been working on dangled from his hands. "We are not from the River, so we do not know how to swim the water's currents well. This makes living in the Marshlands difficult, but we are trying to learn. My friend drowned in water that was no higher than the top of a youngling's head. The waves of the water kept crashing over us—waves like the ones we saw at the main River. A few of the villages we visited have taught us much about swimming. We will go home and show the others what we have learned."

"This is why my brother and I decided to travel to meet the River-dwellers on the east side of the River. We needed to learn and see how it is to live in this land. We carry much knowledge back to our village, and we believe this will make the difference between the Marshland village thriving or dying."

"Has something happened to the Main River?" Le'ana's father asked. "After the storm, our water was healed. It has tasted like nothing I've ever tasted before. And we have seen new plants and animals come to our village after the storm. And the River Monster—that predator has never walked our lands."

F'lorna looked at Lemmeck's parents. She wondered if they knew that his Doublemoon ceremony gift had been returned.

"Something has happened to the main River where it once disappeared under the Desert Plains," Merriton began. "The ground shudders have exposed it."

"Exposed what?" Jaquarn asked.

Merriton looked at Jaquarn. "The entire River down the Desert Plains has been uncovered."

"The River was covered after *The Great Engulfing*?" Le'ana's father whispered in shock.

"It looks like your Ra'ash has uncovered it again," Weston said.

"How far does it go?" T'maya asked, walking to her husband and taking his hand.

"It seems to be endless," Merriton said.

"I sent my falcon over the River. I thought there may be land just beyond the horizon. He soared, disappearing into the Upper Realm. When he finally came back, he had nothing to show from his flight," Weston said. "There is nothing there but Desert Plains and the River."

"Lemmeck was telling me that according to your *Divine Oracle,* the south part of the main River fed into five lakes—the land of the Lake-keepers," Merriton said.

F'lorna realized that Lemmeck had spoken to Merriton quite a lot about the *Divine Oracle* and the history of the River-dwellers. She remembered seeing them engaged in conversation, which was usually when Weston would come chat with her.

"*The Lakes of Domus*," Jaquarn said. "That is where the Lake-keepers lived. They all died in *The Great Engulfing* many, many moon folds ago, just after the Expansion of Jeyshen." He looked at Merriton. "How did you and Weston cross over the River if the River has opened up in the Desert Plains?"

Weston moved toward the fire where the Elders were sitting. "There is a massive waterfall." He looked up the length of the trees around him. "If you took all the Achion trees in this cluster and stacked them from root to the highest branch on top of each other, you may see the height of the drop. But there is now a natural stone bridge that travels the length of the River from west to east. We walked across the River on the stone bridge, but the sprays of the waterfall make the stone slippery. The stone face of the waterfall is much like a mountain. It is a dangerous passage."

F'lorna felt herself become light-headed from the talk of the stone bridge and waterfall. She hadn't told her parents about the Mountain Terror she experienced. She knew for certain that she would never be able to cross the stone bridge without having an immense attack of fear. She needed to calm her breathing and think on something else, but she felt tingling in her hands.

"And you saw this?" Le'ana's father asked.

"We saw it. Smelled it. Felt it. And walked it. The Desert Plains now have the River running straight down it," Merriton said. "My brother and I think that maybe the River runs into the Great Expanse, connecting the north and the south. But we don't know. All we see is the stone bride, the massive waterfall and an endless River weaving through the sand."

278

"It can't connect to the Great Expanse from the north. Those waters are sick. Whatever water flowed from this new Desert River is fresh and healthy," Jaquarn said.

"The River opening up is not what concerns us," Merriton said. He held up the golden stone around his neck. The enormous rock face of the waterfall is riddled with auraium. If Sand-shapers find out, they will want to extract it. And if they do, they will travel south. And if they travel south, they will take our lands."

F'lorna felt her body go completely numb and her vision black, like an Achion hole cover was placed over her eyes. All she could see was the massive rock face of the waterfall in her mind. She fell out of her tree and passed out onto the ground, hitting her horn at the root and tearing it from her forehead.

Chapter 27

THE FORTY-FOUR SYMBOLS

F'lorna awoke. She looked around. She was safe in her Achion tree. The Violet Moon illuminated the atmosphere around her with a soft glow. Her Achion hole allowed very little light in, and she waited for her eyes to adjust. She heard whispering from outside of her Achion hole. She tried to sit up, but her left temple throbbed. She instantly reached up to feel for her horn

280

but cried out when her palm came flat against her head. She only felt a fiber wrapping. Her horn was lost.

She crawled out of her Achion tree. The Violet Moon was still low in the horizon. Nightfall had just begun. She could see the cooking fire burning bright and Merriton, Weston and her father and mother sat on stones around the fire. Out of the corner of her eye, she saw her aunt, Eline. They were whispering under the light of the moon. She looked at them briefly but the pain she felt kept her moving forward. She didn't want to hear their sullen words about the loss of her horn. She needed to talk to the One who foreknew every event of her life. If nothing happened by chance, then He knew this would happen. He knew she would wake one moment missing a horn: a piece of what made her a River-dweller.

She stumbled past the whispers. She heard murmurs about chasing after her, but her mother quieted their speech.

"Let her go," she said. "She must mourn."

F'lorna's feet were bare, and she could feel the spongy forest floor. As she drew closer to the River, she saw violet shimmers of light flickering off the slow current of the tributary. She didn't have to look where she was going. Her feet took her to the Pillar. When she arrived, she fell against the stony wall of the Pillar, her arm resting against the hard rock.

"Why?" she whispered. "Why did you allow this?"

She waited for an answer but heard nothing.

"Why?" she repeated louder, looking up at the Violet Moon.

"Why did you take my friend away from me? Why did you take my horn?"

She pushed off of the Pillar and faced the moon. "Why have you allowed this loss?" she yelled out. She didn't care who heard her. She knew the villagers would treat her differently now—just like her mother.

She brought her fisted hands up to the Upper Realm and shook them at the moon. "You hurt me!" she yelled. "You hurt my mother! You took Raecli! You cause so much pain! Why?"

The ache in F'lorna rose up from the pit of her stomach and filled her lungs. She tried to contain the noise within her, but she couldn't suppress the rage she felt. The pain traveled up her neck and out through her lips, like the rapids of the main River. She yelled out her anger. She could hear her cry tumbling across the water and into the trees around her. She continued yelling, even as her throat began to ache and the empty socket of her forehead throbbed. Finally, her voice cracked and she fell to her knees. The mossy floor was saturated with water from the River. Her shoulders shook with the soft sobs of loss.

"Sing for Me," a voiceless whisper entreated. *"Sing your pain."*

"What do you want from me? To write? To dance? To sing?" She whispered to the grass that she clutched with her fingers. "I can't do anything. I am broken."

"Sing for Me," the voiceless words sounded again.

"I don't want to!" she yelled back. She could hear her angry words echo across the River and back to her. What was she going to do now? She was humiliated. She was deformed. A fresh wave of sobs flowed out of her.

"Sing the *Holy Chant of Jeyshen* when He fell to His knees at the Pillar before His Expansion," the voice insisted.

She wiped the tears from her face. She didn't want to sing but she didn't know what else she could do. She couldn't move her body and no one was coming for her. She opened her memory and allowed the words of the chant to fill her mind. If she could just utter the first word, maybe memory would take over the numbness she felt. She opened her mouth and the first word of the chant stuck in her throat. She exhaled and tried again. This time the word lifted from her mouth and rose up. The next word followed. Then the next. And the next. Her voice drew strong with each word.

She planted her right foot into the grass and stood up. As she stood, her voice became stronger. She could hear her words ringing down the River and dispersing into the trees. She didn't recognize the voice as her own. It had lost its innocence. She continued to sing and a shimmer of peace formed in her belly, like salve being poured onto an open wound. She sang louder. Whatever it was, she needed it. She needed to feel something other than the pain and loss suffocating her. She sang even louder and the peace in her belly spread across her chest and legs. It filled her arms and finally her throat. The heartache was still there, but it no longer smothered her. She could breathe. She could bear the weight of her pain.

The final words of Jeyshen's chant left her lips. The tears were gone. She felt broken but mended, like

283

Lemmeck's horn. She raised her left hand to feel the emptiness on her forehead. She would no longer mourn for it. Her mother had spoken true words. She was still a daughter of Ra'ash. Tiredness overwhelmed her. She wanted to rest. She needed to go back to her Achion tree and sleep. Her feet instantly turned and began to walk the short length to her hearth. She would sleep. She would wake. She would live another day.

"F'lorna," a whisper sounded above her. "F'lorna, will you wake?"

F'lorna opened her eyes. She listened.

"F'lorna, my brother and I are leaving soon. Come out," the whisper sounded again. She knew it was Weston's voice.

She reached up and grabbed the side of her Achion hole and pulled herself up. "I'm awake," she whispered. She crawled out of her tree. She could see Weston in the moonlight. He looked toward the trees where her parents and Merriton slept.

"I wrote you the symbols," he said, handing her a rolled parchment. "I have given you extra parchment with that one to practice. Come with me. We don't have much time."

She clasped the scroll with her right hand, and he grabbed her left hand and led her away from her Achion cluster. When they were several tree lengths away from the cooking hearth, he turned to her. "I want to show you the symbols. I want to write you."

"What do you mean?" she asked confused.

"I'm leaving my arm cover on your tree. Banthem is there now. He will know how to return to you if you keep the covering with you. I want to write to you. I don't want to lose your friendship, but I need to go with my brother. I must return to our village and show them what we have learned," he said. F'lorna noted desperation in his voice.

"But why would you want to remain friends with me?" she asked, reaching her hand to her empty wound. "I am deformed."

Weston shook his head. "No, you are not deformed. You are beautiful. You have something in you that is strong. It is the same thing I had when I helped my village escape the landowners. I care about you, F'lorna. I need to know you will write to me. I will send Banthem to you. He can fly over the River to get to you. Just look for the scroll I attach to the band around his leg, but don't let anyone see you."

F'lorna stared at Weston. His dark, familiar eyes stared back at her. "Show me the symbols. I will try to memorize them." She unrolled the parchments. The one with the symbols was on top of the stack. There were forty-four in all. Weston had written them out in straight, meticulous lines. "Some of them look familiar. I recognize a few from the cylinder Sage gave me."

Weston came beside her, took her hand and brought the parchment into the direction of the moon. "That is good that you recognize them. I will point to each one and make the sound it represents."

As he pointed to each symbol and spoke the corresponding sound, F'lorna could hear the pieces of

285

her language. The words she spoke everyday could be broken down into smaller parts, like the ingredients making a complete meal on a wooden platter. When he finished, she tried to go back to the first symbol and make its sound, but the utterance alluded her. "I can't remember it," she whispered. "I recognize the symbol, but the sound will not stick in my mind."

Weston looked toward the horizon. "The Heat Source will be coming soon. Let me go over the symbols again. F'lorna, you must get this. I can't lose our friendship." He pointed to the symbols and enunciated each sound slowly.

F'lorna went back to the first symbol and tried to remember the sound. "It is not staying in my mind. I feel the relevance of the sounds, but my memory doesn't. It won't let me capture what I hear," she said frustrated. "Ra'ash, help me," she pleaded quietly.

She looked at the parchment. The symbols looked familiar somehow. She stared at the first one. "There are forty-four symbols. Why does that seem familiar?" she asked herself. She recognized the line and swoop of the first symbol. She brought the parchment closer to her face. "I know this symbol," she whispered, opening her mind to whatever it was trying to push itself out. She continued to stare and a spark of comprehension flickered in her Eternal Memory, causing a fire of understanding.

"That is it!" she whispered excitedly.

"What?" Weston asked, staring at her, then the parchment. "What do you see?"

"That first symbol! That is the first Holy Image of Jeyshen!" she looked at Weston. "There are forty-four Holy Images."

"What is that? Your *Divine Oracle*?" he asked.

"It is the part of the *Divine Oracle* that happened during the time of Jeyshen. This symbol," she said pointing, "is the first image. I have danced this image many times." She looked at the next image. "And this one," she said pointing. She scanned the entire parchment of symbols. "I have danced all of these symbols!"

"But how does that help you know the sounds?" he asked, eyeing the horizon.

"There are forty-four symbols and forty-four chants. Each chant begins with a new word." She looked at Weston. "Say the first sound again."

As he made the sound, she thought of the first chant. Its beginning sounded identical to the sound Weston made. "Yes! It is the same! Say the next one."

Weston made the next sound and it began the same way as the first word of the second chant. "It is the same!" She looked at the third symbol and thought of the third chant. She pieced off the first sound of the word and spoke it aloud.

Weston nodded excitedly. "That is it! That is the sound it makes!"

She looked at the forth symbol and thought of the image. Then she thought of the chant that matched it and uttered the first sound.

"Yes!" he whispered. "I can't believe it! You've got it!"

She brought the parchment by her side and closed her eyes. She thought of the fifth chant and uttered the first sound.

"Yes! That is the fifth symbol," he said. He reached into his tunic belt and pulled out his hand. "Open your other hand." She held out her hand, and he placed a sliver of smokestone inside of it. "Here, try to write my name."

She stared at the smokestone. This was the same material that caused Smoke Sickness in her friend's mother, killing her and changing F'lorna's life forever.

"It only harms when it is burned," Weston assured her.

F'lorna tentatively moved the small piece of smokestone in between her fingers. "Which hand do I write with?"

"Usually the hand that you use the most," he said. "It will be your right. Here, let me hold the parchment," he said, grabbing it from her hand.

F'lorna pinched the smokestone with the fingers of her right hand. "It feels soft."

Weston nodded. "It needs to be, so the black will rub off on the parchment. Now write my name. Think of each sound it makes."

She thought of the first sound of his name. It began with the same sound as the twenty-second chant. Then she allowed Jeyshen's twenty-second image to fill her imagination. She could see it perfectly in her mind. She took the smokestone and tried to sketch the image her body makes when she dances the image.

Weston looked at the symbol. "That is very close," he whispered. He brought the parchment to her eyes and pointed to the twenty-second symbol. "You have to make that line longer. Maybe you should use this parchment until your hands become familiar with making each symbol. Now make the next symbol of my name."

F'lorna nodded. She thought of his name and identified the next sound. It matched the first sound of the third chant. She looked at the third symbol again before drawing it on the parchment.

"Yes! That is it! Now there are four more symbols in my name. Hurry! Write them quickly. I must get you back to your tree."

F'lorna thought of the third sound, found the corresponding chant and wrote the symbol. She quickly did the fourth, fifth and sixth.

"You did it!" he said, breathlessly. "You wrote my name!"

F'lorna looked down at the symbols she had drawn. She allowed the image of Weston to fill her mind. "Those symbols say *Weston,*" she whispered. "I have written my mother's symbols."

Suddenly, her eyes flew open. "If I can write your name. I can write anything. I can write one of *Jeyshen's Holy Chants* for my mother!"

Weston thought. "I suppose, but aren't those chants long? You will have to leave a small space in between each word to signify when the word ends and the new one begins. You may only be able to fit twenty or thirty words on one parchment."

She frowned. "Yes, the *Holy Chants* have many words, and the *Sacred Songs of the Prophets* are sometimes longer. They are more like stories that are sung."

Weston looked toward the horizon. "The Heat Source is about to rise. Practice these symbols. I will send Banthem to you. Read my words and write back to me," he pleaded. "Now go back to your Achion tree. Hide the smokestone and parchment. Make sure no one is watching you when you practice writing the symbols. I will stay here until the Heat Source awakens."

F'lorna rolled the parchments into her right hand, clasping the smokestone tightly into her left hand. "Thank you, Weston," she said, facing her friend.

He took her fisted left hand and brought it gently to the center of his forehead. "I am glad your Ra'ash allowed our paths to cross," he whispered.

She smiled and brought her hand back. "So am I." Then she turned and walked quietly back toward her family's Achion cluster. The information inside her Eternal Memory had not changed, but her understanding of those memories had grown to encase two worlds—both the Sand-shapers and the River-dwellers.

Chapter 28

THE LEATHER TUNIC

F'lorna traced the final symbol on the parchment with her finger. She had done it so many times during the last several rises of the moon that she now had the feel of the written symbols memorized. The forty-four *Chants and Images of Jeyshen* had merged into single sounds, encompassing the Rodeshian language. She had used the smokestone a few times while she stayed hidden in her Achion tree. She wrote the symbols Weston showed her on the back of the parchment. Her writing still lacked the beauty of his, but she knew her symbols would get better as she practiced—though she would never have his talent of drawing. Just like learning to dance the images with proficiency, writing them well would take time.

Even though she knew the smokestone wouldn't hurt her, she still felt guilty when she used it. The smokestone was a Sand-shaper's way of making hot, roaring fires. The smoke produced from these large cooking hearths hurt the waters of Rodesh and the Rodeshians with Smoke Sickness. If anyone saw her hiding smokestone, she would come under attack. Smokestone would not be welcomed into their village. She thought of Jeyshen's thirty-fourth chant: the *Chant of Acceptance,* when He told Ra'ash that He would allow Himself to be tied to the sphere. It was the shortest chant and one of the most heartbreaking. She had tried to count all the symbols she would have to make to write the entire chant, but she finally stopped counting when she had ten fingers stretched out—each signifying one hundred.

Weston had written only forty-four on the parchment and there was very little space left. She would either have to get more parchment or make the smokestone thinner somehow. Either way, writing just one of Jeyshen's chants—even the smallest—would be difficult.

"F'lorna," she heard her father's voice call. "It has been three rises since you have gone into your hole. You have only come out to eat and to see Sage and Le'ana when they have come to visit. I think it is time to come out and live life again."

F'lorna quietly rolled the parchment into her palm. Then she fastened a fiber cord around it and placed it above her head on the highest shelf chiseled over her mattress. "Yes, Father," she said. She crawled out of her tree and found her mother, father and her father's sister there to greet her.

"Are you hungry?" T'maya asked.

F'lorna thought. "Yes, Mother.

"Good. I made you a bowl of grain with Charisse jam," she said. She walked to the cooking table and picked up the bowl she had prepared for F'lorna and walked back. "Kytalia has told me that Le'ana brought pouches of Indigo berries. She and her father are at this very moment planting a small crop of them."

"Is the bridge finished already?" F'lorna asked before taking a bite.

"The sinews you brought back were plentiful. Ralona's father is very pleased. The villagers prepared the wood while your group was gone, so all they needed to do was fit the wood together and fasten everything tight with the sinews," Jaquarn said. "The Shoam-sha while you were gone was very tense. Trenton had a lot of skeptical words to offer, but—" he said, grinning widely, "I knew Ra'ash would bring you all back safely."

F'lorna thought of her missing horn—more reasons for Zelara to offer her hateful words. F'lorna chewed slowly and thought. "I fainted," she said simply.

"Merriton told us that you experienced the Mountain Terror," Eline said, walking up to F'lorna and inspecting the wound where her horn had once sprouted. "I've seen the Mountain Terror attack with my own eyes.

The results can be very bad. You started feeling dizzy when Weston was describing the waterfall?"

F'lorna nodded. "Yes, but I didn't think the terror would come back if I was not there."

She finished inspecting F'lorna's wound. "It comes as a smaller attack when you think about it, but I think you were very tired from your journey, which added to your reaction. I will teach you tricks to focus on something else when someone is discussing any large rock cliffs."

"If I hadn't passed out, I would still have my horn," F'lorna whispered. She felt tears stinging her eyes.

T'maya came over and stroked F'lorna dark amber hair. "No, Eline looked at the root. One of the four bulbs of the root had already died, and the other three were very sick. The only thing keeping your horn from coming out was the brace."

F'lorna brought her hand above her left temple. "Then my dance for my Doublemoon Ceremony is what hurt it," she whispered. "You were right, Mother." F'lorna let the tears stream down her face. "Dancing is supposed to be done on the feet, not the head."

"Don't be sad, my daughter. You are still the most beautiful and strong young Rodeshian I have ever beheld. You are my daughter, and I am proud of you," T'maya said. "Now, I want you to finish your food because you are joining Eline to go see the bridge. And she wants you to wear the leather tunic she gave you."

"But we are not celebrating," F'lorna said. "I can't wear my best tunic on a normal day."

Eline came up to F'lorna holding the white leather tunic with colorful embroidery that Vauntan had made. "We are celebrating you and your friends' successful journey and safe return. The bridge could not have been built without the cordage you all offered. Besides, I would love to see you wear the Doublemoon Ceremony gift I bought you. You don't need a reason other than you want to wear it."

F'lorna looked at the supple leather her aunt held in her hands. It would be nice to get dressed up after such a long journey. "Don't they still need me to help with the building?"

Jaquarn shook his head. "Not at all. You, Lemmeck, the twins and the others have been excused from the rest of the duties. You have done more than enough. Even if you wanted to help, the villagers would not let you. They are honored by the sacrifices you all made to harvest so much sinew. Now, I must go. Your mother is helping to prepare the mid-day meal at the Village Achion cluster shortly. I will meet all of you there."

Jaquarn placed his palms on each side of F'lorna's face and bent her head down, so he could kiss the bandage covering her wound. "I have always told you that Ra'ash has a great destiny for you. He would not allow you to experience this unless He knew you were strong enough to handle it. And even if you feel like you are not strong, the Help of Ra'ash will give you all the strength that you need."

F'lorna smiled. "Thank you, Father."

"I will see you at the Village Achion cluster," he said and turned to leave.

295

"Now hurry up and finish your morning meal. I have just made a new lather with the petals of the Rivervalley flowers. I want to wash, comb and braid your hair," T'maya said. "I have already smoothed out a perfect stick for your braid."

F'lorna noticed her mother's chestnut braids for the first time. "You have braided your hair again."

T'maya sighed. "I feel Ra'ash telling me that He loves me with and without the braids, but to make peace with the village, I will wear my hair braided. Besides," she said, grinning, "I miss watching your father lead the Shoam-sha."

"You look lovely, my niece," Eline said, her cobalt-colored eyes beaming with pride. "The tunic fits perfectly on you. Your mother has braided your hair beautifully. You can barely tell the difference between the braids."

"She's had lots of practice," F'lorna said. "She wants us to meet her when the Heat Source is at its zenith for the mid-day meal."

"Well, we had better go. We will go see the bridge first, and I believe they are already working on the pier if you would like to go there next," Eline offered.

An image of Zelara came to her mind. "No, let's just go to the bridge. I want to help my mother serve the mid-day meal."

The two of them left the Achion cluster. F'lorna felt nervous. She tried to calm her breathing using the technique Eline had shown her for the next time she was confronted with the Mountain Terror. Although she had walked the stone path that led to the village all her life, this time the path felt different. Or maybe it was she that felt different.

"I hope you don't mind us going through the village. I know the bridge is being built on the River next to Le'ana's family's land, but I would prefer to walk in the shade. The day is getting too hot for this old River-dweller," Eline said, looking through the tops of the trees at the Heat Source.

"I don't mind," F'lorna said. They walked in silence for several steps. F'lorna looked at every tree and plant along their path, seeing familiar things with new eyes. This was the path she had run along as a youngling. Now she was a Novice Elder and would rather walk and stay aware of her surroundings. She wanted to touch the braid that held the stick to her head, but she resisted the urge. Her mother had warned her not to handle the braid for fear of loosening it. She would no longer be able to carry the water basket on her horns. The stick was not fixed to her head and it would not hold the weight.

"Did your father tell you he will be guiding Blaklin and Jornan's joining ceremony?" Eline asked.

"Sage told me when she visited after my accident," F'lorna said. "Her entire family is preparing. They will be having the ceremony in our Village Achion cluster, so Mother has offered to cook as their joining ceremony gift."

"I am sure Sage's mother appreciates your mother's offering. Not having to cook will alleviate a lot of the burden," Eline said and winked. "Plus, all the villagers know that your mother is the best cook here, and she is used to serving large groups of people. I am sure most of Left River Hook will be here. It will be a large ceremony."

"I am looking forward to it. Blaklin has asked Sage and me to sing one of the *Holy Chants* together."

Eline nodded. "I am glad you are offering song again to Ra'ash and others. I had missed it, but I knew you would find your voice once more."

F'lorna heard noises in the distance and turned her ear to hear better. "I hear the villagers working."

Eline nodded. "Yes, they've been making that ruckus since I arrived. It takes a lot of communicating to build such a large structure."

"Why did you come to visit?" F'lorna asked, turning to her aunt.

"I had helped several villages south on the River, and I began to hear rumors about new animals and plants being found after the storm and ground shudders. I decided I'd better get back and talk with your father. I stopped at Left River Hook, and they told me about the Marsh-landers who came to visit. They told me that the River had been opened and is now running through the Desert Plains. I couldn't believe it. I left the next morning, and thanks to Ra'ash, I intercepted your friends, Merriton and Weston, as they were leaving. They showed me the auraium and described everything in detail," Eline said, looking at F'lorna. "I could see why their description caused you to have another

Mountain Terror. The waterfall sounds just as dangerous as the Northeastern Mountains."

F'lorna instantly felt tingling rising in her hands. She needed to distract her thoughts quickly. "Did you meet Banthem?"

Eline nodded. "Good, F'lorna. You must learn to think on something else when you feel any indication of the terror. Always think on something that is familiar and pleasing to you."

"Yes, I like Weston's falcon very much. He let me pet him, and his feathers felt soft like the underbelly of Achion bark but much smoother. He is a very intelligent bird of prey," F'lorna said.

Eline laughed. "That young Marshlander offered to let me stroke his falcon, and I declined. I am sure that bird of prey is trained well, but I will not be placing my hand near his sharp, powerful beak anytime soon."

The voices in the distance became louder as they strolled toward the River bank. They walked out of the shade of the forest and onto the lush grass that led to the shore. F'lorna gasped. "It is almost done!" The first half was completely done, and they were fastening the second half to the other side of the River. She saw many of the villagers swimming across. She realized they must be breaking for mid-day meal.

"Ralona's father is quite the creator. This offering to Ra'ash is one of the most breathtaking I have ever seen," Eline said, placing her hands on her hips. "The bridge will be a marvel to other villages. Although your father was mainly concerned with functionality, the bridge's beauty will bring many visitors coming to behold it."

F'lorna thought of the Sand-shaper bridge that Weston described to her, connecting the Northwestern Coast to the Northeastern Mountains. It was probably more intimidating than the waterfall she has seen. She was glad she would never have to behold it. She instantly scanned the crowd of villagers, reveling in the familiar faces. She saw one of her birth friends. "Vauntan!" she called out.

Vauntan was working on the sinews they had brought back from the main River. Her flaxen hair—the color of the field grain—was braided at the top and the rest was pulled back at the nape of her neck. Her eyes were a few shades darker than her hair and her skin was fair. She looked up from where she was cleaning the sinews in a large basin of water. "F'lorna!" she called back.

F'lorna and Eline walked to where Vauntan was working. F'lorna appreciated that Vauntan was only a finger's width shorter than she. "How do you like the tunic you made?" F'lorna asked, turning in a circle.

"Doesn't she look as breathtaking as the Rivervalley flowers growing wild in the meadows?" Eline asked.

"Yes, she does! F'lorna, you look amazing! Are you going to the mid-day meal? I would love my parents to see the tunic on you. I am so pleased at how well it fits you," she said, bending over and stroking the embroidery that she had designed. "I was nervous about the black dye I used. It was a new formula that I was trying out, and I didn't want it to bleed into the other colors. I almost didn't use it, but I thought the pattern would have more depth with the black threaded through it."

"I am so glad F'lorna's mother traded for the waterproof leather pouch that Nayran made at the Doublemoon Ceremony. When I realized it was about to rain, I folded this tunic and slipped it right into the pouch. The dress stayed perfectly safe during the storm," Eline said.

Vauntan's smile faded as she looked to the bandage just below F'lorna's left braid. "I am sorry about your horn, F'lorna. My heart aches for you. We heard your cry and then your song echoing through the village that night. I think many tears fell for you and what happened. Almost everyone is sad for you."

F'lorna lifted her left hand and squeezed Vauntan's right shoulder. "I have felt great loss, but the Help of Ra'ash is giving me His strength."

Vauntan smiled. "If there is anything you need from me just let me know."

F'lorna thought of the basket of River Pine Needles Le'ana had given her. "Actually, I have something for you. Le'ana gave me a basket of River Pine needles. I don't need so many. I will give you the rest." F'lorna thought of the needles. If the smokestone was as thin as those, she could write many symbols on a single piece of parchment. Suddenly, a thought came to her. "Can I bring them to you after mid-day meal?"

"I don't mind going to your Achion cluster," Vauntan said.

"No, I'll take them to your hearth because I want you to teach me how to make the black dye you used for my tunic dress," F'lorna said, knowing that her aunt was listening and trying to think of a reason to have dye. She didn't want to lie. "I am creating something for my mother, and I need the dye for it."

Vauntan looked surprised. "I didn't realize you had a desire for creation."

"I don't," F'lorna said, avoiding her aunt's stare. "I just have this one idea of something I believe she will really like."

Chapter 29

THE WRITTEN WORD

F'lorna mixed the ingredients together in the yellow cylinder that Lemmeck had found and given her. She had taken the small parchment out and placed it with another one to keep it safe. She had read all the symbols on each parchment that they had found. It had taken her awhile to understand what was written. She had to imagine the dance of Jeyshen's image and its corresponding chant before she could make each sound. She wondered if she would ever learn to read and write without having to do all three steps.

The smooth surface of the glass allowed the black ink to pool safely at the bottom of the tube. Vauntan had given her the new recipe she created for making black dye—hardened sap, honey, blackberries and ash. The hardened sap had to be pounded into a powder and the berries had to be mashed and the tiny seeds taken out. The ash could be taken from any cooking hearth. F'lorna had played with the recipe. She wasn't dying a fabric thread, like Vauntan used the dye for. She needed the dye to be thicker, so she could dip a dried pine needle into it and lightly scratch the ink onto the parchment.

F'lorna leaned against her mother's cooking table and looked around her Achion cluster. Her parents had gone to Sage's cluster. Blaklin would be joined to Jornan when the Heat Source began its descent the following rise. Her aunt was checking on a few villagers who needed her offering of healing. F'lorna took this opportunity to finish writing the chant that she had been working on for several rises of the Heat Source. She looked at the parchment with rows of small symbols stacked on top of each other. The backside of the large parchment was almost completely filled. She had already covered the front side with the first half of the chant.

Guilt pulled at her, but she ignored it. How could writing a *Holy Chant* for her mother be wrong? Those who offered tanning and creation as their Adoration used designs in what they created. What made this design any different than the others besides the fact it was distinctly Sand-shaper? Her parents had seen the dye covering her fingers. When they asked about it, she had told them she was making a gift. She never said it was for Blaklin's joining, but they assumed it and she allowed their assumption.

She was on the last few words of the chant. She wondered if she should take the time to write them. They were the same words that ended all the chants: *So be it.* She considered not writing the words but quickly decided that she should write every single sound. She felt an importance to writing the chant exactly as it was spoken. Writing was exhausting work. She had to stay very still and bounce her mind from Jeyshen's images, to His chants, to the Sand-shaper symbol and then to the chant she was writing specifically, the *Chant of Acceptance.* It was the shortest chant, but it didn't seem short when she looked at all the symbols needed to write it on parchment.

Finally, the chant was completely written. She carefully lifted her hand so not to smudge any of the dye. She had a clean river rock resting on the top half of the parchment, so the wind would not blow it away. She threw the used needles into the small cooking fire her mother left for her in case she wanted to make hot tea. Then she walked behind her tree and dug a small hole in the ground with her heel. She poured the rest of the dye into the hole and covered it with dirt. She wouldn't be doing any more writing for a while. It was hard work to overcome her restlessness and force her body to stay still for so long. Each symbol had to be exact and her body and hands ached from being rigid for too long.

She walked back to the cooking table and grabbed her mother's water pouch. She poured water over the yellow cylinder, washing the inside of the glass tube. Most of the black dye washed out, but the bottom half of the cylinder would be stained black for good. She stared at her hands. Her fingers were also stained black. She poured the water over them, but she knew the dye would be there for a while. She would have to keep her hands hidden from the villagers.

Once she had everything cleaned and dried, she reached back to her parchment containing the *Chant of Acceptance.* Again, she felt a tug of guilt. "Ra'ash," she whispered. She had given many voiceless words about her writing, but He didn't seem to be answering. Maybe if she spoke aloud. "You are the One who told me I would write. Why do I feel guilty?"

If Ra'ash told her to write, her guilt had to come from another source. She closed her eyes thought about what would happen if the villagers found out that she had written the Sand-shaper symbols. She sensed confusion and fear. An image of Zelara's father came into her mind, and she sensed anger. She thought of her mother and father. Would they be hurt that she had hidden what she was doing? *Confusion, fear, anger and hurt. Ra'ash, why would You want me to write if those are the feelings that I sense?*

"Those are Sand-shaper symbols," a voice said with shock.

F'lorna opened her eyes. Standing in front of her was Zelara holding a large platter with several freshly caught fish. F'lorna had been so preoccupied with her warring emotions that she didn't hear the footsteps coming up to her Achion cluster.

"You are making the Sand-shaper symbols," Zelara said in awe.

"No, I am not," F'lorna floundered.

306

"Yes, you are!" Zelara insisted. "I see black stains all over your fingers."

"What are you doing here?" F'lorna demanded, hiding her hands behind her back.

"My mother wanted me to bring you fish as a peace offering," Zelara said staring at the symbols. She looked back at F'lorna. "You have the Sand-shaper symbols in your Eternal Memory."

"No. I don't. I found this parchment washed up. My hands are stained from a project I'm doing with Vauntan," F'lorna lied, feeling the heat rush to her cheeks. She was horrible at lying.

Zelara set the tray down on the cooking table next to the parchment, then hovered over the freshly marked symbols. "You are lying. They look different than the ones in the cylinders. These are thinner and smaller." She bent down and gasped. "You have written some of the *Divine Oracle* with Sand-shaper symbols!"

F'lorna hurried to find words to excuse what she had done but suddenly stopped. She stared at Zelara and watched as she continued to read the parchment. "How do you know what I've written? You can read the symbols?"

Zelara pushed away from the cooking table, her eyes became watery with fright. "Please, please don't tell anyone. My father can't find out. He will banish me!"

F'lorna couldn't believe it. "How did you learn them?"

"It's all that Sand-shaper's fault! I was just a little girl and a Sand-shaper family moved close to our village. One of them was a girl my age. We met near the River and became friends. Soon I would sneak off to be

307

with her because my father would not allow our friendship. I thought it was only a game. I didn't realize she was using Sand-shaper symbols. I would draw them in the dirt with her and listen to her make the sounds. Now they are stuck in my Eternal Memory for good. I hate her for showing them to me," Zelara said crying.

F'lorna watched as Zelara wept. She could see the burden she had been carrying. She walked over to her and placed a hand on her shoulder. "Does anyone know?"

Zelara nodded. "My mother found me writing them. She told me I must never let Father know. My Eternal Memory has been tainted forever by the Sand-shapers. If the villagers found out, they would see me as an outcast. They must never find out!"

F'lorna shook her head. "The symbols are not to be feared. In fact, they are part of the River-dwellers' lineage as well," F'lorna said, trying to sound confident. If Ra'ash had called her to write them, they couldn't be evil.

Zelara looked up at F'lorna. "What do you mean?"

"I don't have them in my Eternal Memory, yet I can write them. How do you think I learned?"

Zelara looked at the parchment. "Your mother taught you."

"My mother would never teach me the symbols. She fears them just as you do. My Eternal Memory has been shut. The symbols are not in it. I wrote them through the *Divine Oracle.*"

"How?" Zelara asked disbelieving.

"They are the forty-four Images of Jeyshen," F'lorna said simply.

Zelara looked confused but stepped closer to the parchment.

"Your Adoration is dance. Do you not see them?" F'lorna asked.

F'lorna could see Zelara's expression begin to change.

"I see them! But how do you know how the symbols sound?" She said looking up at F'lorna.

"Each of the forty-four Images has its own Chant," F'lorna began. "The first sound of each chant is the sound the symbol represents."

Zelara thought, then looked back down at the parchment. F'lorna watched her as she sounded out the first three symbols. "You are right!"

"Don't you see? The Sand-shaper symbols are also our symbols. We dance and say them every day."

This time F'lorna heard the footsteps coming in through the woods just before she saw Elder Trenton walk into her Achion cluster. F'lorna wanted to grab the parchment and hide it, but she couldn't risk letting her stained hands be seen. She quickly hid her hands behind her back.

He walked into the clearing next to his daughter and briefly glanced at the parchment before quickly looking away as if the symbols burned his eyes. He stared at F'lorna with loathing. "I knew your mother was not one of us," he said coolly. "And you are just as much a Sand-shaper as she. You are an abomination! The village should decide to pull out your other horn to match what you really are."

309

F'lorna wanted to shout back, but she could see his fist were balled like large stones. The intensity surrounding him scared her. She stayed very still and kept her hands hidden.

Trenton looked at Zelara. "Is she polluting your mind with those vile symbols?"

Zelara glanced at F'lorna briefly and looked back down to the ground. "No. Mother asked me to bring fish to the Spiritual Elder and his family. F'lorna had found another cylinder. She was only looking at it when I arrived."

Trenton stared at F'lorna, the force of his glare seared like the light of the Heat Source. "Is your Sand-shaper mother reading those to you?"

"No. My mother has never read them to me," F'lorna said firmly.

"Those symbols are in your Eternal Memory, aren't they? You have been tainted by them. You are trying to stain my daughter's memory too," he said with derision.

"That is not true!" F'lorna shouted. "You cannot accuse me with lies!"

"Father," Zelara interrupted. "She wasn't reading them to me. She was only looking at them when I came. Those cylinders are washing up all over our village."

F'lorna watched as Trenton forced his palms to open and relax.

Disgusted, he looked at F'lorna averting his eyes from the cooking table where the parchment rested. "I demand you burn those Sand-shaper symbols right away. And tell your father that I had come to make peace with him, but now I come to tell him that I will be calling an emergency meeting. This mass infiltration of Sand-shaper influence must stop, starting with you and your Sand-shaper mother. Anyone who opens those cylinders to look upon them grieves Ra'ash and stains the *Divine Oracle* within them!"

F'lorna said nothing. She clasped her stained fingers together behind her back tightly. Trenton's words felt like a sharp river rock jabbing deep within her. She was relieved he did not look directly at the parchment or he may see they were different. She knew now why Zelara carried around her secret so possessively. F'lorna gave voiceless words to Ra'ash that Elder Trenton would leave without prying further.

Trenton looked back at his daughter. "Take our tray with everything on it and bring it back to our Achion cluster immediately. I want you to never speak to that half-breed girl again." Trenton turned and stomped back into the forest.

Zelara didn't move for several seconds. Finally, she slowly walked to the cooking table to retrieve the tray. She stared at the fish before looking into F'lorna's eyes. "Please don't tell anyone what I've told you. My father would disown me. I won't tell anyone you can write the symbols. I promise," she said with pleading eyes. "I'm very good at keeping secrets."

For the first time, F'lorna could see Zelara's vulnerability that she tried so hard to conceal. "I won't say a word."

Zelara breathed a timid sigh of relief. "Thank you."

F'lorna walked up to Zelara and reached out to touch her shoulder again, knowing it may be the last time she would ever talk with her. "The symbols are also part of the River-dweller's history. They are not evil."

Zelara shook her head. "How can you be so sure?"

F'lorna lifted her chin and said with resolve. "Because Ra'ash has called me to a new Adoration."

"What is that?" Zelara asked.

F'lorna presented her stained fingers. "To write," she said.

"Trenton has called an emergency village meeting tonight," Jaquarn said. "Blaklin's family is not happy about it because they were supposed to decorate the Village Achion cluster for Blaklin's joining. Now they will have to wait until the Heat Sources rises in the morning horizon." He paced up and down the Achion cluster. F'lorna, T'maya and Eline were standing at the cooking table.

"I offer you my apology of healing, Father. I did not mean for Zelara to see the Sand-shaper symbols," F'lorna said. She stood with her arms crossed, and her stained fingers tucked underneath the fabric of her tunic. She needed to tell her parents that she in fact wrote the symbols, but she delayed wondering what their response would be.

"I don't believe there is anything wrong with being curious about the Sand-shaper symbols. Trenton's feelings about them are guided by fear. His actions are too extreme. The cylinders are washing up all over the village and there's no harm at looking at them," Jaquarn said.

"It is my fault," T'maya said. "I knew F'lorna had found the cylinders, but to me they are harmless. F'lorna asked questions about Sand-shapers and their work, and I answered them. I'm so tired of being ashamed of my history and the people I came from. I don't want to hide from my past anymore. The villagers put up with me because I try to be like them, but I'm not. They make me braid my hair like I have horns, but I don't have them. And now F'lorna has to have a braid like mine," T'maya whispered. She covered her face with her hands and began to weep.

Eline reached her arm around T'maya's shoulders. "You do not have to be ashamed of who you are. Ra'ash has created you, and everything He creates has value and purpose." She exhaled and looked at F'lorna. "You might as well tell them what you told me and show them the parchment."

F'lorna didn't want to speak what she had been doing out loud, but it was too late. Her mother was right. She didn't want to hide anymore. She uncrossed her arms revealing her stained fingers. "When I received the Indwelling," F'lorna said tentatively, "Ra'ash told me that I would offer Him a new Adoration."

Jaquarn looked at his daughter. "You mean song?"

F'lorna shook her head. "I already offer song. This is a new Adoration. One that has never been offered by any River-dweller." F'lorna thought of Zelara. Would she ever be willing to write for Ra'ash?

T'maya looked up. "What is it, my daughter?"

F'lorna walked to her Achion tree. She reached into the hole and picked up the parchment lying on her mattress. She walked back to her mother and handed it to her. "To write," she whispered.

T'maya took the parchment. "That's impossible," she said stunned.

Jaquarn quickly walked behind his wife. "F'lorna, you made those?"

F'lorna nodded. "Yes, Father."

"But how do you know how to write the symbols?" T'maya asked. "Your Eternal Memory is locked."

"The forty-four Sand-shaper symbols match the forty-four Images of Jeyshen."

"What?" she asked confused.

F'lorna thought and tried to gather what she had been considering about the symbols since she learned what they were. "When the Sand-shapers wrote down the symbols many moon folds ago, they must have used the Holy Images of Jeyshen as their format. Each symbol is one of the images that I dance. I've danced them over and over again, so when I saw them drawn, I recognized them." F'lorna didn't mention that it was Weston who showed her all forty-four images in the first place.

"Astonishing," Jaquarn said, looking closer at the parchment.

"But that still doesn't give you the sound each symbol makes," T'maya said.

"Each *Image of Jeyshen* has its *Chant of Jeyshen*. All the chants start with a different sound. That is the sound the symbol represents," F'lorna finished, hoping her words made sense.

"What did you write?" Jaquarn asked amazed.

F'lorna looked at her mother, feeling tears drip down her cheeks. Her grey eyes darkened, like stones just under the current of the River. Her mother's eyes matched her own. "Read it, Mother. Ra'ash wanted me to write it for you."

T'maya stared at her daughter. "You wrote this for me?" she asked bewildered. She held up the parchment and began to read from the top. As she read, fresh tears ran down her cheeks. She began to read with intensity. When she got down to the bottom, she turned the parchment over and continued reading the other side. When her eyes read the final words, she whispered them aloud: "So be it."

"What is it?" Jaquarn asked, staring at the parchment and then to his wife.

"It is *Jeyshen's Chant of Acceptance,*" she whispered in awe. She looked at F'lorna. "My daughter has given me a piece of the *Divine Oracle.*"

Chapter 30

THE FALCON'S SCROLL

F'lorna listened to her birth friend sing from the platform. The light green tunic she wore looked pretty against her umber skin. F'lorna knew the color of the tunic matched the color of her eyes, but she couldn't see them from where she sat. She was supposed to sing with Sage, but she had been banned from entering the Village Achion cluster for a moon phase. It didn't matter, though. She would be leaving with her aunt when the Heat Source rose in the morning horizon.

Her parents wanted to get her away from the hateful words about her the villagers were filling the forest with. They were scared and confused, and Elder Trenton had made matters worse, describing what happened at his previous village. According to him, the Sand-shapers were a sickness to the community.

F'lorna had crawled up into the shaggiest Achion tree and hid behind the leaves. The Village Achion cluster was crammed with villagers from Left and Right River Hook for Blaklin's joining with Jornan. She would return to her tree after her father joined them when the Heat Source disappeared over the horizon. F'lorna wore a yellow tunic because she knew the glow from Violet Moon would darken the appearance of that color. They were opposites, which is how she now felt. She once was a River-dweller, but now she felt like a Sand-shaper. She no longer knew who she was.

"You are F'lorna of Rodesh," she felt the voiceless words say from within her. "Yes," she whispered. "I am Rodeshian."

Suddenly, she heard leaves swishing quickly around her. She looked down to see black braids. "Lemmeck?" she whispered.

"Yes," the voice came.

Lemmeck quickly made his way up the tree to where F'lorna was sitting.

"Did anyone see you?" she asked.

"No," he whispered. "They are all watching the joining." He looked at F'lorna. "Your hair is down on one side."

She nodded. "Yes, one braid for one horn. I will not braid sticks into my hair anymore."

317

He smiled. "I like it."

F'lorna didn't believe him. "I know that you have admitted that you like me, but it is okay if your feelings have changed. I have changed."

He kept his eyes on her. "I think you are more beautiful now than when you sang with Sage after we harvested the sinews," he whispered without blinking.

F'lorna felt heat rise up into her cheeks. "Even after what I have done?"

"The villagers know that you have been looking at the Sand-shaper symbols," he said. "But Sage and Ralona have told me that you have written them."

"Yes," F'lorna said resolutely. "Ra'ash told me I would write, and I wrote *Jeyshen's Chant of Acceptance* for my mother. She has said it is her most prized possession in all of Rodesh. She keeps it hidden in her Achion tree," she said, waiting for Lemmeck's fearful reaction.

"We must not let anyone else know," he said. "I am amazed by what you have accomplished."

F'lorna's expression floundered. "What?"

"You care for your mother so much that you would compromise yourself to help her. Will you write more?" he asked.

F'lorna looked down at her hands. They still ached from writing so many symbols, the black stains evident on her beige skin. "I don't know. It is very hard work. It takes me several moments to write just one symbol. I don't think it will ever get easier for me. The chant I wrote for my mother was the shortest, but it took many rises of the Heat Source to write all the words. I

318

had to use the River Pine Needles to make them small enough."

They heard pounding and looked toward the Village Achion cluster. Sage had finished her song. She gave a slight smile before leaving the platform.

"She is not happy you could not be there," Lemmeck said. "Many Elders are angry with what they are doing to you. Sage told me that her parents are considering moving to Left River Hook, and my parents are considering it as well. Our land is in between both villages. We could easily provide Left River Hook with the meat we harvest, and let the villagers here eat the foul fish from Elder Trenton."

"Do not do that on my account," F'lorna said. "My intention is not to tear our village apart. I want to come back."

"There is too much fear in our village. The elders are too rigid and unmoving. They care more about following the *Divine Oracle* than really living it. Jeyshen spoke of loving people. What Elder Trenton has done is not love. Your mother can now have some of Jeyshen's chants—something that was once denied her. What if Trenton found out? And now he wants to stop the communal Shoam-sha. He's trying to get your father to step down as Spiritual Elder. He says we don't need one."

"It is sad that they accuse me of making changes, yet Elder Trenton is trying to stop something that Jeyshen Himself established many moon folds ago. It seems that Trenton's version of truth changes with what he wants," F'lorna said. "I don't care what he says. I will not compromise what Ra'ash told me. He thinks he has caught me in one of his fish's traps, but he has only made me stronger to break free."

"You are strong," Lemmeck said. "I like you this way. I will miss you when you're gone."

"I will miss you," she whispered.

"Do you still have the silver mane I gave you from the White Diamond Stag I harvested for our Doublemoon Ceremony?" he asked.

F'lorna nodded. "Yes, I keep it in my tunic belt," she said, motioning to a small pouch with her eyes.

"Can you hand it to me?" he asked.

F'lorna nodded and adjusted her position on the tree. She leaned against a large branch and reached into her tunic belt and felt for the tied strands of the stag's mane. She found it and gave it to Lemmeck.

Lemmeck kept his right hand fastened to a sturdy branch and took the mane from her with his left hand. Then he reached into his tunic belt. He grabbed a piece of fabric from within the belt and placed it on her lap. "Will you open it?"

"Yes." She moved the fabric with her right hand and opened it. "It is a necklace," she whispered. She brought the necklace up to see it. The cord of the necklace was made of thinly worked sinew. But the pendant that hung from it was made of a translucent Sand-shaper cylinder. It was melted and shaped into an intricate design, and the silver hair from the White Diamond Stag was sealed inside.

"How did you make this?" she asked.

"When we were at the main River, there were more cylinders washed up on the shore. I found two smaller ones with no pigment. On the way back to our

320

village, I asked Merriton about them. He told me how they melt old cylinders on stones to make them into other things, like jewelry. I thought I would make you something that would hold the piece of mane I harvested for you, but I didn't want to ask for it back. So I have given you a new piece, and I will make my necklace out of yours."

F'lorna held up the misshapen glass and gently shook the silver mane inside. "Won't you get into trouble?"

"I don't care what the villagers think. Sand-shapers are going to become more prevalent in our lands. We can't hide from them and their creations forever," Lemmeck said. "They are a part of our world."

"Are you speaking of the auraium that Merriton and Weston found?" F'lorna asked. "And the landowners who will want it? They will come down the River once they know it is there."

Lemmeck shook his head. "No, I am speaking about all Sand-shapers—Rodeshians like your mother, like Merriton and the landowners who want auraium, even Raecli and her grandfather. We must be able to communicate and identify with them. Our village is trying to hide from the fact that not all Rodeshians look and act like us. But the landscape of Rodesh is changing, not just physically but socially too."

"You think the Sand-shapers would want to read the symbols of the *Divine Oracle*?" she asked.

Lemmeck stared into F'lorna's grey eyes. His emerald eyes shone brightly in the Violet Moon. "I think many of them will, and I think Ra'ash wills it. He loves all Rodeshians the same."

F'lorna heard a voice she recognized coming from the platform of the Achion cluster. She turned quickly to see her father standing in front of Blaklin and Jornan, wrapping the joining vine around their clasped hands. "You are now joined in Ra'ash," her father shouted for all the villagers to hear.

F'lorna smiled as she heard the pounding of the table and calls of favor and blessing to the new husband and wife. "Blaklin will be pleased that her joining is so well received."

Lemmeck nodded. "Now she has another story that she can tell the villagers."

"Did you know that they are serving a honey custard as the joining desert?" F'lorna asked. "One of my mother's favorite recipes. And guess what is sprinkled on the top of the custard?" F'lorna asked, playfully.

Lemmeck thought. "Could it be Le'ana's Indigo berries?"

F'lorna nodded. "Yes. Those berries will definitely be a part of Blaklin's joining story," she said.

"The villagers will all have blue lips, but the taste of those berries is worth it," Lemmeck said smiling.

"I better get back to my Achion cluster while the food is being served," F'lorna said. "It is dark now, so I won't be seen. I don't want to cause a distraction for Blaklin's ceremony." F'lorna grabbed a lower branch and stretched her body off of the tree, dangling just a few inches above the ground. She released her hands and her feet nimbly landed on the mossy, forest floor. She heard a thump on the grass next to her.

"Let me walk you back to your hearth,"
Lemmeck said.

F'lorna shook her head. "No, please stay here and
enjoy the ceremony for me. They have all worked hard
to make it special. My mother has seasoned and smoked
the Wood Deer. I want you to sit with your family to
taste all the foods."

"I will," Lemmeck said. "But let me put your
necklace on first."

She handed him the necklace and lifted her dark
amber hair. He stood behind her with the necklace and
reached his left hand around her neck. He brought the
necklace's ends together and tied the sinew. When he
was finished, he turned her around. "It looks beautiful on
you," he whispered.

She clutched the small glass pendant. "Thank
you," she said reaching her left arm out and squeezing
his right shoulder. "I will see you when I return." Then
she turned around and began her walk back to her
Achion cluster. She hid the pendant under her yellow
tunic. Even though the path was dark, she knew the way
well. She felt like she was walking the path to her
Achion tree for the last time, and in a way, she was. The
River-dweller she used to be was quickly fading. She
now had to embrace the Rodeshian she was becoming.

F'lorna's feet finally brought her into her Achion
cluster. She walked to her tree and sat in the hole.
F'lorna looked at the cooking table. She saw the bowl of
soup her mother had left for her. She wasn't hungry. She
reached for the pendant and caressed the glass that hung
from the sinew around her neck. She liked how it felt—
smooth yet misshapen. Lemmeck's gift honored her. It

felt like Ra'ash was telling her that He was proud of what she sacrificed in order to learn to write. However, the thought of writing more symbols caused tension to rise through her hands, up her arms and into her shoulders. She let go of the pendant and tried to rub the tension out of her neck with her hand. "I do not want to write anytime soon," she said to herself.

Suddenly, she heard a screech from above her. She jolted up and looked into the branches of her Achion tree. Two piercing eyes stared down at her. It was Banthem. Weston had kept his promise. He sent his falcon to her. Banthem made his way back to the arm covering Weston had secured to a branch on her tree. He held a large wooden cylinder. F'lorna squinted. Weston must have wanted to write more because the cylinder was so big that Banthem clutched it in his powerful claw. She went to her tree and placed her foot on the bottom rim of the hole, lifting her body up. She grabbed the first branch and made her way up to the falcon. When she came eye-level to him, she stopped and nodded at the powerful bird.

"Hello, Banthem. Is this for me?" She gently reached toward the falcon and unfastened the cord securing the rolled parchment to the band around his leg. Then she gently reached to his chest and stroked his silver and tan feathers. He seemed pleased with the attention. "Don't go anywhere," she whispered to him.

She carefully climbed down the tree and opened the parchment. It was a letter from Weston. He couldn't fit many symbols on the parchment because of the thick smokestone. F'lorna held the parchment and gave a mischievous grin. She reached into her Achion tree and

324

grabbed the small pouch that contained her needles. He needed to know how to write smaller symbols by using River Pine Needles. He would also need the ingredients to the black dye she used. She looked at Banthem. "I guess I'll be writing sooner than I thought."

"F'lorna, are you ready to go?" Eline asked. The Violet Moon still hung in the horizon. The Heat Source will rise soon. "I want to leave before your parents wake. You said your goodbyes after the joining, and your mother has already shed too many tears. We will be traveling slowly. My body is old and there are many plants I want to show you along the way. I would like to reach the traveling Achion cluster before the Heat Source makes its way to the evening horizon."

F'lorna held her traveling bag and stared at her Achion hole. There was so much left inside that she was unable to bring. Her youngling memories filled the hollowness of the tree with life. She had set her left horn on the highest shelf that was chiseled above her mattress. Her mother told her to bury it, but she had washed it and kept it instead. She would leave it behind and create new memories as she journeyed south with her aunt. She would learn the Healing Adoration from the best healer on Rodesh. "Let me put my Achion cover on," she said, placing her bag to the ground. She reached her head and arms into her tree and grabbed the hole covering under her mattress. She took the left sinew of the covering and anchored it. Then she took the right sinew and stretched it until it was anchored. She gently removed her hands and allowed the cover to rest against the tree, safeguarding everything within. She knew her mother would be looking toward the tree. She wanted her mother to see that the tree was not empty—it was merely waiting for her return.

She looked to her aunt who was waiting for her. "I am overwhelmed with sadness. I feel like my life as a youngling had died," she whispered.

Eline walked toward F'lorna and squeezed her right shoulder with her left hand. "Not at all," she said. "Who you are now will always be a part of you, like a seed that grows into something beautiful and useful. You may look and feel different, but the F'lorna inside of you will always be there."

"Do you miss being a youngling?" she asked. Her aunt had seen Twofolds of the moons. Her hair was white, but her cobalt blue eyes still shone with vigor.

"My body may be aged, but the spirit within me still feels like a youngling. The spirit that Ra'ash gives each Rodeshian is eternal. Though our bodies will eventually return to Rodesh, our spirits will enter the Eternal Dwelling of Ra'ash forever. There you and I will be about the same age—young and energetic—and the sum of who we are on Rodesh will follow us."

F'lorna nodded. "Yes, I do understand that, but leaving is still difficult. I know I can't stay, and I am honored and excited to travel and learn from you. Yet, I feel the same sadness as I did when Raecli was taken from me, like I have lost someone special."

Eline took F'lorna into her embrace. "You are so much like your father. You feel so deeply and love with

326

intensity. You will have many heartaches in life because you give so much of yourself to others."

"Should I not?" F'lorna asked, coming out of her aunt's arms.

Eline stared at F'lorna for several moments. She softly swept her deep amber hair away from the wound that had closed above her left temple. Finally, she exhaled. "Love Ra'ash with all that's within you, and He will lead you into a life filled with both joys and sorrows—and they are both valuable, as long as neither takes your eyes away from Him."

F'lorna knew that her aunt had much more to say, but she guarded her words. "Yes, Aunt. I am ready to leave with you."

Eline nodded. "Good. We will go to the new village bridge, fill our bota bags with water and begin our journey to the southern tributary villages. I have many friends south. Their villages are much different than Right River Hook. I believe you will flourish like I did." Eline adjusted the travel bag on her back.

F'lorna looked at her Achion tree one more time, glancing up its full length. Suddenly, she saw Weston's thick leather arm covering that he wrapped around a low branch for Banthem. She had attached the scroll she had written to the band around the great falcon's leg before her parents returned home, and he had slept peacefully on her tree through the Violet Moon's course across the Upper Realm. He must have flown off before her aunt had woken her. "I forgot one thing," she said and instantly went to the tree.

She jumped, catching the low branch and pulled herself up. She wrapped her legs around the branch and brought her hands toward the arm covering. She quickly untied the sinews that held it in place and grasped the heavy material in her hand. She released her legs and allowed them to dangle before freeing herself from the tree. She landed softly on the forest ground with a thump. She walked back to her travel bag, bent down and untied its sinews, sliding the tightly rolled leather deep into the opening. Then she retightened the bag and swung it onto her back as she rose. "I am ready for my next journey," she whispered, following her aunt beyond her Achion cluster.

Raecli looked out the opening of the traveling case. She could see her grandfather speaking with some of their servants. She didn't understand why they were traveling south. She felt uncomfortable being so far from their estate on the Northwestern Coast. She adjusted the turban covering her horns. Her grandfather wanted to extract them, but she couldn't bring herself to losing her horns, even if they were frowned upon by the other Sand-shapers. She wasn't willing to give up who she was to make others feel comfortable.

"You should close the curtains, my dear. I wouldn't want the Heat Source to burn your young skin," her grandfather said. He seemed in a jovial mood, which was not common when he was working with his servants.

"Did you find what we came here for, Grandfather? Are we able to go home now?" Raecli asked in a sweet voice. She had learned over a moon turn ago that her grandfather responded better to polite, demure speech.

Her grandfather held up something that looked like dark yellow sap trapped within a stone. "I did indeed find what I wanted," he said allowing the light to reflect off the treasure he held. "And there is a lot of it. We may have to stay here for a while yet. But don't worry, my dear. I will procure us a temporary home while we are here. You can wait a little while longer, can't you?"

Raecli nodded. She could sense the command imbedded in his rhetorical question. "Yes, Grandfather. I don't mind waiting."

A smile spread across the old man's face and his violet eyes refracted the light of the auraium he held.

WRITER

Alisa Hope Wagner loves deep simplicity. She is home most days, but if you do see her out and about, you may actually be face-to-face with her extroverted identical twin sister. More than anything, Alisa adores being a wife to her high school sweetheart (Daniel), mother to her three awesome children (Isaac, Levi and Kiki) and daughter of the Most High King.

After hours of writing and editing at her computer, Alisa cannot wait to workout in her garage gym. When the day's work is finally done, she listens to smooth jazz and gets creative in the kitchen. But before she begins to write each morning, she sits with her Bible and journal and chats with God, letting the Holy Spirit encourage, correct and guide her.

Alisa is an award winning writer of Christian fiction and non-fiction books. She has been writing for 13 years and has written and published 17 books across all genres, including her speculative fiction books, the _Onoma Series_. She lectures at churches and colleges about her four favorite topics: faith, family, fitness and fiction. Additionally, she writes about the topics on her blog, www.alisahopewagner.com.

Alisa competes in bodybuilding competitions and is a retired MMA fighter. She shares her health passion and knowledge in her 2 fitness books. She can be found on Instagram, Twitter, Facebook and Goodreads with her username: @alisahopewagner.

Alisa is the creator of *enLIVEn Devotional*: a writing ministry that brings the words of diverse writers together in order to support world missions. She and her co-coordinator, Holly Smith, produce devotional anthologies with proceeds going to the poor and needy of this world. You can find out how to get involved in this ministry at www.enlivendevotionals.com.

The most important thing Alisa would like to tell her readers is that God loves you so much that He sent His Son into this world to claim you as His brothers and sisters. No matter who you are or what you have done, Jesus loves you and died to have a supernatural relationship with you in this life and the next. Don't waste one single day. Ask Jesus into your heart, make Him your Lord and Savior and begin really living!

ARTIST

Albert Morales is an accomplished illustrator and painter with credits spread across the art board. He was a nominee for the 2018 CARTOON CROSSROADS Cartoonist of the year, where this year his strip joined the BILLY IRELAND CARTOON ART MUSEUM's collection of original art since the 1900's. His work is now curated and collected next to the likes of Charles Schultz (Peanuts), Bil Keane (Family Circus), and Bill Watterson (Calvin and Hobbes) to name a few.

Albert's creator owned comic strip SUPER IMPACTO VS. THE WORLD has also been recently published in a collection along with fellow cartoonists entitled TALES FROM LA VIDA by THE OHIO STATE UNIVERSITY.

Albert has had the opportunity to work with the HERO INITIATIVE on several of their 100 book projects including: Wolverine 100, New Avengers 100, Fantastic Four 100, Walking Dead 100, Hellboy 100, and TEENAGE MUTANT NINJA TURTLES 100.

Wrapping up his run with MARVEL / UPPERDECK as an official MARVEL - UPPERDECK artist (with SPIDER-MAN: Homecoming and FLEER ULTRA X-MEN), Albert is continuing doing creative projects in the way of publishing creator owned books. Slated for 2019 and already catching fire is his new book ANNIHILATION JONES and his just announced illustration duties for ALISA HOPE WAGNER'S new VIOLET MOON SERIES starting with *F'lorna of Rodesh*!

You can find Albert Morales at the following social media sites.
artwise310@hotmail.com
https://www.instagram.com/angryroosterstudios/
https://www.facebook.com/albert.morales.5477

ALISA'S OTHER BOOKS

Onoma Series:
Eve of Awakening
Bear into Redemption
Mark within Salvation
Hunt for Understanding (coming 2019)

Fitness Books:
Fearlessly Fit
Fearlessly Fit at Home

Vessels Series:
Imperfect Vessels
Broken Alabaster Jars
Gathering Empty Pitchers

Following God Series:
Following God into the Cage
Following God onto the Stage
Following God across the Page

One Year Devotional:
Slay the Day: Your Daily Dose of Victory

Faith Books:
Our 6 His 7: Transformed by Sabbath Rest
Simple Musings
Why Jesus? (coming 2019)

Devotional Anthologies:
Granola Bar Devotionals: Spiritual Snacks on the Go!
Get to the Margins: A Devotional Anthology of Writers on the Edge

Made in the USA
Columbia, SC
25 September 2019